TOOTH

AND

NAIL

SUMMONER FOR HIRE
BOOK ONE

Domino Finn

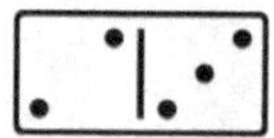

Published by Blood & Treasure, Los Angeles
First Edition

Cover by James T. Egan of Bookfly Design LLC.

Print ISBN: 978-1-946-00841-1

DominoFinn.com

Demons are Real

Not only that, they're everywhere. Shadows, secrets, strangers. Dark beings with mythic powers every bit as dangerous as their legends.

Opening your eyes to this reality isn't easy. Devils are crafty. Supernaturals hide in plain sight. Even wizards will do anything for power.

What you need is a professional. Someone with nothing left to lose. A tour guide to Hell who packs enough smarts and resolve to handle anything in your way.

What you need is Shyla Crowe, a smooth operator on a very bumpy ride.

Welcome to the thrilling world of *Summoner For Hire*. It may not be virtuous, but it's a living.

TOOTH & NAIL

SUMMONER FOR HIRE

BOOK ONE

The Hire

"I hear you have a set of abilities that could be useful to me," said the old man who identified himself only as Lambert. He was a regular enough man, if a bit old fashioned, wearing a textured sports coat with a patterned gray ascot. His thinning white hair was parted over a pair of coarse muttonchop whiskers, with his chin and lips clean.

"Sure," I said, casually leaning the wooden chair against the wall. "Sneaking, B and E, safe cracking."

"Commendable, I'm sure, but I'm not speaking of those particular skills. It's said you have connections with... spirits."

The man was gaunt, in his seventies, but extreme age only accounted for half his stark visage. There was a coldness about him that came only with exposure to harsh, undeniable truths. This man didn't read storybooks or engage in trivialities. He was the type who knew what he wanted and went for it.

I shrugged dismissively. "I get paid for results, not my

life story."

His sharp lips curled into a smile, but my eyes were on his muscle, some kind of radicalized biker gang. An odd escort for a dignified man. They definitely weren't from around here.

The Downtown-adjacent warehouse was their idea. Nondescript. Empty, except for a table and two chairs. I sat across from Lambert with my back against the wall so I faced the room. Besides the boys outside with more testosterone than brain power, two bikers stood several paces from us. For the old man's protection.

The first was a tired stereotype. Big bald guy with a ruddy-brown beard and 'stache, a broad frame of fat competing with muscle. The shirt under his vest rode up and revealed tattooed script on his white belly. Four-to-one it was a misconstrued Bible verse. A silver cross hung from his neck. He stood immobile, watching me through black sunglasses, chewing on a toothpick.

The girl was the odd man out, so to speak. As bald as the other skinheads, she had piercings on her tongue, lips, ears, and eyebrows, and not a single tattoo in sight. Dark-blue eye shadow splashed over green eyes, staring me down for one wrong move. Between the bikers and myself, there was a lot of black leather in the dusty warehouse.

For his part, Lambert appeared neither threatening nor threatened. Like I said, he was experienced and knew how the world worked.

"Humor an old man, Miss Crowe," he said with a self-deprecating chuckle. "I'd like to know if the stories are true.

Can you do it? Can you make contact with the beyond?"

I huffed, thinking I'd wasted my time. "I don't do seances, if that's what you're after. Find a teller with good reviews on Yelp."

"I'm looking for the real thing."

I pursed my lips. "And who told you that was me?"

"An old associate."

"Who? People shouldn't be talking."

"Neither should I."

I twirled the iron coin in my fingers and frowned. I didn't like that strangers knew my intimate business. And he was searching for more. Between my fingers rapping the table and the other hand toying with the coin, the old man took every opportunity to snoop. I had a feeling he didn't miss a detail.

"No rings on your fingers, I see."

I slammed the coin to the table before he remarked on my age. The sudden clap made him twitch. "Keep this about the job and the money," I warned, "or I walk."

The big guy with the sunglasses spit out the toothpick and grumbled. He puffed his chest out or sucked his gut in —I couldn't tell which—and approached with a sneer. Pure intimidation, plain and simple.

Lambert allowed the charade to play out an extra second or two. I was unfazed, my eyes never leaving the old man's. He was testing how cool I was under pressure, and I didn't disappoint.

My potential client raised a hand. "That will be enough, Grady."

The big baby stopped and crossed his arms, revealing a Celtic cross tattoo just below one glove. I'd seen animists wear similar runes relating to their true origins, but this meathead was miles away from that meaning.

"Never mind the true believer," tempered Lambert, catching my gaze. "They do good work for me."

I nodded like it was nothing, eager to get a move on. "The job."

The old man rested his elbows on the table and steepled his fingers. "Yes. What do you know about the Crown of Aevum?"

I pocketed the coin, pulling my unzipped leather jacket open and revealing the Led Zeppelin T-shirt underneath. "I haven't heard of it, but I know the Latin."

Look up aevum in Google Translate and it'll tell you it means age, but that ignores the Latin's philosophical roots. The word has a connotation of aging eternally. Or living forever.

Lambert's eyebrows shot up. "I'm surprised you aren't aware of such a crown in the city. It's surmised to have been worn by two popes. I was under the impression holy relics were your bread and butter."

I cleared my throat to cover my discomfort. There had been a time, back when I played sidekick to my father, when I specialized in antiquities. But that was Dad's deal. I was alone now, and a girl had to put food on the table.

"Sorry to disappoint you," I answered coolly, "but I don't care if the crown's made of gold or cardboard stamped with a Burger King logo. I can get it for you if the price is right."

The skinhead woman narrowed heavily painted eyes. Lambert only chuckled. "All business. I appreciate that. I'll get right to it, then. Tomorrow night, a foreign dilettante is throwing an upscale soiree in a high-rise hotel. Important people will be attending. Investors, well-to-dos, you know the type."

He said all this as if he weren't the type, which was interesting given his apparent means.

"The host of this party likes to show off," he continued, "and everyone knows the true show of wealth isn't money, but access. Who you know. Where you go." Lambert leaned forward. "What you acquire."

"The crown's on display?"

"His own personal museum. The private viewing room is located centrally in the hotel room. The walls are custom built, with barred windows. It's a small space, maybe fifty square feet, not much more than a cage, really. There's a single entrance, leaving only one way in, and one way out."

"A safe room," I said.

He nodded. "The only object in the room is a central pillar with a velvet pillow. Resting on top is a crown of golden laurel leaves."

"And how do you know all this?"

Lambert's eyes flashed. "Because I attended last week's soiree."

So, my client considered himself a well-to-do after all. I cocked my head. "The room itself shouldn't be a problem. It would be more secure without windows, barred or otherwise. What's the tech situation? Where are the cameras?"

"I'm afraid that's where I'll be relying on your expertise. An old man's eyes aren't what they used to be." He smiled, suddenly a model grandfather.

I didn't buy the doddering act but this was what I signed up for. "I can work with that. What *can* you tell me?"

"There's a full security detail. At the elevators, and in the hall at the front door. Everyone going inside the room is vetted. Absolutely no entry without a proper invitation. The good news is, the host doesn't want his guests harassed. Besides a guard at the door to the cage, they remain outside." He turned to the woman. "Teegan?"

She walked over and placed a paper on the table. It had an address and a room number. It also had a name: Ahmad Kahn.

"And the offer?" I asked.

"One hundred thousand. Double that if you vet the crown's authenticity."

"I'm not an expert, Lambert."

"No, Shyla Crowe, but I'm relying on your ability to *contact* one."

I sighed. He really believed this thing was real, and he wanted me to check with the entities who might know.

"For my money," he added, "I expect any insight you can glean."

Which would require an extra ritual after the heist was done. I bit down. Depending on the forces at play, that might be the hard part of the job. But I'd do what I could, within reason. How far he wanted to go didn't concern me.

I wasn't making Faustian deals over mythology.

"I'll look into it and let you know if the price is fair," I said, which was part of my usual due diligence. "Who am I stealing from?"

"Someone who deserves it."

I flinched at the words that were practically snatched from my thoughts. It was one of my rules. I didn't steal from anyone who didn't have it coming. Not that I was a patron saint of righting wrongs or whatever, but pocketing someone's life savings didn't sit right with me. So I preyed on scumbags and outlaws and predatory business people. Bonus points if they were involved in criminal activity. Lambert had done his homework on me.

"Mr. Kahn is a secretive host. An expert in speaking generalities without revealing anything at all. He doesn't say it, but everyone knows what he is: spoiled Arab royalty who flaunts his wealth at every opportunity."

"Right. Showy." Which made him a prime target. Even if he happened to be a good person, he was rich enough to shrug off the loss. That was good enough for me. "The party's tomorrow. After it ends, does the crown stay in the room overnight?"

Lambert shook his head once. "I don't know."

"Is it already there now?"

"I don't know."

"Do we have any intel on where the crown is other than when it's on display?"

"We don't and it doesn't matter," he stressed, "because you're going to steal it as the guests are leaving."

Talk about showy. "That's an unnecessary risk."

"It's quite necessary, I'm afraid. It's the only time we know precisely where the Crown of Aevum is, and Mr. Kahn could hop on a jet and disappear the next morning. But there's more to it than that. When someone of such importance loses something so valuable, it's not the money that vexes them, but the affront."

"You're talking about payback," I said. "They'll never know it was me."

"I'm counting on that. Throughout the night, our host will take his guests to the crown room, one by one. As the festivities end, he sees them all out at once, all the way down to the ground floor, for a final sendoff. I want the crown stolen in that precise window, before he returns to his room to lock it down."

I cracked a smile. "He'll assume one of the night's guests lifted it."

"More importantly, he won't suspect any of his guests from the previous week."

I nodded. It was classic misdirection, with the added benefit of not casting any specific person as the patsy. "It's a workable plan, but it comes with increased risks. We don't know what the guards are doing after the guests leave."

"I'll pay extra, of course, if you need to put someone down."

"I'm not a killer," I said firmly enough that he wouldn't ask again. Apparently Lambert hadn't done all his homework on me. This was the biggest line I drew. I was a thief, not a murderer.

He took a measured breath. "Well, I'll leave that to you. The compensation is there, if it comes to it."

But I knew it wouldn't. I'd be invisible, moving in and out like a ghost. "Sounds like we have a deal."

We stood and shook hands. Teegan led Lambert from the warehouse, but the bear of a biker lingered as the car outside started. Grady sneered at me. I crossed my arms and waited for his petty posturing to end. A troupe of Harley motorcycles roared to life, announcing the club's readiness to depart.

The biker pointed at me. "You be good now, you hear?" He backed up like I had a gun on him before turning and exiting the warehouse.

I shook my head idly, wondering why I subjected myself to these people. The engines outside blared, combining into a unison of buffeted screams, and then faded into the distance like a speeding tornado.

From the shadows of the warehouse interior, radiating golden eyes blinked open. A beast stepped out on all fours, demonic face and angled horn stubs catching the light. His body, clawed hands, leathery wings, and serpentine tail were made of stone.

"You should've let me kill him," he grumbled.

"That's what you always say, Bernard."

"Are you trying to stifle my feelings? Because it sounds like you're trying to stifle my feelings."

I snickered. Bernard was a hellion. His preferred conflict-resolution methods tended toward the extreme, but I was his summoner and he was loyal to me. In other words, he was all talk. Kind of like a lovable dog. A big, three-hundred-pound demon of a dog.

Links of chain rattled through metal, sliding loose and hitting the pavement. My eyes shot to the open sliding door. "Bernard!" The gargoyle slunk back into the shadows so he wouldn't be seen.

I stomped over as a single engine started. By the time I hit sunlight the skinhead woman was straddling her Harley, watching me over her shoulder. She winked blue lashes, flicked her helmet shut, and gunned it down the street to catch up to her crew.

I scowled, eyes dashing to my black Ducati. A piece of paper flapped in the wind, pinned under my helmet. I snatched it and read, "Nice bike." On the flip side was a contact number.

I hissed, wondering how much she'd seen. It was delicate work, being a summoner for hire, but a girl with my upbringing didn't have a lot of options. It was either this or shovel beauty products on Facebook.

The Hotel

The Ducati Monster hummed between my thighs as I navigated the downtown streets. The Stealth trim sported a matte-black body and components, with stylized red and gray accents. It was a naked bike, stripped down and minimalist, known as a modern cafe racer.

Despite the impressive horsepower and torque, the 821 was the mid-level model. I was a small girl who relied more on zip and maneuverability than raw output at the track. As it was I didn't get enough opportunities to take the Monster out of urban mode.

I parked at a meter on Olive Street across from the historic Commercial Exchange Building. I killed the engine and rested on the bike, taking my helmet off and then my calfskin riding gloves so I could manage my phone and do a little intel gathering.

The old office building was now a newly restored boutique hotel. Their website didn't include mention of special exhibition or event spaces, but I did note the top floor had enlarged suites with open floor plans. It was possible our upscale host had temporarily converted the space to a showroom.

I also searched for news of famous royalty or expensive antiquities in town, but didn't come up with anything. That wasn't much of a surprise. Although these guys flaunted their wealth and were the opposite of low-key, the circles they ran in were so exclusive that the non-elites like us barely got a whiff of them.

Instead I sent a text message. "Need some background." Then I listed the basics of what I had. Ahmad Khan, the crown, and the hotel. With that, I slipped the phone in my back pocket, popped a couple of quarters into the meter, and crossed the street into the belly of the beast.

Most of the ground floor was a well-lit bar with mid-century wicker chairs and numerous plants lining the broad windows. A cozy reception area was tucked off to the side, blending into the same space but with a separate entrance. That suited me since I wasn't planning on announcing myself.

Still, the location posed some difficulties. The downtown area had been revitalized over the last ten years. Even at night, the streets would see generous foot traffic. Hotels were regular with people coming and going at all hours, and bars attracted even more within my precise time window.

I made my way to the elevators tucked in the far wall. Just for kicks I pressed the button for thirteen. It was Khan's floor. The button's glow immediately went black as I released it, which meant a key card swipe was needed to unlock hotel access. Not one to be put off, I found the single button above the top floor labeled "Broken Shaker." The elevator accepted the input and carried me to the roof.

The door opened to sunlight and a skyline of buildings. I followed the elevator wall around to the attached tiki bar, the only structure on the roof. Beyond were tables with pink umbrellas and a rooftop pool deck with pink lounge chairs.

"Hey there!" called a bright voice behind the bar. "Can I get you something?" She slid a menu my way.

There was only one guest sitting at the bar, a man in a Hawaiian shirt and flip-flops watching a video on his phone. Probably temporary respite from the wife and kids at the pool. The bartender was waiting on me and I didn't want to make a lasting impression, so I sidled up to the bar and picked the first thing on the menu.

As she made my drink I eyed the pool area. A young couple sunbathed. Two families played in the water. An older woman with a straw hat read a book. The roof was a nice midday escape, though a little busy for my tastes.

"Here's your trash-tini," said the bartender, placing the stemmed glass on the bar.

I paid in cash. The drink looked like a martini, with a toothpick spearing an olive and cocktail onion. The gin and vodka mix was strong and had a distinct smoked flavor. I nodded thanks and wandered away with an idle taste. As soon as she turned around, I slipped past the bar area and followed the small structure around to the lonely corner of the rooftop.

I was finally out of sight.

I sipped my drink and leaned against the wall with a sigh. My phone buzzed and I checked the text message from Trap.

"I'm guessing you want a rush on this?"

Trap was my computer guy. He got me background, papers, and various little things I needed. The fact he was following up with a timetable meant he hadn't found much at first glance. I was confident he'd come back later with something solid. I replied, "That's what I pay you for."

Background was invaluable, but some things required a personal touch. I moved to the edge of the roof and waved my arm. The smell of sulfur drifted on the breeze. A face resembling a monstrous bat peeked over the building's outside wall. Bernard's wings were tucked over his back as he gripped the building's brick with four paws.

"This is a lovely perch," he remarked, gazing at the open sky. "I rarely do building hopping these days."

I leaned over the edge to peek down but it was a hard thing. The walls were built to discourage that sort of behavior. "I need you to get a look in the windows down there. See what we're dealing with. It should be a loft with a central safe room. And watch out, there might be guards."

The gargoyle glared. "My senses are more acute than yours. I heard the details the first time."

"Just a friendly warning."

"If anyone needs a warning it's—"

Bernard ducked below the lip of the wall as a woman strolled around the corner. I was still holding my phone, so I picked it up to my mouth like it was on speaker.

"Okay," I said loudly, "talk to you later."

The woman's eyes followed the tiki bar's wall behind me to the edge of the building. It was straw-hat lady, the one who'd been reading a book by the pool. "I'm sorry," she said, slightly put off. "I thought the elevator was here."

I hiked a thumb backward. "Other side."

"Ah, thank you." She lingered a nosy moment before moving on.

I toyed with my phone a few minutes, knowing the gargoyle was already scoping the rooms. As his summoner, I needed to be in his vicinity. It was sort of like a leash, albeit a long one. It was smart to keep hellions on leashes. They tended to garner a lot of attention when left on their own.

Bernard had free rein to easily circle the building. The real trouble were the cars and pedestrians below. Luckily, this edge of the building was flush with a low parking garage, and its roof was empty. Bernard returned as I was finishing my drink.

"The room's on the corner overlooking Olive," he said, pointing toward the pool opposite the bar. "Three men with guns inside, but no royalty. I saw the safe room. It had drapes over the windows so I couldn't confirm the crown was there."

My lips crooked. "The men have to be guarding something."

"My thoughts exactly. And I found a way in. That end of the building has a series of metal balconies."

"I saw those when I parked," I said. "They're just for show. Or maybe they were functional in 1924. I don't know.

I wouldn't stand on one of those things now."

"Don't be a baby."

"They're not fire escapes. There's no ladders connecting them. We don't know if the windows even open."

He shrugged. "The street's too visible to come from the ground, but that end of the rooftop is closed off to house air conditioning compressors. It's just a little hop over the edge."

I scoffed. "Easy for you to say. You have wings."

"And you, my dear, have a gargoyle. As for the window, I can take a closer look during the night."

I worked my jaw. A broken window was a sign of forced entry, which would point to an outside suspect rather than a guest from within. I was gonna need to find a way to work around that. Maybe, if I threw a rope down from inside, it would look like one of the party guests lowered the crown to an accomplice on the street.

As far as a plan, that was probably as good as it was gonna get without further information.

"See you back at the house," I said. I dismissed Bernard with a wave of my arm. He broke apart into a wash of black ashes that caught in an updraft and spread across the sky.

Home Sweet Home

I lived in an industrial section of Downtown currently undergoing a renaissance and now known as the Arts District. My building used to be an old bread factory. Like the Commercial Exchange Building, everything around was getting trendy makeovers and second lives. Within a short walk I had a go-to wine bar, coffee roaster, and brunch spot that made A1 crepes. Still, the functional chic came packaged with streets that were as gritty as ever. These days, that authenticity was part of the allure.

My building was six stories high and I was on the top floor. Aaron waited in the hall by the front door of my loft.

I froze, panic turning into guilt. "One o'clock," I said sheepishly.

He flashed a dry smile while his head cocked to his watch. "One fourteen, actually."

I huffed. "I'm sorry, Aaron. I was just planning on picking up a job but decided to scope the place out at the last second. I thought I had time."

"Then why do you look so surprised?" He straightened, holding a bottle wrapped in a brown paper bag. "I'm guessing you forgot about our custodial meeting completely."

My eyelids fluttered, verging on a full roll. Our boss had code names for us. I was the Handler, a reference to my skills with hellions. Aaron was the Custodian. He took care of the money and coordinated the various team members. He even managed city connections in the rare case we needed them. There were others. The Lead was our actress, when a job called for the role of a beautiful woman. The Wire was our technician. It went on and on like that.

The code names were a way to insulate us from each other. Each operator had their own job and we were called on as needed, all parts of the greater whole. It was a stupid formality but it served its purpose. I didn't know most of their names, and they didn't know mine.

Aaron was the exception. Other operators came and went, but the Custodian was the foundation of our group. We'd worked together so closely that we'd shared moments of raw honesty, even when it was against the rules. He was Aaron Scott and I was Shyla Crowe, but in front of the others it was the Custodian and the Handler.

Aaron had soft gray eyes and a long face that some might associate with rugged handsomeness. A strong nose and jaw capped with a cleft chin. His eyebrows were intense, and he styled his brown hair in a modern wave. Even his wire glasses were worn well.

That said, Aaron was anything but rugged and outgoing.

He acted more lawyerly than spontaneous, always cool and collected. He never went anywhere without a button-up shirt. He wore a jacket when it was cold but usually skipped it in the daytime. The tie was hit or miss. Today he sported a silk number with a forest print. It was clear by looking at him that he was the guy who crossed the Ts and dotted the Is.

"Welcome to my humble abode," I said, pushing open the oversize door.

The industrial loft was large and stylish. High ceilings with exposed pipes and air ducts decorated with hanging lights, concrete pillars and finishing, and large steel windows across the back wall. It was a place of modern lines, its cold aesthetic sharply contrasting with the ample sunlight streaming in. It was one of only three units in the building with a private patio balcony, which spanned the entire length of the loft and overlooked a community pool.

The open floor plan meant the kitchen and dining room were in one corner and the couches in another, with only a bookshelf divider separating my bedroom. For most, it would be nineteen hundred square feet of paradise, but for me it was just a place to work.

"I was wondering," I said as I headed to the kitchen, "why don't we ever meet at your place?"

Aaron snickered and looked around. "My skill set doesn't warrant a spacious luxury loft, apparently."

He said it like he was annoyed, but it was a common game we played. He knew the loft wasn't mine. According to the deed, it was owned by a gravel company headquartered in the mountains. Part of the Custodian's job was handling construction contracts for Bedrock, the code name for our boss.

Yes, that meant I didn't even know who I worked for. More on that later.

I pulled two wine glasses off the rack and set them on the glass dining table. "What are we celebrating?"

He paused, dumbfounded. I nodded to the bag in his hands, from which he pulled a bottle of red. "A Zinfandel from Paso Robles." He handed me the bottle so I could admire the label. I handed it back to him along with the corkscrew.

As he opened the bottle, I trudged over to the bedroom on the other side of the loft. There was a steel safe in the wall alongside the master bathroom. Despite the open space, Aaron respected my privacy when I went into the bedroom. It was a little gesture I appreciated, and not just because I didn't want anyone peeking at the combination safe while I opened it.

Most of the stuff I kept here related to my work or my craft. Iron coins, pendants, and other trinkets. Various fake IDs, documentation, and books. Some spare tools of the trade, like lockpicks. Stuff I didn't want anyone else seeing.

I zipped open an empty leather handbag and loaded it with two five-inch stacks of cash. Two hundred thousand dollars, just like that. I sighed at my remaining reserve funds: not even an inch of money. This was the first time in a year and a half that I didn't have next month's payment already in hand. Which wasn't an emergency. It just meant I needed a sure score this month. The Crown of Aevum only got me halfway unless I could verify it was the real deal.

I zipped the bag, locked the safe, and returned to the table, setting the money bag down beside a newly poured glass of Zin. We raised a toast and drank.

"What do you do with all that money, anyway?" I asked.

Aaron didn't bother looking inside the bag to count it. He'd long ago stopped worrying about my ability to pay the monthly sum, which had started at fifty grand but worked its way up to two hundred as I proved my ability to pay. No good deed goes unpunished, and I was very good.

"You know I can't tell you that," he said.

"I know."

I wandered to the windowed back wall. Beside my wine cooler and glass rack was a media center with a vintage wood-framed record player. I slid open a drawer and leafed through the sleeves.

"Day-drinking goes better with music, don't you think?"

I dropped the needle on the record and the signature sounds of Bob Dylan came through the Sonos speakers scattered throughout the loft.

"An oldie but a goodie," I said with a sigh.

The vinyl collection and player were my mother's. I had never met her, and my father hadn't been big on music, so it was up to me to carry the torch. It was an act of reverence by me, to surround myself with the same songs that had once enraptured my mother. I grew up referring to this stuff as classic rock, but nowadays that meant Nirvana and the Pixies.

Crazy how the world slowly changes, and all the while I was stuck.

I took a big gulp of wine, killing off the starter glass and returning to the table for an encore.

Aaron pressed his lips tight in concern. "Shyla, do you really not know what we're celebrating?"

"What, two hundred K doesn't cut it anymore?" I finished my pour and topped off his glass too.

He nodded in thanks and held the glass before me. "We're starting a new year together. Our tenth."

I set the bottle back on the table a little too loudly. The glass rang out, and I blinked, eyes scrunching. "That can't be right." I leaned against the tabletop and did the math. "But somehow it is. This is the anniversary of our ninth year in business."

He clinked his glass to mine, since I wasn't doing it. "I prefer to see it as the start of a new year. Number ten. The beginning of the end. We have just over a million dollars left to pay off. At this rate, you'll have that in five months."

I sat in silence, aghast at having the finish line in sight. Because the surface of this was simple. Aaron and I were operators and Bedrock was our employer. But the truth was much more grim, and I wasn't sure it could ever end.

You see, my mother may have been dead, but my father wasn't yet. Not exactly. He was trapped in Hell and I was in hock over his debts. Which meant the surface of our employer-employee relationship with Bedrock was a lie.

The truth was, this was our ninth anniversary in servitude to a demon.

Debt

The biggest burden in life is family. Don't let anyone tell you different.

My dad started me off early. Paulson Crowe was a collector of antiquities, but as he couldn't afford to buy them he turned to thievery. He taught me a lot. How to get into a locked room, how to move unseen. He taught me the value of money and other people's stupidity. Most of all, he taught me the importance of knowledge and control.

My father's collection was ephemeral, often being sold off to fund the next acquisition. He began taking money to obtain hard-to-get items for investors. It was an exciting cat-and-mouse game, flying around the globe in high-stakes heists and subterfuge. Paulson was a stern man but not a severe one, expecting the best from me not out of cruelty but because it was vital to our professional survival. It wasn't a warm relationship but I loved him.

My father was the type of guy who never blamed his innocent daughter for her mother dying in childbirth. The kind of guy who fought tooth and nail for me, no matter what. It was just the two of us most of my life. And it was only in recent years that I began to wonder if it was me that had been the burden.

But now it was my turn to pay the Piper.

In my early twenties, my dad disappeared. I still wasn't sure exactly what had happened, but it was clear he started messing with forces he didn't fully comprehend. It's a bad cliche, for summoners to get into trouble with demons. There were good hellions like Bernard who you could count on not to screw you over. There were bad ones you had to meticulously protect yourself against, as when handling a loaded weapon. And then there were those whose names should never be uttered aloud.

At first, Paulson vanished without a trace. For years I continued working, taking whatever jobs would pay the bills, afraid for my life and staying under the radar.

Until one day I was found.

Maybe it was inevitable as my skills leveled up, or maybe it was a chance meeting with a stranger that did it, but I was tracked down and cornered by a demon named Bedrock. And he had a lot to talk about.

At some point, my father had crossed a line. He wasn't dead but he was the demon's captive in Hell. I saw it with my own eyes. That was all it took, and from that moment on I was in hock to a demon.

Trust me, when it comes to debts, none are worse than those of your father. Doomed by conception, I never had a chance to be responsible for myself. To be my own person.

But that could soon change, in a matter of months and with a number of dollars shoveled to fund whatever malicious empire Bedrock orchestrated. And that was terrifying to me.

Because the only way I'd gone on so long was by compartmentalizing absolutely everything. Putting my head down and doing the jobs. I was the Handler. I couldn't afford to care where the money was going, or who the other operators were, or what Bedrock had on them.

I didn't even know anything about Bedrock himself. Demons often changed names and countenances and specialized in subterfuge. It was more difficult to fight an enemy you didn't know.

But now that I was on the cusp of freeing Paulson Crowe, of absolving the sins of the father, I was forced to consider all the moving parts as a functioning whole. I had to blow up all the compartments, all the walls, and put the jagged pieces together in a way that started to make sense.

In the end, could I really trust a devil to make good on his deal?

"I—" stammered Aaron. "I'm sorry. It was a mistake to bring it up. I thought you'd be happy."

Dylan crooned, "The times they are a-changin'," and I sighed.

"It's not you, Aaron. I'm just being confronted by my life's choices all at once."

He stood awkwardly close to me, obviously uncomfortable by my sudden mood change, not knowing what to say. Even after a glass of wine, Aaron couldn't loosen up. I gave him a good-natured shove in the chest. He moved a little less than I'd expected, and my hand encountered solid muscle.

I cleared my throat. "It's my professional opinion that you need another glass of wine."

He chuckled but didn't move for the bottle.

It was weird. In the past I'd always been into outwardly tough guys. Maybe it was packaged with my bandit lifestyle, a two-for-one deal. Trouble was, over time, most of the outlaws I met were more like this morning's heavy-handed biker.

Aaron was a sort of put-together everyman, which was a little boring for my tastes if I was being honest. Not that I had time for my tastes. I put that stuff behind me a long time ago. Real relationships, like the rest of my life, seemed unrecoverable.

"You okay, Custodian?" I asked with a soft smile. "Need another shove?"

I didn't remember having been physical with him before. Admittedly the trash-tini at the bar was a lot stronger than I'd assumed, but it didn't seem like something to fret over. But instead of having loosened him up, he scratched the back of his neck uneasily. I caught sight of a block of metal in his right hand, and I realized it was part of his ring.

"Is that a signet ring?" I asked. "How come I've never noticed that before?"

Aaron shoved his hand to his side. The ring I'd often seen on his right ring finger was turned upside down, with the blocky flat end in his palm. He set his nearly empty glass of wine on the table and fingered the ring with a frown.

"I shouldn't talk about it," he said.

I drew back and shook my head, unsure how to respond.

"It's not that I don't trust you, Shyla." He frowned momentarily. "The ring is a reminder of my wife."

And I had a new moment of clarity. The Custodian was a victim too, of course. I was the one with the hellions, but he helped work off our mutual debt in his own way.

"I... I'm sorry," I said. Then I swallowed. "Did she die?"

He shook his head once.

"Is she... like my father?"

He gave a curt nod, making it clear we weren't supposed to be talking about this. But then, we'd already traded our names and little bits about each other in the past. Bedrock wasn't an all-knowing entity, after all.

Aaron cleared his throat. "I know about the records, your mother's things, but do you keep something to remind you of your father?"

I hiked my shoulders and set my glass on the table. I wanted to mention the book. It felt wrong not to tell him the truth in this tender moment. But we were all obligated to Bedrock, and I didn't want Aaron on the hook for withholding information for my benefit.

"This job is my reminder," I said drily.

We both stared at the floor. It was a moment even Bob Dylan couldn't salvage. Always punctual, Aaron checked his watch.

"I need to get moving," he said, and I nodded quick agreement. "You said you picked up a job?"

Which was the way it usually worked. I had a debt to pay off, but it was up to me to come up with the money. It was only rarely that Bedrock or one of the other operators brought something to me.

"A supposed crown of immortality being shown off by a Middle Eastern royal," I answered. "Some old man who kind of reminds me of my father if he was rich and heartless and ten years older." I wasn't sure why I'd added that last part. It hadn't been a conscious thought, but I supposed it had to do with the intensity and love of antiquities. "He wants me to lift it from a cocktail party."

"A party? We should put the Lead on it."

The Lead was an expert in social engineering, otherwise known as soshing. If someone needed to be flattered, schmoozed, and distracted, it was her who did it.

I clicked my tongue. "I don't think there's a need to cut Blondie in."

"Please, Shyla, there's enough money to go around."

I was friends with Aaron but didn't want to advertise how empty I was. Call it professional pride. "It's not that. The heist is after the party ends, and I'll stay out of sight the whole time. It should be a quick hotel job tomorrow night."

Aaron's face tightened. "That's not a lot of time."

"What can I do? The client set it up for me to steal the thing from the party to cast suspicion on the guests. It pays well." Which was all that really mattered, he knew. "Don't worry, I already put Trap on it."

At his mention, Aaron frowned. I wasn't supposed to work with operators outside the group, and it was the

Custodian's job to coordinate operators. But Trap was an old friend. From before. I trusted him even if it made Aaron uncomfortable. Besides, what didn't make him uncomfortable? As long as Bedrock didn't get wind of particulars and got his money, we were golden.

"Just be careful with him," warned Aaron. "I still haven't met him."

"That's a good thing," I reminded, both of us knowing why.

"It's just hard to trust a guy who doesn't meet face-to-face."

"Is that why you're here in person? Checking me out face-to-face?"

He smiled. "That and our employer doesn't like direct deposit."

My jaw instinctively clenched. In a professional setting, in front of other operators, I had no problem calling Bedrock my employer, but here, after talking about my father and Aaron's wife... He was a full-on devil.

"The last million," nudged Aaron, recognizing my anger. "That's all we need, and then we're free."

"And then we're free," I repeated, but I wasn't sure I believed it.

Josalie

I opened the door to let Aaron out and he stopped short of walking into my neighbor. Josalie wasn't so deft on her feet. She slammed face-first into his tie. Her arms splayed out, having just barely saved a cupcake from certain destruction in the collision.

"I'm sorry," hurried Aaron.

"My pleasure," said Josalie, pulling back with a lingering hand on his upper arm. "Tom, right?"

Josalie Cruz was my friend, but she wasn't allowed to know Aaron's real name or his code name. He'd introduced himself once as Tom and I've had to stick with it since.

"Wow," she drawled, giving his arm a pinch or three. "Don't think I can't see those biceps you're hiding under there."

Aaron was uncomfortable, as always, so I stepped in to help him out. "Don't harass my associates, Josalie. Tom was just leaving."

Her eyes widened with mischief. "Don't go on my

account. I'll come back later. Put a sock on the doorknob so I know when to knock."

I pushed Aaron out the door before I turned beet red. "See you later," I peeped. He turned, unsure what to say, but I shut the door before the moment got weirder.

Josalie burst into laughter that I was sure Aaron could hear. I flashed intense eyes, grabbed her by the shoulder, and dragged her to the living room. "You love to embarrass me," I said curtly.

"I'm not embarrassing you, honey, I'm helping you! You need to have a little fun in this life. You mean to tell me that man comes around your place like clockwork and hasn't made a move on you yet?"

"It's not like that."

Josalie had a strong personality. She was a heavyset Filipina with a sunny disposition and a dirty mind.

"I don't accept that," she said. "That man is too proper. You know what he needs? For you to rip his shirt off, pull down his pants, and give him a sloppy blowjob. You know, just slobber all over him and your hands. He'll love you forever."

I could barely breathe through my constricted throat, half out of laughter but the other half fearing Aaron was listening at the door. "You're not working today?" I asked, if only to change the subject.

Josalie was a nurse, which was actually how we'd met five years ago. With my arm in a cast, we chatted in the hospital and discovered we lived in the same building. We'd been fast friends ever since.

She wasn't like me very much. In fact, she was the polar opposite. I think that's why we got along.

"Of course I don't work today, girl. It's Glada's birthday."

I immediately remembered, in case the cupcake in her hand wasn't clue enough. I didn't remember who Glada was, but that was par for the course because Josalie attended a *lot* of birthday parties. She had a huge extended family. It was always a cousin or sibling or relative or something.

"Sorry," I started, feeling like I was apologizing a lot today.

Josalie swiped her hand in the air. "Don't even worry, girl. I know how you're always getting up to stuff. I didn't bother calling when I didn't hear from you. But I saved you this."

I took the cupcake with an appreciative smile. It smelled like caramel espresso. "You're the best."

"I know I am." She pulled out a joint and a lighter. "Believe me, I know how you feel. There are a lot of kids in my home right now. Mind if I smoke this here?"

"Knock yourself out," I mumbled, half the cupcake in my mouth.

Josalie strutted to the window and swung a panel open, taking a drag of the joint and watching the record spin. "You know this is some white people music, right?"

I smiled and nodded. "You're damn right."

She laughed. "Okay, as long as you know that. You want a hit?"

"I'm good."

I finished off the party favor, went to the kitchen to wipe my hands and mouth, and made a pit stop at the table for another glass of wine.

"Drinking early," teased Josalie.

"You smell like tequila."

"I'm at a party."

"You're hiding from a party while smoking pot."

I joined her at the window and she shrugged. "Just wanted to check in on my bestie."

She knew I hated that word. But she was my best friend, more or less. And a very normal friend. She had a husband and kids and a job. Not only did she know I was into some shady stuff, she knew better than to ask about it.

"You have too many windows in this house," she said after blowing smoke outside. "Aren't you afraid of people looking in?"

"No one can see at this angle. And the windows are tinted."

"But what about if I wanna sunbathe topless?"

"Stay low?"

"Screw it. I have other things to worry about. Like Tom." She winked. "Do you ever catch him looking at you? You think he thinks you're cute?"

"Ugh," I scoffed. "The best way to piss me off is to call me cute."

"What?"

"I get it. I'm five feet tall. My lips aren't full enough, my breasts aren't big enough. Guys think I have a pretty face, go with cute, and call it a day."

She laughed. "What's wrong with that?"

"I don't wanna be cute. I wanna be hot. A stunner. A bombshell."

"Ooh, you wanna be *sex-say*." Josalie puffed her chest out as she said it. She didn't dress glamorously and was pretty well covered up, but she knew how to move her body. "Don't worry. You definitely make a statement in those biker leathers. It was the first thing I noticed about you. Those giant boots."

I chuckled. "Keeps the douchebags at bay."

"That and never smiling," she said. "I can't believe you're complaining. I wish guys told me I was cute."

"They'd be crazy not to." Josalie was a working mother of two kids, and definitely overweight, but she was pretty, with slightly chubby cheeks and those full lips I was just yearning for. Most striking were her eyes and eyebrows which she painted sharply.

"Nope," said Josalie after an extended toke, "all guys say is I'm cool."

I shook my head. "Cool is good. All I get is bitchy."

"Because you don't smile," she teased. "And, you know, you could ease up a bit sometimes."

"Fuck that."

We giggled like teenagers for a minute. I sipped wine to the music until I got a phone call.

"I gotta take this," I said, walking away.

"No problem." She extinguished her joint. "Mind if I use the bathroom?"

I waved her to my bedroom, which was the much nicer

bathroom she was gonna use anyway, and answered the phone on the way to the couch. This was the call I'd been waiting for.

Trap finally had some answers.

Trap

"Tell me something I wanna hear," I said into the phone.

My couch was a low-slung sectional with thick-woven white fabric. I hugged one of the oversize pillows like it was a giant teddy bear.

"What is that?" he asked. "Dylan?"

"You can recognize that from two seconds of music?"

"The man's voice is unmistakable."

"I just didn't think you'd know him."

Trap chuckled. "I'm a Renaissance man, Shyla."

"You're a boy. You're too young for Dylan."

"So are you."

I smiled. "Okay, that's one thing I wanna hear. Hold on." I pulled the phone from my ear and went into the music app to lower the volume. But not too much. "Back to business."

"I got you."

I didn't know about Renaissance man, but Trap was quite a character. His personality fit his voice, smooth and low. He was an old soul.

"So the first hit is our royal," he said. "I checked local airports for arrivals and purchased some hacked manifests. It's not the kind of thing that's advertised so it's no surprise I couldn't find anything. But Ahmad Khan is an alias, as I suspected. The name's commonly used by one Prince Fahd Al-Assaf of the House of Saud."

"A Saudi prince, huh?"

"Through and through. But don't get put off by the label. The family is fifteen thousand strong, and most of them don't have meaningful power. I'd say Al-Assaf sits just on the cusp between the haves and have-nots."

"I don't know if you can call even a poor Saudi prince a have-not."

"Fair enough. So Al-Assaf, he used to come around all the time, treating our country like his own personal Disneyland. A few years ago he supposedly sexually assaulted a staff member of his swank New York hotel. He flew the coop before formal charges were brought up and hasn't been around since."

"Until now."

"Hey, money buys a lot of forgiveness."

Access, I thought, remembering Lambert's words. Okay, this mark definitely deserved a little burglary. "Wouldn't a prince be staying in a more exclusive hotel?"

"I did think that was odd. Guys like this prefer uber-exclusive joints the business refers to as six-star hotels. Thing is, these hotels share a blacklist. You see, one guy's money is never enough to counter all the rest of the money they're making from everyone else. They need to keep the peace."

"And their reputations," I added.

"There might also be something in it for him. So as to avoid another international incident, Assaf's been keeping a low profile for years. Maybe staying at smaller boutique hotels keeps him under the radar. Who knows how long he's been doing it?"

I nodded. We weren't likely to dig up a lot of details on a Saudi prince who avoided the spotlight. I was half surprised we got a real name.

"I also dug up some pictures," he said. "Some from his last-known visit. They're part of the packet of files I'll send over after we talk."

"What about the Crown of Aevum?"

"This one's a miss as far as specifics. No matches for the Latin name applying to a crown or wreath. It could be a new title that sounds old. Something forgers like to do.

"That said, crowns of immortality are old concepts. The idea's usually metaphorical. Religious stuff. There are also a lot of jumbled meanings depending on which culture you're looking at. Laurel crowns have been associated with Greek gods, Charlemagne, Napoleon—you name it. The Romans awarded them as triumphs in sports or the arts. Some even considered them the ultimate triumph over death." He took a breath, probably ticking down his list of notes. "Christians, too, associate the symbol with the resurrection of Jesus."

Trap wasn't telling me anything I didn't already know,

but I paid him for the research and let him disburse it. As he spoke, Josalie exited the bathroom and proceeded to go through the clothes in my closet. She was already high.

"The big takeaway is that these things were huge status symbols. It makes sense why our prince might show his off. You know that saying, resting on your laurels? It comes from this. It means resting on your old achievements."

"Old triumphs," I wondered aloud.

It wasn't a lot to go on. Both the mark and the package were appropriately mysterious. At the same time, the background info tracked enough to be legit. There was a lot of money at play here. Still, we hadn't yet tackled the biggest wildcard in the equation.

"What about the old man?" I asked, waiting for the bomb to drop.

"Lambert Pemberton. He's a cagey type too. Isn't seen in public a lot, but he's a well-known patron of the arts. He owns a compound outside Phoenix."

That struck me as interesting, but not odd. I'd grown up in several places. Phoenix was one of them.

"He sponsors a foundation for young artists, but besides art for art's sake, Lambert's also a collector of antiquities. He owns original canvases and sculptures spanning the Middle Ages and the ancient world. This crown is right up his alley."

"Maybe, but something gives me the feeling his interests are more than scholarly."

"Trap paused a second. "What, like he actually believes the crown has powers?"

I pondered the question a moment. I wasn't sure what I thought. "This thing can't be real, right?"

His voice came through smooth and confident. "Are they ever?"

I snorted. "Right."

Josalie was giggling, and I craned my neck to see what she was up to, but didn't have a clear view through the bookshelf.

"Anyway," finished Trap, "I'll bill you my minimum rate for this one. Besides IDing the prince, nothing was a strain on my network."

"Thanks, Trap."

I knew he was disappointed in the intel, but it was along the lines of what I was hoping for. When it came to scores, surprises weren't good. Normal and boring was the best kind of money.

Josalie must've heard me hang up because she ran out of the bedroom with my bathrobe hooked over her shoulders. The gray silk streamed behind her like a cape. "I never understood what these things were for," she laughed.

But I tuned out her words. "Give me that," I snapped.

I hopped off the couch and tugged the robe away. Josalie's jaw hung open as I marched to the bedroom. My wardrobe doors were flung open, revealing a large standing mirror within. I hurried over, trying not to gaze into the reflection, and threw the bathrobe back over the mirror. After making sure it was properly covered, I shut the doors.

"I'm sorry, Shyla," said an oddly demure Josalie. "You always let me go through your clothes."

"It's nothing," I said, waving a tense hand. But I noticed how crestfallen she was, aware and apologetic that she had crossed a line. I sighed. "Look, don't worry about it, okay? You can go through my closet all you want, but the wardrobe's off-limits. Deal?"

Josalie hiked a shoulder and quickly nodded. I went over and gave her a hug, which she happily reciprocated. When I pulled away, she was smiling like her old self.

"Still besties?" she asked with a smirk.

I rolled my eyes and went in search of my wine glass.

Light Reading

I relaxed for the next hour after Josalie left, and only part of that time was occupied with feeling sorry for myself. I may not have been a bubbling cauldron of optimism, but I didn't wallow in depression either. I was jaded, sure; cynical, you bet your ass; but my feelings strayed toward the practical. If I wasn't going somewhere with it, I left it behind.

By sheer force of will, I drank slow enough to leave half a glass in the bottle. I corked it up and returned to my wall safe. It was no longer crowded with money, but there were some other objects of note. Trinkets personal to me or related to my craft. From the bottom shelf I pulled out a heavy wrap of leather and placed it on the bed.

My loft was stark and modern. The polished concrete floor was cool to the touch. My tight leather pants and riding boots were still on, probably a defense mechanism. All that aside, my king-size bed was the warmest place in the world. I'd splurged on the soft sheets and fluffy blanket. Their orange and brown tones gave the room life.

It was welcome comfort for what I was delving into.

I unfolded the leather and exposed the book. It was old, but not as old as many books of magic. This one was from the nineteen-fifties, created with the utmost precision and care. The pages were of thick stock with gilded edges, bound in the Byzantine style. The hard cover was marbled goatskin. Embossed in gold across the face were the Latin words *Semitas Daemoniorum*, which translated to *The Path of Demons*.

This was a book that was built to last centuries. A modern-day grimoire.

Grimoires are books of magic that often deal in arcane spells, witchcraft, and other occult secrets like the orders of angels and demons. As far as accuracy goes, they're a mixed bag. The first thing you needed to watch out for were the forgeries and fakes. There was a time when these books brought fame and fortune, at least in some circles, and many opportunists crashed the party without an invitation. They didn't know magic, but they sure could spin a tale.

And then you had the dabblers. You know that saying, those that can't do, teach? It was sort of like that. Why promote a book revealing the secrets of the universe if you really know the secrets of the universe?

Lots of grimoires were based on earlier grimoires, outright stealing and changing information to suit the politics of their time. Further problematic was the age of these texts. Just because Decarabia was an archon of Hell in 1577 didn't mean he was still one today.

Which all meant a good summoner needed to be

intimately familiar with the reputable grimoires while taking their combined bodies of knowledge with a hefty grain of salt. Education, as always, involved picking out the truth among the fabrications.

I took a slow breath and reverently opened the cover. The first page had a handwritten name at the top. My grandmother, Estever Crowe.

She had been an accomplished summoner herself, by all accounts better than my father, though much of that was my own speculation. Filling in the blanks between what I'd been told and the little I'd seen. I directly remembered very little of my grandmother. Estever was the sweet old lady who handed me treats or gave me a feather before my father parked me in front of the television and spoke with her on private matters.

I never knew what happened to Estever. She died when I was a kid, and my father never went into details. His name was written below hers. Paulson Crowe had assumed the *Semitas Daemoniorum*.

Below his name was mine, Shyla Crowe, the book's current owner. This was my father's possession that I kept secret, even from Aaron. I couldn't let anybody know I had access to the information within these pages, because unlike many other grimoires, this one was the real deal.

Estever had recognized the failures of the books from the Middle Ages and the liberties taken in their nineteenth-century counterparts. *The Path of Demons* was an attempt to modernize the current thinking, to map out the rings of Hell and their archons, and to pass the secrets down the family line, summoner to summoner. This text would never grace the shelves of a Barnes & Noble. It was for family.

I paged through the planar catalog that opened the book. It explained how our world is the Material Plane, and how there are others.

The High and Low Elemental Planes, sometimes called the Aether and the Nether, are where many summoners get their starts. There are dangers to avoid, as with anything, but summoning airy wisps and earthy spirits is kid stuff. Armed with the proper tools and knowledge, almost anyone can pull it off.

A bit more horrific is the Spectral Plane, but that's mostly because people fear and romanticize death. This is where people go when they die. It's not a permanent destination, though. More like a pit stop before moving on. The Spectral Plane is variably called the Murk; or the Dead Side; or Sheol, Limbo, Purgatory, Barzakh. This one has the most names because it's the closest to the living, almost in reach. People brush against it every waking day.

This is also the plane that inherently belongs to the Earth. Angels and devils have no access to it. It's only for the remnants of those who once lived here, ours and ours alone. So you see, not so scary.

It took a different skill set than mine to contact spirits in the Spectral Plane. I wasn't a necromancer. Besides, I often didn't see the point since spirits didn't linger there. Estever was long gone, and my father was somewhere else entirely.

I paused on the pages of the Abyssal Planes. Hell. This was where things got frightening.

The secret has more or less been out for a while now that Hell consists of nine rings. Each level has its own name, and each one in succession leads deeper.

The first four rings are destinations for humans. It's not really eternal torment so much as a place to reside. These spirits of the dead are in a strange boat: neither accessible by summoners such as myself nor by necromancers channeling the Spectral Plane. When you talk about Aeternus, Erebus, Kur, and Gehenna, you're talking about places like Hades, real lands of the dead.

Which isn't to say proper hellions don't live there too. You'll find as many beings as you take the time to look. Summoners commonly interact with the inhabitants of these realms, each increasing in difficulty and danger.

Stygia is the fifth ring of Hell, and it's a Goldilocks zone: an appropriate mix of foreign and familiar. Not too hot and not too cold. It's full of hellions possessing great power but still similar enough to humans to find common ground. At least you hope.

I didn't do deeper than Stygia. You go deeper and you start getting into the royalty of Hell. The legends.

That said, every ring has its own devil king known as an archon. Even the human rings. Nothing stops hellions from playing in the human territories and nothing stops humans from descending deeper. I didn't know where my father was, but after all my searching, I knew he had to be deeper.

The archons of Hell are their own kind of royalty, their own kind of power. Although I would never attempt to summon one directly, within the proper rituals, their names are a literal form of currency.

I brushed up on what I knew of Stygia and its denizens, double and triple checking my research for good measure. You don't want to be caught unawares when dealing with demons.

After I was satisfied with my plan, I left the book on the bed and returned to the dining room. I picked up each chair and set them aside in the kitchen. The corked wine bottle also had to go, leaving the glass tabletop empty. Then I bent to the rug and overturned each edge.

Unlike my other room rugs, this one had a custom bottom. It was smooth and untreated except for the edge, where a heavy rubber-gripped liner ran along each side. This kept the rug weighed down and prevented slippage from stray kicks.

Beneath the main bulk of the rug was another pad, but this one was all cushion and no grips. With the edges of the rug overturned, the rest of it slid easily with a bit of lateral pressure. The modern table had a sparse metal frame, heavy enough to stay put but light enough to move if needed.

I pulled the rug with the entire table across the spacious concrete floor and revealed lines of metal shaping an encircled hexagram. The ultra-high-purity copper-iron-zinc alloy was a professional install, permanently embedded into the polished concrete. This was the main reason Bedrock paid rent on the desirable loft. You could call it a work-from-home situation.

Welcome to my office.

I set down a circle of lit candles, knelt before the six-pointed star, and pulled the pentacle from under my shirt. The amulet was a Sigillum Dei, a gold disk meticulously inscribed with an ornate diagram. It wasn't the same one my father had worn—his went missing along with him. This piece was custom-made to exact specifications from *The Sworn Book of Honorius*. It was a complicated sequence of nested circles, a pentagon, heptagons, and a familiar five-pointed pentagram in the center.

Pentacles were a measure of protection. Every time I used mine, I tried not to think that my father's had failed him.

I closed my eyes and focused, breathing the scent of the candles, and called to Stygia. Despite the sun still hanging in the sky, the room darkened. The smoke in my nose turned to burning pine. I opened my eyes to a massless drift of gray smoke formed above the hexagram. Rounded ears perked out.

"I am here," something whispered, wispy snout testing the substance of its new environs.

The head rotated in place, slowly, like a baby using eyes for the first time. As it did, the smoke materialized into a furred bear head. Its features were indistinct, surrounded by a mass of rising smoke continuously billowing from its mouth and ears. It was a bonfire without fire, except for the piercing light of its two glowing eyes. They focused on me.

"Who are you, summoner?" it requested.

I made sure the Sigillum Dei was in plain view. "You know better than to ask that. You're a smoke devil, right?"

The demon snorted, pushing enough smoke from its

mouth to flash a set of teeth. "I am as you called."

I nodded with certainty. "A test, then. Are you familiar with a man named Paulson Crowe? It is known he currently resides in Hell."

This question was standard operating procedure when I summoned a new demon, part of my endless search for answers. I never expected much from asking, but I had to try.

The ghostly demon studied me a moment. "I know of none by that name, but Hell is a many-layered place."

"Fine. I have a simple job for you."

"Blood requires blood," it said.

"There's no killing. I need perceptive eyes with driftless form. I want you to confirm an artifact is where it's supposed to be, and I want you to do it without being seen."

Smoke devils were notoriously cryptic and difficult to tame, like keeping a puff of smoke in your open palm. The simpler the job, the better, otherwise you'd have a wild card on your hands. I was keeping things as rudimentary as possible.

"What is the artifact?" it asked with apparent curiosity.

"A purported crown of immortality. Gold-leafed laurel. When I get to the site, I need to know it's there."

"Shall I fetch it for you?"

"No touching. See if it's there. Report on cameras and guards and traps. Any countermeasures you detect around the crown. That's it."

The smoke devil made a strange whinnying that bordered on disappointment. "This is an insufficient challenge to my skills."

"Which leaves no room for error," I asserted.

I caught a toothy smile behind the smoke. "And what is my payment?"

I produced an iron coin engraved with the seal of Balam, the archon of Stygia. The devil's eyes gleamed brighter than before. "If you're in and out without incident, it's yours."

A low growl filled the loft. The bear's ears turned back and its head went low. I'd pulled out the big guns with this coin. It was valuable, and a consumable resource, created through intense research and ritual. But I couldn't afford the job to go sideways. I didn't want things to end up the way they did the last time I'd dealt with a smoke devil.

"I await your call," it said and hastily disappeared, the smoke dispersing in a puff.

The Scope

After the toll of the ritual and the wine, I took a two-hour nap. It was one of the perks of working nights. By early evening, I felt refreshed and eager to get out.

I rode the Monster back to the Commercial Exchange Building, this time parking a block away and walking the rest. The first thing I did was book a hotel room with a credit card linked to a fake identity. The subterfuge was almost overkill, using an alias to check into a room when it wasn't even the night of the heist, but it was safer to cover my bases. Besides, the bills for work expenses went to Bedrock.

I asked for a higher floor, though didn't pay for a loft on the thirteenth. Key card in hand, I took the elevator up to ten. I tested the thirteen button and it lit up. Perfect. My key card granted access to all floors. I exited on ten and let the empty elevator continue up.

I scoped out the hall, getting a feel for the layout of the building. There was one camera on the elevators, but that was it. The hallway ended at the window facing Olive Street. The metal balcony appeared solid, but the window was permanently secured in place.

I swiped into my hotel room next. The lock was a single bolt, nothing fancy. I looked both directions down the hall, making sure it was clear, and closed the door. Using tools from my jacket pocket, I went to work, sliding them around the door jam. It took a bit of leverage but the angle worked. My pick bent around the frame and clicked the door open.

I closed the door to practice again when someone came down the hall. I put the tools away and followed him to the elevator, satisfied I had it down. I wouldn't be subverting any locks tonight or tomorrow anyway. I had just wanted to check.

I went to the ground floor and found a spot at the bar with a clear view of the front desk and the windows to the outside walk-up. The elevators were out of sight but I had eyes on the path toward them. I sat with a cocktail, not really drinking but getting a feel for the place. The bar was slightly crowded, and I tried guessing who was a hotel occupant and who'd come off the street. It wasn't too hard, but there were no Saudi princes.

There was one guy, however, who was definitely out of place. A boy, barely twenty-one, with stubble on his head and cheeks. His black jacket didn't sport gang colors, but I thought I recognized him from outside Lambert's warehouse. A member of the motorcycle club. Our eyes locked across the room before he looked away.

I snorted. It made sense the bikers would be watching

out for Lambert's interests, protecting his investment. What I didn't like was the feeling they were watching me. This kid was definitely low on the totem pole, so he wouldn't know anything. And maybe they were just keeping eyes on the prince.

I sighed and pulled out my phone, going through the packet Trap had sent me, realizing I should've included a background request on the bikers. It was an oversight not to.

I ignored the info on Lambert for now and focused on Prince Fahd Al-Assaf, or as he preferred to be known, Ahmad Khan. Not a prince at all, just a rich vacationer. I studied the closeup of his face intently, as if the photo had captured his essence and I could soak it up if I stared long enough.

"Hi there," said a man wearing jeans and a button-up. "Mind if I sit for a minute?" He pointed to the stool beside me currently occupied by my boot.

I glanced at the empty seats on both sides of me. "Sorry," I said, "I'm waiting for someone."

I learned a long time ago not to smile out of politeness, since a smile often invited interest. Still, I kept my voice light, remembering my conversation with Josalie. My goal was to come across as firm, not bitchy.

"Really?" asked the guy slyly. "Because it looks like you've been waiting a while." He motioned to my cocktail on the dregs of the crushed ice. "You sure you don't want me to sit? You're too cute to get stood up."

Ugh, that word. What was wrong with me that I hated

it? I had long black hair. Dark makeup and leathers. I projected a tough loner image. Did this guy not get that or didn't he care?

Across the room, the biker boy stiffened. His eyes shot to me and he turned around, trying his hardest to be inconspicuous but only calling extra attention to himself. I pulled my boot off the chair and sat up as Al-Assaf and his contingent of bodyguards strolled past from the elevator. My eyes darted outside to the waiting limousine.

"You see what I mean?" said the guy hitting on me, capping off a statement that I'd missed while offering me a shiny black paper.

I took it and my confusion grew. It was a business card for a talent agency.

He smiled. "Here, I'll make you a bet that I can buy you the perfect drink. Taste it and tell me I'm wrong." He pointed to the now-empty stool. "If I may."

"It's all yours," I said.

As he moved in and signaled the bartender, I hopped off the stool and headed to the exit. I used the bar entrance, which was separate from the desk entrance the prince used. We exited the building at the same time, thirty feet apart.

The crew wore traditional red-and-white-checkered head coverings and dressed in dark colors, including the prince. I turned on my phone's video camera and strolled down the sidewalk, holding my cell to my ear while pretending to be on a call. A Saudi bodyguard opened the door to the limo and they began to load up. I quickened my pace ever so slightly to get a better shot of the mark.

One of the guards keyed on my movement. Although his head was averted, facing the car and the prince, he nervously eyed me. It was weird because I wasn't being forward or intimidating. Just one of several pedestrians passing on the sidewalk. I took no outward notice of him and continued walking, oblivious.

The guard relayed some information to his crew in a language I didn't understand. Although he moved to stay between me and the prince, blocking my view as he entered the car, none of the other bodyguards seemed to notice me. The entire crew loaded in, and I caught a flash of Al-Assaf's face.

I continued down the block, gabbing on the phone without showing interest. The limo pulled away from the curb and drove off in the opposite direction. I rounded the corner of the building into a well-lit alley, leaned against the brick, and took a relieved breath.

That little jaunt had been strange. Despite me not doing anything overt, the guards were wary. Had I spooked them or had it been something else? After careful thought, I concluded it was a case of simple paranoia. That was never a good quality in a mark, not unless there was a way to take advantage of it. The bodyguard was just being thorough. They couldn't have known I was more than a random person going about my business.

I checked the video. The opening was my cleanest shot, before the guard sensed me. Unfortunately that was when I was furthest from the prince. His head was turned away from the camera. He held something shiny in his hand as he approached the car. No, after reversing and rewatching, he wasn't holding anything. The sun was reflecting off a gold ring.

Afterward, Al-Assaf was obstructed by his crew. The video just captured his security team listening to orders. None of them glanced after me as I passed, which reinforced my conclusion that I hadn't been noticed.

I got lucky at the end of the video, when Al-Assaf peeked from the car. A nice head-on shot of his face. My lips pursed.

I paused the video, opened the image packet from Trap, and studied the close-up of the prince. It was an older shot, from a few years ago at least. Al-Assaf looked different in person, with a trimmed goatee instead of the full beard. All the pictures from Trap had beards. I wondered if the trim was part of the new alias.

I turned back around the corner. The street was no longer notable so I re-entered the hotel, this time by the desk entrance. The biker stood there glaring at me. I stared back on my way to the elevator. He was too nervous to say anything, but his boots kicked after me when I passed.

"Uh... Uh..." he stammered as I pressed the elevator call button.

"Don't bother." The door opened. I entered, swiped my key, and pushed thirteen.

The biker hesitated a second before taking a step toward the open door.

I held my hand in his way. "We're full up."

He straightened and watched the door close on him.

I shook my head. What had that been about?

The layout of the top floor was similar to mine, but not exactly the same. There were a lot fewer doors because each room was larger. The hallway didn't run all the way to the window overlooking Olive Street either. I had known this because Bernard reported that window led straight into the mark's room.

Around a bend in the corridor was the room in question. I turned the corner casually, half expecting to run into a guard in the hallway. That might be the case during the party, but it wasn't now. The entrance to Al-Assaf's room was clear. Even better, this strip of hallway was essentially private, with no additional cameras or rooms in sight.

I pulled the Balam sigil from my pocket, flicked it spinning into the air, and snatched it back into my grip. "All right, Smokey, you're up."

Smokey

A puff of burning evergreen flashed before my eyes, leaving a hunched figure of a bear at my feet. "Named me, have you?"

"Only *you* can prevent forest fires."

The demon sighed. Now that he was fully material, I could see his entire body, and everything about it was off. Aside from the glowing red eyes and the limitless head-smoke, his torso was skinny for a bear, missing much of its fur, with skin a dead gray. Smokey's forearms and hind legs both ended in pointed talons, similar to those of an eagle but mammalian in nature.

"Behind this door is a caged safe room. There's a pillar with a pillow. I want to know if there's a laurel crown there."

The demon bear stared at the door idly.

"Remember my instructions. Keep an eye out for countermeasures, and stay out of sight. There may be people in there. No contact."

The red eyes returned to me and the iron coin in my hand. I didn't need to directly pay all hellions like this. Bernard, for example, would never accept any tribute from me. But some demons were all business. And yet others still, like smoke devils, treated these transactions more like a game.

"It will be done," he said.

The bear dissolved into wisps that joined the billowing smoke around his head. Instead of drifting to the ceiling it curled around and shot under the door, vanishing.

I waited a few yards out of sight of the peephole and listened. Everything was predictably quiet. With any luck there was only a dozing guard or two to avoid.

As the moment drew longer, I wondered if the crown wasn't in the safe room at all. The soiree wasn't tonight. It could be somewhere else on the property, like in an actual safe. That's where I would keep it. I should've asked Smokey to search further if needed. Then again, I didn't want to complicate his parameters. The more free rein the devil had in the room, the more trouble he could cause.

The ding from the elevator came down the hall. I was around the corner so I couldn't see anyone, but there were few enough rooms on this level that any approach made me nervous. What if the prince had forgotten something? What if the guard detail was changing?

I approached the corner with a makeup kit. I snapped it open and peeked the mirror around the wall. A single Saudi guard was coming this way. I pressed my lips tight and looked to the end of my hall. There was a lone door with a sign reading, "Exit Only."

I hurried over, confirmed it wasn't alarmed, and silently opened it. There was no key card scanner for re-entry on the outside. I picked out the business card from the douche at the bar and stuffed it into the strike plate box. With the bundle of thick paper obstructing full closure, the spring bolt couldn't engage. The door appeared shut but allowed re-entry.

I waited at the edge of the reinforced window as the guard turned the corner, checked the hall, and entered the prince's room. Once again, the Saudi contingent appeared capable, on top of security even without cause for suspicion.

As far as developments went, this wasn't much of one. Still, I didn't like it. Smoke devils had the power of full invisibility so a single guard should be easy to circumvent. I was more concerned about the slight change in situation that might encourage Smokey to go off-script. He was bound to follow our agreement to the letter, and I'd been pretty firm, but demons had a way of using your words against you.

A door below closed heavily. My brow furrowed. That wasn't a good sign considering I was high up in an exit-only stairwell. Stomps echoed on concrete. They were coming upstairs.

I grumbled inwardly and peeked down. Thick fingers slid up the railing a few flights below. It was the big biker from this morning, Grady. Not only that, he'd come from the tenth floor. *My* floor. I backed away from the banister before he could see me.

Now *this* was a wrinkle I hadn't counted on.

The stairwell door was reinforced metal. Even a big guy like him wouldn't be able to force himself inside. I pushed back through the door into the interior hall. The business card fell away and the door caught, suddenly shoving me back and clicking loudly shut.

Through the small window fluttered the painted blue lashes of Teegan. The bitch just locked me out. Her sharp brows arched playfully. I scowled and looked to the door past her, where Smokey was still searching. Her smile faltered as she followed my gaze. When she turned back to me, I pulled away.

Damn. I didn't want her to know what I had cooking with Smokey. Meanwhile, Grady's heavy footfalls were getting louder. The two-bit bikers had successfully cornered me.

If I really wanted to, I could get the door open, but it would take time. It was an exterior door, metal and with a solid lock. I'd never be able to beat the big dummy wheezing up three flights of stairs.

I considered dispelling Smokey, but a few extra seconds could be crucial. I had to buy the demon as much time as I could, which meant potentially loosening his leash. The bald guy with a beard came around the last bend and faced me, ten steps down.

"Strange place for exercise," I said, leaning against the top of the banister like I'd been waiting for him.

His face hardened between breaths. "You're not supposed to be here."

"What's the problem? You're paying me for a job. I'm doing it."

"No. The job's tomorrow. Lambert was very specific about your window. If you blow this thing early, the whole plan is shot. Your contract is void."

I sneered. I didn't like threats of withholding money, especially when I hadn't violated any explicit terms. If they were Lambert's words, I would've given him a piece of my mind. But this oaf didn't know what he was talking about.

"You're the one threatening to blow our cover," I said snidely as I descended the steps. "You're making a small racket."

"I don't take orders from you."

"Same here. Little tip," I said as I passed. "If you're not the one with the money, you're not the boss."

His hand came down hard on my shoulder. I spun and punched him dead center in the chest. He was shocked by the immediate counter and paused a second, but he hadn't budged.

"You little bitch!"

His knee hammered into my stomach, doubling me over and sending me down a few steps.

I groaned, the wind knocked from me. I wasn't a stranger to a scuffle, but I was a small girl when it came down to it. Besides, I usually had Bernard for these situations. I struggled to breathe and stretched my fingers, ready to summon help.

"I was just gonna warn ya," spouted Grady. "Make sure you know you're not runnin' things. But you had to get smart." He took a step down toward me.

I debated enlisting Smokey's aid. It wasn't a good idea. Not only was the smoke devil in the middle of a job, but he was an unknown quantity. If I called him to me, there was no telling what he'd do.

My other option was to dispel him and call Bernard. That was the natural option but it also cut Smokey short. It would effectively null our contract, requiring a renegotiation to get it in place again. With a longer window that was doable, but the job was tomorrow. And I already had a biker gang on full alert.

I slowly closed my fingers, deciding to tough it out. It was what professionals did.

I pushed to my feet, gripping my aching stomach. "Fair enough. We each got a lick in."

"That wasn't a lick," he laughed, still approaching.

"This is a mistake, Grady. Lambert's not gonna like this."

"Let's just keep this our little secret then."

He took an overconfident step toward me and swung his fist. I ducked beneath the telegraphed blow and shoved a stun gun into his gut. He thrashed at the contact, belting forward and headbutting me. As I staggered, his knuckles came around and knocked the side of my head.

I hit the wall. The stun gun clattered away. I blinked, desperately trying to refocus the scene.

"You are a feisty one. I'm gonna have fun with this."

I leaned on the railing and retreated down the stairs, but his boot caught me and sent me down another half flight. I hit the floor in a daze.

Pain and anger flowed into me. This piece of shit needed a lesson, and Bernard was too good for him. Thoughts of the Dark One flooded me, an arcane being who came packaged with power and toughness.

I banished the thought from my head. That hellion was dangerous. The Dark One was summoned *into* me. She was a possession who granted supernatural strength and endurance. Basically, she could handle my biker problem without a stray thought.

But I couldn't do it. Even in this much pain, I couldn't bring myself to resort to her. The Dark One was evil, willing to kill and maim with abandon. It wasn't just a mean streak, either. Every time I used her she threatened to take control, forcing me to go through with horrible acts, forcing me to break my code.

It was a line I wouldn't cross.

I continued down the stairs and Grady followed. He was faster because I was shaky on my feet. At the next flight I checked the hallway door. Locked.

"That's far enough, little lady."

He lunged at me. I fell backward, sliding toward the stairs, sticking my boot between his as he pounced. He tripped forward and I rolled aside. Grady tumbled headfirst down the next set of stairs. You know that saying, the bigger they are, the harder they fall? Even I cringed as he bounced to the flat turnaround.

We both panted on our sides. He groaned and cradled his shoulder. When I sat up, I saw it was dislocated.

"I told you to leave it alone," I spat. I was still shaking at how close I'd come to invoking the Dark One.

I descended, staying out of reach as I sidestepped him.

"This isn't over," he called after me.

"It is for now." I massaged the welt forming on the side of my head and continued to the bottom.

I was angry. Lambert using thugs for protection was his prerogative, but they had no business interfering with my work. They shouldn't be loitering anywhere near the mark. Biker tough guys were ten times more likely to blow the lid off this thing than I was, and there was a gang of them.

I cursed and kicked outside on the ground floor, finding myself in a darkening alley between the back of the building and the parking garage. It was a nice spot, quiet, absent bikers and pedestrians alike. I trudged toward Olive Street with an eerie feeling following me. I spun and caught the glow of yellow eyes in the shadows.

I recoiled and readied my spellcraft to call Bernard to my aid, but the eyes were gone. I breathed hard, wondering if they were ever there to begin with.

"Forgetting something?" asked a voice behind me.

I spun again, nearly having a heart attack. A black bear sat hunched at my side.

I exhaled, relieved. "Smokey."

Fiery eyes studied me with curious disdain. "Expecting anyone else?"

I cleared my throat and pulled the iron coin from my pocket. "Report."

"The crown's in place, just as you said it would be. There

are no cameras or guards in the room. No countermeasures to prevent your access to it."

I twitched at that. Something about the specific wording he used. "Are there any traps or situations I should be aware of?" I explicitly asked.

Smokey smiled, baring his teeth. "None at all, summoner. I swear it on my archon, Balam the Great and Terrible."

I stared at him a moment. His report was done, and he'd come through. I had what I wanted.

"Good work."

I flipped the coin into the air and he hungrily caught it with deadly talons. "Be seeing you again..." he whispered as he dissolved into nothing.

I stomped to the street toward my bike. When you dealt with Hell as much as I did, you needed nerves of steel.

Coffee

Later on, I left my local coffee roaster with a vanilla latte at my lips. I was used to late bursts of caffeine. They kept me sharp at night.

I was down the block from my loft, just a short walk, so I'd left the motorcycle at home. The bit of exercise was good for me. It loosened me up after taking a pounding. It also helped me think. About Smokey, the Saudis, and the bikers. The crisp air felt nice, and I pulled the jacket tight when I got a chill.

I checked up and down the block for any interested parties. I didn't like the thought of being followed. The loft, the utilities, the bike—none of them were in my name. I effectively lived off the grid, as a good criminal should. I took care to make sure no one followed me home. The last thing I wanted was a Nazi biker at my doorstep.

But no one was watching me. No one accounting for my movements. It might only be for now, but the thought was comforting.

An hour ago I'd fully expected a call from Lambert, a warning to someone he saw as a bumbling amateur. The call hadn't come. I started to think maybe the bikers realized they'd been overzealous in their protection duties. Or maybe they had different motives than Lambert. They were mercenaries. They weren't loyal to him but to his money. All it took was someone to come along with a little more.

I reminded myself to watch out for them. Criminals were only as good as their code. Lambert was in danger of getting in over his head. One wrong move and the bikers would cross him.

I flinched as my phone rang. My fleeting satisfaction at the situation waned. But the call wasn't coming from Lambert.

"Aaron," I answered, "I didn't expect to hear from you tonight."

"Don't get excited, Shyla. I'm afraid I have some bad news."

I licked some latte foam off my lips. "Hit me."

"I spoke with Bedrock. The usual updates and all that. I mentioned your little soiree tomorrow night."

"Uh-huh." That was usually how these things went.

"The party is a no-go."

I stopped in my tracks and raised my voice. "WHAT?"

"Word from the top," he said. "You're not to steal the crown."

I shook my head in a moment's hesitation. "How do you expect me to secure money if I can't steal valuables?"

He sighed. "It's not me, Shyla. My role as Custodian

entails looking out for the interests of the team."

"You mean *his* interests."

"We're under strict orders for the party to go off without a hitch. Important people will be in attendance. Bedrock wouldn't appreciate one of his associates being included in your burglary's suspect pool."

I grunted. Lambert's plan didn't involve any specific patsy, but a theft at the end of the party, as the guests were leaving, was meant to throw suspicion their way. It wouldn't work if one of the Royal-We's friends was in attendance. "Who is it?" I growled.

"Who is what?"

"Who's Bedrock's favored guest? Because he's costing our *employer* a lot of money."

A relaxing breath came over the line. "I can't tell you that."

"Come on, Aaron. If you keep things from me, how the hell am I supposed to look out for his interests?"

"I'm the Custodian," he said firmly. "That's *my* job. You're the Handler. Go find something else to handle."

I scoffed. "Don't give me that line. I deserve to know who's robbing me of my biggest score in a year."

"If I told you, I'd be dead. And you might be dead too. It's the same for all of us. You know the deal. *We don't draw the ire of Hell.* I won't risk my—"

He stopped short. He didn't need to remind me his wife was at stake. In that moment, he also knew I was thinking about my father. Both of us had dragged this conversation all the way down the drain and now neither wanted to continue.

What a crappy anniversary. What a crappy end to a job that was just starting to get interesting. One I'd already spent an iron coin on and taken a couple of punches for.

After a minute of silence, Aaron sighed again. "I'm sorry, Shyla. I—I know this isn't what you wanted to hear. My advice is just to cool off tonight and start fresh tomorrow. In the grand scheme of things, it's only one day of wasted work."

"I'm not worried about the work," I said under my breath.

I frowned, all my thoughts focused on what a stickler for the rules Aaron was. If only I hadn't given him the specifics of the job. It was almost unheard of for me to go through with a score without giving him notice, but this one was on such an accelerated timeline that I could've gotten away with it. If I'd never mentioned it this morning and given him the heads up right before taking the crown tomorrow night, the whole thing would've been done before Hell was ever aware of it.

And hey, if in the process I'd accidentally drawn their ire, and Bedrock's specifically, then all the better.

But that was now over with. I couldn't go against an explicit directive from my employer. Not with my father at stake. I would simply need to find another way to come up with next month's money.

"This sucks a bag of di—"

"Shyla?" interrupted Aaron. "Remember what we talked about this morning. Let's just keep our eyes on the prize.

We're almost free."

I took a calming breath. For some reason the hope in his voice saddened me. I nodded silently and ended the call, unable to vocalize anything positive.

Start fresh tomorrow.

Cool off tonight.

That was easy for Aaron to say. He wasn't the one waiting on a midnight appointment with a demon.

Bedrock

I opened the bathroom door and a rush of steam escaped over my shoulders. Strolling into the bedroom and rubbing a towel through my hair, the cool air nipped my naked skin. The stark contrast from warm to cold prickled my arms and legs. It invigorated me.

"You can't trust smoke devils," chided the bat-like gargoyle on his haunches beside the bed. "They thrive on treachery."

"You're still on this, Bernard?"

"I am and will be until you admit the obvious." He waited with a self-righteous glare.

I rolled my eyes. "I've dealt with smoke devils before."

"And we all remember how that turned out. But why listen to *my* opinion? You're an all-knowing summoner. I'm merely an actual denizen of the World Below."

I snickered. Bernard could be whiny sometimes, which was totally unbecoming a three-hundred-pound death machine. "You're from Kur," I pointed out. "That's two rings away from smoke devil territory." I pursed my lips. "Remind me again how much you know about Stygia?"

Bernard didn't care that I was naked. He didn't particularly look at me, and he didn't avert his eyes either. He was very much like a loyal doggo. The matter of clothes was trivial.

Without a care in the world, I walked into the living room. One of the loft's central features was the wall of windows. Even at night, whether on the pool deck or in a distant building with binoculars, nobody could see in from the outside. Exterior lights shone away from my windows, lighting the pool below, and blinding anybody trying to catch a peek.

In the summoner business, workplace privacy was a necessity.

I found my half-full coffee cup and took a sip. It was cold now. I was a slow drinker. Nothing wrong with enjoying a leisurely beverage every now and then, except the hot ones always got cold too fast. I usually ended up microwaving them several times before finishing. This time I didn't want the hassle.

I returned to the bedroom, Bernard's tail flicking hypnotically, and stretched out on the bed. It would've been nice to fall asleep, to forget about the worries of the day, but it wasn't possible. My heart was beating a million times a minute.

My eyes fell on the *Semitas Daemoniorum*, open on the appendix of demons at the back. There was a new entry for Smokey, my latest encounter. I read over it to make sure I didn't miss any details. Satisfied, I idly browsed the appendix, not looking for anything or anyone specifically. Just brushing up.

A summoner had to arm themselves with as much information as possible. You never knew when you'd spot a detail, an offhand mention or notable mannerism that gave you an edge against a demon. When it came to the summoner-hellion relationship, identity was paramount. Knowing a demon's true name, sigil, and home made it a lot easier to protect yourself. And I was sick of only knowing Bedrock by his code name.

My phone chimed. I swiped off the alarm and sighed. It was time.

"That's my cue," muttered Bernard, rousing from the floor and stretching.

I scratched his stony chin. "Sorry, boy." He disappeared in a puff of ashes. They swirled on the floor a moment but ultimately vanished without a trace.

I closed the grimoire and locked it in my wall safe. Took an extra look around the room to make sure nothing incriminating was lying around. After that I approached my mid-century wardrobe, opened the doors, and sighed. I delayed a moment to strengthen my resolve.

"Eyes on the prize," I whispered, repeating Aaron's sentiment.

I yanked the bathrobe off the standing mirror inside the cabinet, putting my back to it, and slipped my arms through. The gray silk was soft against my skin. I tied the front closed and turned to the mirror, coming face-to-face with my employer.

Bedrock was a young guy, if only in appearance, with a long nose and strong brow that left his eyes in caverns. His skin was thin, possibly a sign of his true age, and he had a brown mustache and goatee, on the thin side, with spiked ashen hair.

"Your hair's wet," he said in annoyance.

"Is it?" I blinked, picking up the towel and dabbing my head a few times before returning it to the bed. "Sorry, I hadn't realized."

His lips pressed into a silent grumble. As demeaning as my relationship with Bedrock was, the hair was one of my few weapons against him. He could insist I bathe before meeting him, but it hadn't been an accident I didn't fully dry off.

"It's no matter," he said, pretending not to be bothered. "I'm pleased to see you." He watched me and waited.

It was my turn to hide *my* annoyance. "Pleased to be here."

"Are you?" he asked pointedly. "We've known each other nine years, Shyla. We shouldn't deal in deceptions."

The blackness of the mirror's background was unnerving. So were the glimpses of his serpentine tail darting about in anticipation.

"You're right," I said, plastering my face with a light smile. "We're practically friends. What was your real name again?"

The demon chuckled. "You wound me, Shyla. My alias is hardly a deception. I'm upfront about the need for security.

But that's not what's really bothering you."

My smile sagged. "No."

Bedrock crossed his arms and settled closer in the mirror's frame. "There, you look more honest now. Falsity does not suit you. Never smile on my account."

I wet my lips, uncomfortable under his piercing stare. His eyes were like black holes. "I'll remember that."

"You are such a beautiful creature, my dear. I wonder if you know it. Eyes full of fire. Heart full of passion. It runs through your veins. It is stunning. It is maddening. Men must erupt at your boldness."

My eyes flashed. I stretched my neck to break his gaze. Bedrock was quite passionate himself when he wanted to be.

"I will not stand for your unhappiness," he said.

"Then give me back my father."

"In due time." He smiled as black swirled across the pane of glass. "You see our agreement as a burden, but it is in fact a boon. Not everyone gets the chance to correct a mistake. You may never understand how much I help you, but in this I don't blame you." Bedrock whisked a pointed finger through the scruff on his chin. "There's something else troubling you."

I swallowed. If I was gonna subject myself to this, I might as well be honest about it. "You took me off my job."

The devil backed away and nodded. "Are you having money problems, Shyla?"

I snorted. "Didn't the Custodian pass on my tribute?"

"He did, and I am pleased."

"It doesn't matter how much money I already have. This

job is more."

"We must be careful with greed, my dear. It has dragged down the greatest of men." He twisted with snakelike grace, and I wondered if he was talking about my father.

"I don't mean it like that. But this job is a windfall. It's a simple lift and the client's overpaying."

Bedrock pondered my statement. "Does that not sound any warnings?"

I shrugged. "Nothing I can't handle."

He snickered in amusement. "That's what I like about you."

"What's your interest in the Crown of Aevum?"

Bedrock yawned, appearing anything but interested. "I know of this particular relic."

My eyes narrowed. "Is it real? Does it grant immortality?"

"Do you imagine your prophet wearing it? Rising from the dead wearing a golden treasure?"

Bedrock knew by this point I wasn't very religious, but he often took jabs at Abrahamic faiths all the same. It was something personal with him.

"Honestly?" I said. "I think it's a phony."

A set of perfect teeth grinned back at me. "In some contexts, yes. This one's an artifact from Ancient Egypt. A crown of justification. A wreath for the dead. Actual leaves coated in gold in honor of the sun god Re. As some went on to believe afterward, the crown represents victory over death."

I almost staggered in place but held strong. Bedrock had

just given me the second half of my score, verifying the artifact's authenticity, and he'd given it to me for free. That was unheard of when dealing with Hell. Maybe it wasn't a crown of immortality as Lambert believed, but a genuine Egyptian funerary relic was invaluable.

Which meant the job was now worth two hundred thousand dollars.

Bedrock watched me with a curious expression. "You are pleased, yes?"

He knew the information helped me. I didn't want to give him the satisfaction of gratitude. "That knowledge only makes the situation worse."

"Knowledge, my child, never makes one worse off."

I huffed. "What good is identifying the crown if you've prohibited me from stealing it?"

"A predicament, no doubt."

Which was a strange thing to say, considering his study of my reaction. It could be that Bedrock enjoyed seeing me squirm—you should never put that past a demon—but my instincts told me this was something else.

And then he hit me with a question out of left field. "Do you trust the Custodian?"

I stiffened, wondering at the trick.

Of course I trusted the Custodian. Aaron and I were in this together, more so than the other operators. I was careful that my answer didn't come too fast or too earnest. Bedrock was testing me. He didn't know we were friends, but perhaps he suspected it. Perhaps Aaron had accidentally let something slip.

I took a measured breath. "I don't trust anybody, but I trust the Custodian to follow your orders just like I do."

Bedrock nodded as if the answer satisfied him, though he wasn't finished with the subject.

"Give me your honest opinion," he said slyly, "so I can get inside your head." The wording made me shiver, but he couldn't really get inside. Bedrock licked his lips, taking delight in forming the question. "Which of my operators do you believe I rely on most?"

I pursed my lips. My employer was asking me to compare myself with my coworkers, the Custodian and the Lead and the Wire and the others. Like a literal performance review from Hell.

And once again I got the feeling Bedrock was playing at something, pitting me against Aaron. He definitely knew something.

But his question was an interesting one, because I had sometimes pondered the same thing myself. Not out of malice or in preparation of political machinations, but due to the primal urge of survival.

Where did I rank in Bedrock's empire?

Aaron was important. His custodial duties, his coordination, was a vital component of the team. Above that, Aaron was good at what he did. I didn't fear for his future, at least not as long as our contract was ongoing.

My summoner skills were likewise unmatched. It may have been a cocky thing to think, but I had job security. Bedrock couldn't simply replace me, not without his tool set in the Material Plane taking a major hit.

Some of the other operators, unfortunately, were eminently expendable. The Lead was a good social engineer, but it was easy to find another pretty face willing to sell her soul. The Wire had computer skills and connections, but it wasn't a stretch for someone else to fill that role.

The demon waited patiently as I came to my decision.

I cleared my throat. "I don't *think*," I said firmly. "I *know*. You rely on me and the Custodian over the others."

His question hadn't been explicit about naming a single one of us, for which I was thankful. He didn't smile or frown, but he nodded, satisfied enough with my answer.

I sighed. "Bedrock, do you think we can get a move-on tonight? It's been a rough day."

He smirked playfully. "Shyla, I can go whatever speed you're comfortable with. You want to get this over with?" His image in the mirror leaned close. "Show me what I hunger for."

I pressed my lips tight and dropped my bathrobe to the floor.

The Terms

Demons were creeps, and Bedrock was no exception. His eyes traced up and down my nude body. As strong as I was, I quivered involuntarily. His desire was like a physical thing, poking and prodding my exposed flesh.

"Yesss," he murmured in pleasure. "It has really been too long, my dear."

My face scrunched up. "You better not be touching yourself."

He laughed. "I wouldn't dream of it. When finally our pleasure becomes physical, it will be your flesh against mine."

I objected to him calling this "our" pleasure, but I didn't say anything. Apparently, even devils had hopes and dreams, but I wasn't looking to hook up with one.

Bedrock lifted a finger and twirled it in a circle, requesting me to spin around. I did so, slowly, rolling my eyes hard as I faced away. When I stopped square with him,

I scowled.

"Are we good? I'd like to see my father."

"Almost, Shyla. For someone who wants to take things slow, you sure like to go fast." He let out a long predatory breath as he admired my body. I still wore the Sigillum Dei, which didn't seem to rankle him.

"The Custodian is a good worker," he said idly. "He does what he's told. He follows the rules, as you say. But you, my little Crowe, have more individuality than that."

The hair on my neck perked in sudden nervousness. "I never go against you," I hurried.

"You don't," he said knowingly, "but you understand the world of gray. You deal in it every day. You're dealing in it this very moment."

He was talking about my nudity, the exchange for him allowing visits with my father. It wasn't enough that my family was trapped, indebted, and that I was working it off. Bedrock wanted to shame and break me.

I played his game out of necessity. Everything I did was for my father.

"Paulson," he mused, "might be saved much quicker, you know. Would it not please you twice to sleep with me and see his freedom?"

I contained my glower with a neutral face. I wouldn't let Bedrock see the guilt I felt for not freeing my father faster. What was a night of sex for freedom? I wouldn't blame anyone for doing it.

But me, I couldn't bring myself to. Even if it was selfish, if it meant my father would suffer for years.

But I had every reason to avoid an act so intimate. It wasn't rational to believe a night of passion would be limited to a moment, that consequences couldn't spill over into the coming days and years.

And when you were dealing with a demon, that warning applied tenfold. I wasn't about to have Rosemary's baby.

I shook my head, letting him know my position was firm.

"I didn't think so," conceded Bedrock. "Not yet. But I bring up your individuality in a world of gray for an altogether different reason."

I stood upright, showing him his games had no effect on me. "Spit it out already."

He eyes hardened ever so slightly. He liked me strong, but only to a point. "As the Handler, you juggle many competing interests. You must please your client, please your *real* employer, please your demons, and please yourself, in one fell swoop if possible. Such a feat is often impossible without a bit of wiggle room."

My breath held a moment. I forgot I was naked, forgot I was speaking through a window to Hell, thoughts circling around Bedrock's point like a frenzy of hungry sharks. What exactly was he getting at?

"You still want me to do the job?" I asked in confusion.

"I have said what I have said."

"Yeah, about pleasing my client."

"Lambert is none of my concern, Shyla. How you please him is entirely yours. But blaming someone else for your losses is not the best path."

"You mean blaming you for taking me off the job."

"Perhaps, or perhaps I was speaking in generalities."

I stood there, mind churning on Bedrock's cryptic comments. He was pushing me just a bit out of my comfort zone, saying enough to know he meant something, but not enough to know what. And now that the message was delivered, the thrust if not the meaning, he was already backing off.

"Next time," he said curtly, "dry your hair first. You have five minutes with Paulson."

And the image on the glass immediately flickered to my father, standing in a dark room with chains on his legs.

My eyes went wide. I scooped up the bathrobe and dove over the bed, crashing unceremoniously on the far side. I blinked away the tears of shame already welling up. Damn Bedrock. How dare he fucking do that to me. My own father.

I hurried my arms through the robe and closed it tight before rising from behind the bed. My father gazed distantly to the sky. He hadn't noticed my nudity. Or, more likely, he was pretending not to have.

Who was I kidding? My father was in Hell. He must've witnessed horrors on a daily basis. Bedrock's trick was meant to shock *me*; it would have little effect on my father.

"Dad?" I said, voice cracking.

Paulson turned, eyes focusing, his natural wits and sharpness returning at the sight of me. He was a robust man in his late sixties, with a mind like the point of a nail. Close-cropped white hair, stubbled cheeks, and a healthy build, he was my own personal Indiana Jones. He wore a navy wool jacket with the collar up.

"Shyla!" he cried, joy overtaking his face. "I see you're still out there making moves."

Smiles rarely came natural to me, but I was beaming now. "I learned from the best."

"Nonsense," he said. "You're better than I ever was."

I laughed, and just like that, my daddy was back, and for a minute we chatted about nothing at all. Sometimes those conversations were the best.

Aside from that scary first moment of him appearing in a daze, he was the same Paulson that had raised me. To some extent I'd been exaggerating about him witnessing daily horrors. Hell couldn't have been a pleasant place, especially whatever prison he was in—I didn't know what he'd endured before Bedrock had tracked me down—but over the last nine years of our working relationship, my father wasn't treated to torture. No intestines endlessly drawn from his stomach or boulders being forced uphill. This wasn't torment in the biblical sense. A deal was a deal, and a large part of these check-ins was to confirm that.

My father's spirit wasn't broken, and neither was mine.

We caught up, gave each other encouragement, and reminisced about better times. When we hit a lull in the conversation, he worked his jaw a moment and grew serious.

"I need to know, Shyla—"

"Dad..." I whined in a child's annoyance.

"I know you hate my pestering, girl, but I need to know you're not doing *anything* that would compromise your soul. Not even for my sake. I could never live with myself if you ended up like me. I would take my own life before I allowed that to happen."

My father. He was all business, even when that business was family. Every single time we spoke, no matter how much I assured him, he needed to go over the deal again. Just bookkeeping, he called it.

These visits of ours, I knew, weren't just about me making sure he was okay. Paulson needed these moments, needed to see his daughter thriving so he had the will to continue. And I would be here throughout, giving him whatever assurances he needed, right up till I paid the final dime on his debt.

"I summoned a smoke devil today," I said idly, changing the subject.

"Stygia," he groaned, both unsettled and impressed. "You know you can't trust them."

I chuckled. "That's what Bernard says."

"Mm-hmm. And he's still treating you well?"

"Always." Part of the arrangement with Bedrock was he couldn't listen in on these visits. This was private. "I have a good team, Dad. You'd like them. Even a couple of friends, like the Custodian."

My father didn't immediately respond. We were in the last minute of our talk and he was starting to go sullen. The irony of having so little time is we waste so much of it with worry.

"No need for concern," I said with a grin. "I'm not getting too close. You taught me to look out for family above anyone else."

His lips crooked against his will. "You remember that, do you?"

"Forever."

Cancellation Policy

The next morning, I called the number Teegan had given me to contact Lambert. Twice without answer. I was still pissed about the fight the night before and again the bikers were failing in their duties.

I headed out on the Monster to blow off some steam, troubled by my conflicting goals and feeling sore. My phone buzzed and I quickly pulled over and answered it. No one spoke.

"Put him on," I hissed.

There was no direct answer, but I heard footsteps on tile and the background noise of a public place. My patience was wearing thin.

"Hello," came Lambert's voice.

"We need to talk."

"We are talking."

"In person," I insisted.

He waited a beat. "I suppose I can find a spot in my schedule, but shouldn't you be preparing for tonight?"

"The job's off. Do you wanna talk about it or not?"

The statement was followed by a protracted silence and then some whispers. Finally, Lambert said, "I'll see you immediately. My associate will give you the address."

The phone was handed off to Teegan who gave me the location of a downtown French bistro. They were nearby. I gunned the bike several blocks and parked across the street from the restaurant.

I crossed between light traffic, assured of my righteousness but dreading the meeting all the same. It wasn't easy telling someone you had to cancel a job, but I was a pro. If circumstances arose beyond my control and I couldn't follow through on an offer, I delivered the news face-to-face.

As I approached the corner entrance, Teegan rounded the building. Bald with blue eye shadow, she wore spiked armbands today that accentuated the studs on her ears and face. At least two other bikers waited further around the corner.

I grumbled. I'd assumed the motorcycle club had slept in, but they were awake and escorting Lambert. That meant she'd been dodging my earlier calls. I didn't let it bother me. This was the last time I needed to suffer her presence.

She stopped in my path. She wasn't well muscled, but she had a good six inches on me. Being short, I was used to it, but the last thing I wanted was a repeat of last night.

"You better hope the old man doesn't want you dead, because it would be my pleasure to oblige."

Was anyone in this gang not a posturing shitbag? I didn't

show fear. If I was bigger, stronger, I would've decked her right here. As for now, with her friends, that was probably a losing proposition. The restaurant was a public meeting place in broad daylight so I couldn't bring my pets out to play.

"You're taking trophies now?" she growled. "You're a thief to the core, aren't you? You just couldn't resist."

I sneered defiantly. "I don't know what you're talking about."

"The silver cross you stole. I want it back."

She really was a crazy person. I ignored the accusation and looked past. "He here?" I asked gruffly.

"Table in the back," she groused. Then she leaned close. "You better play nice." Teegan retreated around the corner in a huff.

Someone was a little manic today. I scowled. Lambert needed to find better grunts. I eased the tension in my face and stepped inside the restaurant, boots clacking on antique hex tiles.

A marble bar and glass displays with fresh breads surrounded an open kitchen. Booths lined both windowed walls. Lambert sat at a table beyond the bar. The club members were on the sidewalk outside, keeping eyes on me through the window. I could live with that.

Lambert stood and motioned me to a chair. He was in the middle of a plate of poached eggs. An extra mug of tea was set opposite him. One sugar caddy, but two stacks of creamer cups.

"Someone else here?" I asked.

"Someone else *was* here." He motioned me again to sit and I did. He followed after me, folding his napkin across his lap. "I was in the middle of brunch with an associate, but your hysterical call forced a premature end to our business. Can I get you anything?" He waved a waitress over.

I resented his depiction of me as hysterical. Then again, I had pressured him into this meeting. Probably just my calls being ignored that had set me off.

"I won't take up too much of your time," I said, pursing my lips at the coffee pot behind the bar and then smiling at the waitress. "But I will have a coffee." I checked the table. "And can I have an extra mug with a raw egg in it?"

The waitress hurried away as Lambert stared oddly at me.

"Breakfast of champions."

He nodded, too polite to say anything.

"So I was busy yesterday," I started, "getting background on our royal, scoping out the hotel."

"I'm sure you found everything to your satisfaction."

"That's just it. I've hit a bit of a snag, and it's something I can't work around."

He tapped his fork on the plate. "I find that hard to believe. I made sure everything was in order before I brought it to you."

"It's not that. Your information was good. Except for Ahmad Khan. It's an alias for a Saudi prince. One Fahd Al-Assaf."

His eyes lit up. "That sounds like progress to me."

"All up to the part where I can't get the crown for you. I

need to turn this one down."

Lambert set down his fork and steepled his hands on the table before him, staring at me a moment, features stern. He'd used the same gesture when he first hired me, except he was now wearing a ring I swore I hadn't seen yesterday. It was gold with a fancy design on its face.

"Shyla Crowe," he murmured, "you disappoint me."

"You wouldn't be the first guy."

He sneered at my flippancy.

I kept my eyes on his ring. It had an upraised cross adorned by six colorful gemstones. In my research, I'd come across some Christian depictions of crowns of immortality represented by a ring of stars.

Lambert saw my attention and covered the ring, voice going hard. "Do you know what the world thinks of thieves?"

I leaned back and crossed my arms over my chest. "Probably the same way it thinks of the people who hire them."

"There are countries today that still sever hands that snatch things that aren't theirs. There are places where, when a robbery is thwarted, entire communities of bystanders join in to beat the perpetrators to death. These are unremarkable people, going about their daily lives. Thieves are universally condemned, but it's not due to the simple act of theft."

I rested in the chair, debating whether I should just walk out right then and there. The waitress made my decision for me. Lambert quieted as she set two mugs down. I thanked her and used a spoon to whip the raw egg. I then poured it into the coffee and stirred in some sugar and cream. Lambert waited patiently with a look of disgust so I played it up. I pointed to one of his butter packets.

"You using that?"

He quietly slid it over. I took a bit in my spoon and mixed that in too. My concoction finally complete, I took a heavenly, glorious sip, refusing to allow him to kill my mood.

Lambert frowned and his voice lost its edge. "Have you read the *Inferno*, Miss Crowe? I imagine, in your line of work, you have a penchant for old things."

There he was, dropping hints at my history again. But the coffee was good and he'd regained his calm. I was curious to hear what he had to say.

"History is familiar with Dante's nine circles of Hell. Thieves, I'm afraid, do not fare well in the narrative. They're thrust deep into the eighth circle known as the Malebolge."

The *Divine Comedy* got some things right about the nine hells, but it's mostly an allegory for the seven deadly sins. A gross oversimplification of a vast swath of territories and politics, viewed through a Christian lens.

The eighth ring of Hell is indeed the Malebolge, but you're unlikely to find human thieves there. After the first four rings, human presence is sparse. The eighth ring is a place of dirt and ditches and clinging mud, populated by only the most hardy of hellions. It's the wild fringe of the World Below, and we can only speculate what happens there.

For a perspective as close to the truth as I can figure, refer to none other than Dungeons & Dragons. I'm not even kidding. The game creators invented their planes of Hell to serve their fiction, but their ideas of competing factions and motivations and subterfuge were spot on. Hell is both an ordered and lawless place, far from a mere receptacle for sinners.

"Even below the Malebolge," continued Lambert, following Dante and Virgil deeper, "is the ninth circle, the frozen lake of Cocytus, reserved for the worst offenders: those committing treachery against their fellow man." His face lightened at his point. "You see, Miss Crowe, there's a difference between an honest thief and a dishonest one."

I sipped my breakfast silently. Rather than an emotional outburst, the old man was zeroing in on something I very much believed in.

"There's a difference in taking someone's livelihood," he stressed. "Their means. Their sentiment. These are personal things, and they drive personal emotions."

"I agree," I said bitterly, not happy to concede the point but knowing it in my bones.

Lambert, surprisingly, smiled. He nodded softly. "I had a feeling about you."

"You sure it was just a feeling?" I asked in challenge. "Or have we run into each other before? Because I also looked into you, Lambert. I'm sure you realize I used to live in Phoenix."

His brow wrinkled. "Is that so?" He shook his head. "A

coincidence, nothing more. My estate isn't even in city limits. It was your work that drew me to you."

"If you say so."

I wore my skepticism plain, but I'd lived several places and didn't remember him. It very well could've been a coincidence. The old man didn't betray any nervousness so I didn't press the issue, though I remained wary. Lambert did, after all, know a bit more about me than he should have.

"You have a personal code," he said, highlighting his point. "That's not just something I respect, it's the sole reason I hired you in the first place. This is why you and I are going to work something out."

The Worm

Despite my best efforts, the old man was finding a way to ruin my coffee. He sat there, suddenly pleasant, acting the nurturing grandfather.

"I can't help you," I said as plain as I could.

"Come now. Hear me out. I'm sure your professional courtesies require it."

I swallowed another bitter sip. He was still trying to worm me into the job.

"You must, from time to time, find yourself working alongside those whose rules aren't as... stringent as yours?"

I sighed. "I'm only accountable for myself. Other people do what they do without my say so. Life's complicated and I'm not about to fix it all. But yes, I do work with other people. Which is why I'm here." I took a breath, realizing I was being too roundabout. "Look, you're free to hire someone else for the score if you want, but I have a network in this town, and I'm not able to act against them without repercussions. Anything you paid me wouldn't be worth my while. I'd be ruined."

"I see."

The man went silent for a minute as he picked up his fork and resumed eating his eggs. My shoulders relaxed, the tightness in my neck eased. All hostilities at the table were done, and I'd explained the situation as clearly as I could. I sipped my coffee, suddenly hungry and wondering where I would stop for food on the way home.

"What did you find about the crown?" he asked, curious.

I might as well tell him. It seemed the professional way to end this relationship. "It's not what you think it is. It's an Egyptian funerary wreath."

"So it seems you know something of antiquities after all." Lambert grinned slightly.

The bastard had known. The sparsity of information had been a test.

"Amazing," he said, eyes shining. "You found that out without even entering the room."

Which of course he also knew. His biker gang was keeping tabs on the crown, preventing me from doing any more than sniffing around.

"That's all I have," I said. "I'm sorry I can't give you more."

Lambert finished his food. He placed the fork and knife on the edge of his plate and slid it to the side of the table. "I won't hear of it. Relics are like people. Their origins are only a part of the puzzle. They're able to grow in power, transform themselves, just like you or I."

"You really think it has magical properties?"

"I do. The Crown of Aevum has evolved past its Egyptian beginnings, just like I hope you can evolve past your limitations."

"If you really want immortality so bad, they're advertising this new app called Haven. Supposedly you can upload your consciousness to the cloud."

He scoffed. "I have no use for games. Death isn't a problem technology can solve."

"And the crown can?"

"*You* can, Miss Crowe, by completing a modified contract. There must be a way we can all be happy."

"I—"

I swallowed my words as his sunk in. The sentiment was eerily similar to Bedrock's advice. Please the client, please the employer, and please myself. All I needed was wiggle room.

My chin bounced from side to side as I pondered the tangled mess.

"Miss Crowe, I'm satisfied that your hesitation isn't a cheap ploy to extract additional funding from me. I also think I understand the precarious environment in which you operate and the complications at play. Now understand me. You are in a unique position. One I highly value. I am prepared to double your compensation, upon delivery of the crown."

Damn. Four hundred total. Lambert really wanted this thing.

"I can't get you the crown tonight," I said with a heavy sigh.

"But—"

"Tell me the truth, Lambert. Are you purposely implicating someone at the party?"

He appeared indignant. "Of course not. I neither know who's attending tonight nor do I care."

"Okay, so if this crown can really do what you think it can, you can wait a few days."

"And we may miss our opportunity. This moment has taken heavy planning and investment to reach."

"It's a risk you're gonna have to take if you want me involved. Even if the crown leaves the city or the country, I'm an international gal."

"The expenses could be exorbitant."

"The price of immortality," I returned.

The old man frowned. He was more aware of the stakes than I. "I'll only agree to it if I know the Crown of Aevum is genuine."

I arched a brow. "Don't you?"

"I know what it is purported to be, Miss Crowe. I need you to tell me if it's real. If I should continue spending my fortune chasing this particular piece or if I should look elsewhere." He waved for the check and straightened his jacket collar. "If you cannot acquire the crown tonight, then you can certainly inspect it for me. I have given you the time and place where you can vet the crown unmolested. There's a bag with two hundred thousand dollars waiting for you outside, an advance if you agree to take this on. But you need to be at that party, *tonight*, and putting your hands on the crown so that you can tell me, beyond a shadow of a doubt, that it's real."

I followed his eyes through the window. The biker woman held a backpack and winked.

Easy money and I didn't even need to steal anything yet. Who said you couldn't please everyone?

"I'll figure it out," I said, standing and gulping my coffee while the waitress placed the check on the table. "But keep your thugs out of my way." I stormed away before I had time to second-guess my decision.

Outside, I grabbed the bag of cash from Teegan. "Looks like you guys need me alive a little longer. Where's Grady?" I gloated. "Called in sick?"

Her eyes turned to daggers. "That's not funny."

"Give me a break. He got what he deserved."

"You bitch." Her hand went to the gun tucked into her waist, but she didn't draw. The two bikers at her back straightened and opened their jackets, revealing more firepower. "I know what you did," she growled, "and you're gonna get what's coming to you."

I blinked at her, dumbfounded. "It was a few bumps and bruises."

"Teegan," barked Lambert, now on the sidewalk. Her eyes shot past me and I stepped out from between them as he approached. "You will do as I say or I'll find someone else."

"We're good," she snorted, frustration evident. "We were just trading war stories." She spun her finger in the air and the three of them loaded onto their curbside bikes. They gunned the engines, sneering at me before riding off, leaving me and Lambert alone.

"This needs to stop," I warned him. "They're gonna blow the job. This stuff takes finesse."

"She's not a problem," he assured. "She's noticeably shaken after last night."

"Last night?" Now I wondered what Teegan and Grady had reported about our confrontation.

"Of course, you wouldn't have heard."

"Heard what?"

He coughed lightly and composed himself. "One of their club members, the big man with the beard you met yesterday, was found murdered last night two blocks from the Commercial Exchange Building."

My whole body went numb. "How... ?"

The old man pondered the question with a frown. "He was eviscerated, Miss Crowe. Eyes removed, intestines strung over the asphalt. From what they told me, Jack the Ripper would've been proud."

Lambert clenched his jaw and strolled away on the sidewalk, leaving me behind. For a full minute, I couldn't move.

The Tail

I returned to the Ducati looking over my shoulder. I'd left Grady in the stairwell. He was breathing and smack-talking. What had he said? That our business wasn't over. Except it had been, in my mind at least. I had no reason to go after him, much less kill him.

What other trouble had the big idiot gotten himself into?

I was now understandably paranoid. I started the motorcycle and slipped on my helmet and gloves, wishing I'd turned down the job after all. But the two hundred Gs in my backpack were plenty consolation for one dead meathead, and that was only half the score if things went my way.

As I pulled into the street, a dark gray Mercedes delivery van did the same. Maybe it was my heightened state of mind or maybe it was the paranoia, but I couldn't immediately dismiss the possibility I was being tailed.

I made a couple of turns over the next few intersections,

checking my mirror to see the van matching my movements. There was no doubt it was following me. I wondered how long this had been going on. Did someone just pick me up after meeting with Lambert, or had the van been behind me beforehand?

One thing was sure: it was hard to get far tailing a motorcycle with a van. Not if there was any evasion involved. I stopped at a red light behind some city traffic. I could slip between the lanes right now, cut to the front of the line and turn off without the van having a chance to follow. Then I'd have shaken the tail and missed my chance to get answers.

I didn't like the idea of adding yet another mystery to this case.

Instead I resumed with the traffic as the light turned green and pulled into an underground parking garage. It was a large building with an exit on the other side if I needed it. I collected my parking stub from the machine and pulled forward, waiting at the bottom decline.

The gray van turned into the lot. I smiled and slowly rounded the turn. The first two levels had a decent amount of parked cars, but the third level was a ghost town. I veered the bike across the middle of the lane, set the kickstand, and took my helmet off. After surveying the lot, I settled against a cement column between parking spaces, away from my Ducati.

The delivery van turned onto my level, moving slowly to gauge the tight ceiling clearance. They hit the brakes when they saw the Ducati in their path.

I waved from their flank and crossed my arms, in a casual lean like I was meeting old friends.

The van shifted to park and the side door slid open. Three men leapt out, two with machine pistols. They spoke in a foreign language, Arabic maybe, but their dress was decidedly Western. They hurried over with weapons pointed. I avoided making sudden movements.

"I figured introductions were in order," I called out. "I'm Shyla Crowe, but you already knew that. And you are?"

"Don't move!"

They converged and spun me around roughly, planting my face on the pillar. They held my hands tight, checking my palms and fingers, then running up my arms. One pulled the Sigillum Dei from under my shirt. He scoffed and released it.

"Where is it?" the one without the gun demanded. His English was good but there was some kind of accent.

"What are you talking about?

One of the gunmen unzipped my backpack.

"That's my money."

After checking the multiple pockets, he said something in his language that sounded like a curse. They spun me around to face them again and checked the jacket pockets. They hadn't taken my money.

"I usually don't let guys get to first base without a little small talk," I muttered. "Buy me a drink, a coffee at least. Really, I'm a cheap date."

"Where's the ring?" demanded the boss. He had a mustache without a beard, tanned skin with black hair.

"You guys are gonna need to slow down. I waited for you to see what you wanted. What ring are you talking about?"

They traded uncertain glances. I searched them for identifying objects. A silver bracelet, a wedding band. The boss had a large gold ring, just like Lambert.

"What is that?" I asked, nodding toward it. "A cross with six gems?"

Another curse. The man pulled his hand to his side. "Who we are is not important. You have something that belongs to us."

"That's doubtful."

"Where is your father hiding?"

"What does my fa—" My face flushed red. "Don't bring him into this."

"You're coming with us."

"I am most definitely not—"

They yanked me hard. One gunman grabbed my wrist while the other pointed the machine pistol at my back. The boss led us back to the van, into the open side door.

"Let's talk about this like civilized people," I urged.

"No more talk. You come now."

"I really am trying to warn you."

They shoved me into the van and jumped in behind. I scanned the interior. Another man sat at the wheel. The van was empty of personal effects besides a bag and some power bar wrappers. It looked like a rental to me.

As the door slid closed, it bounced off the reinforced shin plate of my boot stuffed in the way. "I'm warning you guys. I'm here willingly. Don't close that door."

One of them laughed and kicked my foot out of the way. "You do what we say and we'll not hurt you." The door slammed shut.

I sighed. "I think you have that backwards."

I waved my hand and the vehicle interior darkened and filled with sulfur. The van listed as Bernard slammed one gunman into the wall. The other machine pistol came up and a stone tail lashed it from his hand. Harried cries rang out as the gargoyle grabbed both guns and crushed them.

The boss went for the van's back door but I pounced on him. "You're not going anywhere."

The van shifted into reverse and gassed backward.

"Bernard!"

"I know."

The gargoyle pawed toward the panicking driver. The van starting turning to face the exit ramp but was going too fast and overran it. It slammed into the garage wall. All the loose passengers in the back, including Bernard, were thrown into the back door. The weight of a boulder hit us.

The van peeled out and headed up the ramp. Despite my tight grip on the boss, his hand clicked the back door handle. The double doors swung open. Bernard and one of the gunmen fell from the speeding van and tumbled along the incline.

I gripped the swinging door as the van rounded toward the exit. My other arm was around the boss' neck. "Who are you people?" I demanded. "What's that ring?"

Bernard loped up the parking structure behind the van. He'd left the gunman behind to get to me. The other one in the van was just regaining his senses.

I grabbed the boss' hand and pulled it close with a threatening growl. "What is this ring?"

"It's for my position as a Knight of Solomon!" he cried. "Please! I'm nobody!"

We were on the second level of the garage, moments away from the busier level one. I didn't want to bring Bernard up there.

"What do you know of my father?" I demanded.

The other man in the back rose to his feet and drew a dagger. I kicked my boot to stymie his advance.

"My father?" I prompted.

"He was a thief."

I shook the man. "How do you know him?"

He swallowed, desperate to get out of the headlock. "He worked for us!"

The other man knocked my boot away and advanced. I shoved the boss into him and rolled out the open back door, spinning on the concrete. The van swerved around the up ramp and out of view, squealing tires echoing throughout the garage.

Bernard's paws stomped beside me. "Shall I give chase?"

"Too many eyes," I groaned.

His golden eyes lit up. "There's one downstairs."

I nodded and Bernard reversed back down to the third level. I forced myself up with gritted teeth, even more sore than before. When I got my feet under me, I walked lightly to the staircase between the levels, going down and approaching my bike.

"He's gone," reported Bernard.

I nodded. "Figures. Let's just get home."

I gingerly lifted my leg over the bike and reached for my helmet.

Keepsake

I pushed into my loft ready to sprawl across the couch but immediately sensed something amiss. Bernard materialized at my side and emitted a low growl.

Objects on bookcases were shuffled and out of place. Furniture was shifted. My place had been tossed.

I hurried to the wall safe in my bedroom as Bernard rushed to check the bathroom for intruders. The safe was closed but the dial wasn't pointing to the same number I'd left it on. I opened it and found everything where it was supposed to be. I breathed a sigh of relief.

"They couldn't get in."

"Who says they're finished trying?" Bernard cleared the rest of the loft as I loaded my new stacks of cash into the safe. With everything that had gone wrong, it was a small miracle I'd held onto the money. Mission accomplished. I was good for another month. I closed the safe and set the dial. Maybe all this hassle had been worth it.

"It looks like we're good," I said as I emerged from the

bedroom.

Bernard was sniffing the rug under the dining room table. "It smells like Hell in here."

"Smoke devil, remember?" I lifted the rug and found the hexagram undisturbed. "The intruders didn't find this either."

"Yes, but what were they after?"

I frowned. "Money? I'm more concerned with how they know where I live. My name's not on any papers and I'm careful about being followed."

The gargoyle chuckled. "As evidenced by today. Although careful isn't the word I'd use."

"Do you always have to rain on my parade?"

"Whenever possible. Do you think someone's going after Bedrock?"

"That would be something. I think someone else thinks I have something of theirs."

"What did the men in the van want?"

I shrugged. "A membership ring? I don't know. Those guys are part of a secret society, I think. He said he was a Knight of Solomon."

Bernard's stony face went solemn. "Must I state the significance of King Solomon in this context?"

"No."

Solomon, the son of the Warrior King David, was a ruler famous for his riches and wisdom. He lived in the tenth century BC and built the First Temple in Jerusalem, and legend goes he had help. He was a famous magician and exorcist with an army of demons and jinns. In other words,

King Solomon was a summoner.

"The ring," I said, dumbfounded. "It's a golden cross encircled by six colored gemstones. I was thinking of it as a circle, but it represents the six points of a star."

"A hexagram," muttered Bernard. "The Star of David. The Seal of Solomon."

We shared a minute of stunned silence. The whole thing was ominous, I had to admit, but I wasn't sure what it meant. Lots of secret societies based their histories on biblical stories. Even the Freemasons. Their name stemmed from their apparent assistance in building the very same Temple of Solomon.

When it came down to it, so-called secret societies may have been mysterious, but they weren't very mystical. Most of them amounted to little more than ceremonial dressing for drunken orgies.

"You think they're clueless zealots," said Bernard.

"I don't know what I think. I normally wouldn't put a lot of stock in it, but they said my father worked for them. Lambert wore the ring. And the video's too grainy to get a good look at it, but I'm pretty sure Al-Assaf had one as well."

I prepared another message for Trap, collating and logging supporting data. The video of the prince. The description of the ring and the title Knight of Solomon. This time I wanted Trap to have as much information as possible upfront so I wasn't gonna send the request until I had a good hour to consider the angles. There was a whole history's worth of stuff to look into, possibly even personal history with my father. It felt like I was just getting caught up at the end of things.

But I couldn't dwell on the puzzle too long. The crown job was tonight. I wouldn't steal it, but I needed to get close enough to examine it. I'd already taken the money for that much so I was committed. Whenever Trap got back to me, I'd decide if I wanted to continue with the rest.

Until then, I just needed to be extra careful.

I moved to the bedroom, picked up a pillow from the floor, and sat down. I had to come up with a plan for the heist-turned-snoop-job, but all I wanted to do was clean up my place and rest. Bernard paced around the bed until something caught his nose. He sniffed at the wall.

"It smells of Hell in here," he said again.

"It's just Smokey."

"No, this is sweet, like flowers." He stopped at the safe. "Are you sure nothing's missing?"

I almost assured him but had a troubling thought. I crouched beside him and opened the safe, skipping past the cash and charms and checking the inventory of iron coins. Various demon sigils had been engraved into each one, coupled with a heavy dose of spellcraft. I paused.

"One's missing."

"I knew it," snapped Bernard.

"But that would mean someone got into the safe. They didn't take the money."

"Not someone, Shyla. A hellion. And they have little use for Earthly money. Which coin did they take? It will be a clue to their allegiance."

I drew away from the wall slowly. "Paimon."

Bernard's eyes went to full alarm, and there was a good reason for it. Several reasons, actually.

Paimon was the archon of the City of Dis, a series of towers and gates reputedly guarded by the furies and fallen angels. Dis was a prison of the worst kind. It was also the sixth ring of Hell. It was beyond my abilities to summon a devil from there.

Paimon's coin was a notable treasure of my collection, the only one of its kind, having been personally fashioned by my grandmother, Estever Crowe. It was beyond my abilities to replicate.

But worst of all was the insinuation of allegiance. Whatever demon had ransacked my place had taken the coin as some sort of tribute to his archon. Paimon himself was a grand king, but he bowed to another. One that went by the name of Lucifer.

No one bothered Hell's king of kings. No one dared. Grimoires and legends often conflated the names of Satan, Lucifer, and the Devil, but they weren't all necessarily the same. But Lucifer was real, one hundred percent, and even King Solomon wasn't powerful enough to command him.

I trembled at the thought that he was somehow connected to this, not directly but through several degrees of separation. Someone here was playing a deeper game than I'd assumed possible, and I was beginning to wonder just what exactly this Crown of Aevum could do.

Appraisal

I worked a bit on tidying up the home front. I was used to having demons in my loft, but not uninvited ones. The thought of shadowy fingers on my stuff was icky. Luckily, nothing besides the coin was missing or damaged.

I filled a freezer bag with ice, wrapped it in a dish towel, and pressed it to the bruises that were forming on my back. At this point, I had plenty of bumps to go around. Maybe I'd find time for a spa treatment after all this was over.

For now, there was work to do. I dismissed Bernard, made sure I had ample iron coins in my pocket, and summoned a helper hellion.

A small furry creature rolled onto its back on my glass table. Fleshy hands and feet scraped the sky, frantically seeking traction. The fingers were like toothpicks with knobbly knuckles. Finally, with the assistance of a furless length of tail, the demon rolled onto its butt and sat upright, legs splayed comfortably to both sides of a fuzzy pot belly.

Two giant, bulbous eyes opened, taking up two-thirds of

the creature's face. Besides the hands, feet, tail, and eyes, round pink ears and a tiny fleshy snout also seemed glued to a giant poof of fur.

"Shyla, you ungrateful hussy," grouched the miniature crone. "It's been a while since we spoke."

I answered with a pleasant smile. "How're you doing, Feifei?"

"Fine, fine. Feifei's always fine. Always hungry too."

I grabbed a saucer from the kitchen and filled it with a carton from the fridge. When I placed it on the table, the hellion's eyes somehow opened wider. She fervently sniffed the treat with her pug nose before leaning in and licking at it like a cat.

"This is good! What do you call it?"

I chuckled. "It's sweetened oat milk."

"They make milk out of oats now? Ridiculous. Delicious but ridiculous." Feifei slurped at the dish while I patiently waited with an amused expression.

Whenever dealing with dangerous or unfamiliar demons, it was always smart to summon them into a circle. It was the safe option for a first-time meet and greet, similar to going on a daytime coffee date. Circles made sure demons behaved and kept them from escaping. They were a safeguard used to come to terms and lay ground rules for future relationships.

When those relationships evolved, direct summoning was the easier and less ritualistic way to deal with them. It was important, however, to only perform that with hellions you considered friends. Or at least compliant.

Feifei was a friend. She'd been in the family longer than any of my other familiars, Bernard included. And she was most definitely harmless, as long as you ignored her constant insults.

The furry little cross between a monkey and a gerbil finished the saucer. As she leaned back, a skinny tongue licked the last of the milk from her pink nose. She tapped her belly in pleasure. "Ah, humans may be raving, incomprehensible idiots most of the time, but no one eats better than they do."

"I think that was almost a compliment."

"It's not my fault. You drugged me with food. That hag Estever never gave me stuff like this. Thought it would spoil me."

I always loved being surprised with little tidbits about my grandmother, but they were never useful. Hellions were forbidden from discussing business with their summoners. It was part of the contract's fine print.

I sighed happily. "But you were good friends, right?"

The critter smiled. "She was a hardheaded, difficult witch of a woman, but she was the best."

It filled my heart to hear that. I needed to make sure Feifei had plenty of oat milk from here on out.

"So let's talk business," she spat. "How did that Kwakiutl mask treat you?"

"Eh, it didn't fetch as high a price as I'd hoped."

"I told you. Humans never listen to Feifei."

"I know. I have something new I want you to appraise for me. But we'll only have a minute or two tonight."

"A little nighttime sneaking, huh? You know I don't like trouble. I'm from the first ring of Hell. Everyone's peaceful there. No one has time for trouble."

"Ah yes, the Asphodel Meadows don't leave you with a lot to worry about, do they?"

"It's nothing. We're all resigned to it. Stay on topic, slowpoke. Will there be drama over there or not?"

I shook my head. "Would you relax? I'll be right next to you, and Bernard will clear the room beforehand if needed."

"Great, that brute. Might as well set fire to the place while you're at it."

"It'll be fine."

She snorted. "There you go. Never listening to Feifei. Okay, what am I appraising?"

"It's an Egyptian funerary wreath that goes by the Crown of Aevum."

"Never heard of it. Let me guess: a crown of justification turned into a crown of immortality."

"That's the current thinking. It's made of gold and should be horseshoe shaped."

"I don't need those details. I have extremely perceptive eyes. Even a bumbling dullard like you might've noticed." Her head bent sideways as she curved a leg behind her ear to get at a deep itch. "I'll tell you what. I'll do it, but I'll need three coins as payment."

"Three coins?!?"

"What? It's a reasonable ask. If this thing is real, it'll need knowledge like mine. Show me someone else who can do what I do, in two minutes no less."

"But three coins—"

"Is proper recompense considering you're gonna put me in a room with hostiles. Humans are always bickering and fighting, especially where immortality's involved."

I took a measured breath. She wasn't wrong, but I held firm. "I'll give you two coins, one for each minute of your time."

"Fine, but I want them in advance."

I rolled my eyes. Feifei was my friend, but she was also a shrewd businesswoman who knew her value. "Deal." I placed two iron coins on the table, bearing sigils of minor demons, and slid them over.

Grubby paws snatched them up and brought them to her nose. "Yes," she said, sniffing, "these will do."

"While I have you," I hurried, stalling her as she prepared to go, "I had a random question. You've often given my family advice on dealing with demons and the various rings."

"I can't handle another question about Paulson," she groaned. "I don't know anything. I told you that."

I put my hand up. "It's not that. But I have had a coin stolen."

"What kind of dimwit would steal one of those? That's bad juju."

"It was Paimon's coin."

For the first time, Feifei was stunned silent. One of her eyes twitched closed and her tail went back and forth in irritation.

"That," she said after a moment, "is not a detail I

appreciate hearing after we settled our contract."

"It's a separate thing," I said. "It's unrelated to the job."

"Nothing's unrelated, Shyla. If I wasn't such a pacifist I'd leap onto your face and give you a good thrashing."

I grumbled at the tough talk from a tiny furball.

"You want to know who took the coin," she deduced.

I nodded.

"And you'd like to know what they want with the coin. And what Dis is up to."

"Yes."

"Well, I don't flaming know. You know why? Because I don't sniff around Dis. You know why? Because there's even more drama there than on Earth. You know why? Well, actually, I couldn't tell you. BECAUSE I DON'T SNIFF AROUND DIS."

I huffed. Feifei was pragmatic. Not looking for trouble among the hellions of Dis was the smart play. But what if they were coming to me?

"Look," said the miniature hellion, "you're a good kid. Too distracted to see the nose on your own face, but a good kid. Let me give you a little free advice. Don't associate with Dis. Good summoners have gotten into a lot of trouble for a lot less. Listen to Feifei."

And with that, the furball rolled forward and disappeared.

The Job

I started the night early. That meant sending Trap the full details of everything I had before hitting the street and scoping out the Commercial Exchange Building.

It was a crisp night. My eyes were peeled for anything. Gray delivery vans, Harley motorcycle clubs, Saudi bodyguards.

Just like I always did, I went through my rules. The habit was ingrained by my father, and even though I was long past needing it, the repetition was a ritual with me. It calmed my nerves.

Rule number one: no killing. Rule number two: steal only from someone who has it coming. Rule number three: be a professional. It was that simple.

After discovering the easy exit the night before, I passed through the same back alley. Another alley intersected this one at a T-junction, heading away from the hotel down a double-long block. I rode this way, past dumpsters and storage sheds and locked doors at the rear of stores on either side. It was a nice private strip with no people or security cameras all the way to Ninth Street. I parked the Monster just outside the mouth of the alley and put enough quarters in the meter to cover me until the cutoff. Then it was a quick stroll on foot back the way I came.

I didn't take a lot of gear with me and I didn't need to. The best part about demons was they were always with you. And on that note it wouldn't be anyone but Bernard and Feifei tonight. Too much at stake to risk using one I didn't trust.

So I was traveling light. I didn't even have my cell phone on me. That was rule number four. Don't take phones on crime sprees. They're mobile tracking devices on every citizen, and we do the government the favor of keeping them charged. So my phone was on the sofa bingeing Netflix, exactly where I'd say I was if anyone asked. The streaming data and phone location would back up my story.

I lapped the hotel twice, checking if anything was out of place. On my second pass I saw some definite hoity-toities exiting a car and heading to the elevator. I wasn't sure when the party started but it looked about time. That left me plenty because my role didn't call for a stage presence until the last act.

I sat at a cafe across the street and sipped coffee as I watched the other guests arrive. Since there were no Saudi guards and thus no one to greet them on the ground floor, I couldn't be sure who was headed to the soiree, but certain people had that look of class I didn't otherwise see patronizing the hotel.

After some time I figured the party was in full swing. There was about an hour left on my clock and nothing else to see down here. I entered the hotel from the bar, stepping through and scanning the crowd for anyone that stood out in the wrong ways. It pleased me to see the bikers weren't in attendance tonight. Perhaps Lambert had heeded my warning. Perhaps tonight was too important for them to screw up.

I entered the empty elevator and hit the button for the roof. I no longer had hotel access as I didn't have a room tonight. Current occupants would be suspects for any intrusions, and that was a list I didn't want to be on, alias or no.

On the roof, there was a decent bit of business at the tiki bar. I moved toward the pool without letting anyone see my face. A couple sat in a quiet spot by the sparkling water, but no one was swimming or tanning at this time of night. I passed them by, pretending I was taking in the skyline. When they were deeply distracted by each other's tongues, I hopped the vinyl fence in the back and landed in a farm of air conditioning compressors.

From here on out, I'd be a ghost.

Several strides saw me to the far side of the roof, opposite the elevators. I leaned over the edge. Just as Bernard had said, the metal balcony was a short drop down. Unfortunately, it overlooked Olive, a busy street. We'd need to minimize exposure from this side.

I navigated to the side wall, skirting around whirring machines. Al-Assaf's was a corner room, sharing a border with the overground parking garage in the back. That was where Bernard had scoped the windows before, and it was where we'd wait now.

With a wave of my hand, the gargoyle appeared on the side of the building, motes of ash swirling off his stone skin. He nodded my way and proceeded down to the windows, carefully peeking within. After spying the event from several angles, he returned to report.

"Full swing," he said. "At least a dozen guests, but I can't see them all. The crown's on display."

I grinned. "You see him performing any supernatural feats with it?"

He arched a devilish eyebrow. "What, like making bunnies disappear?"

"You know what I mean."

"Nothing of note. Just that decrepit Egyptian mummy he raised from the dead to drink the souls of the damned."

I rolled my eyes. "I need to find me a new gargoyle. Mine's broken."

"I kid, I kid. It's just a fancy piece of gold, Shyla."

"It's *my* fancy piece of gold." I frowned. "Just not tonight. We'll get in quietly and summon Feifei for her appraisal."

"Ah, yes, how could we exclude the ornery gremlin? You didn't feed her after midnight, did you?"

"I let you watch entirely too much TV." I snickered. "She's an academic, behind the coarse facade. That's why we need her."

"I wasn't protesting."

Although true, Bernard's tone was off. It wasn't like the protective gargoyle to be nervous before a job. "What's with you tonight?"

His sigh came out like an annoyed growl. "I don't like this one. It's too easy for too much money."

I blinked. "You're hanging on the side of a building thirteen floors up. That's easy?"

"For me it is. We're not considering something. Don't you find it odd that our prince wears a gold ring too? They're on to you."

I'd pondered that but hadn't heard back from Trap yet. It was still a piece of the puzzle I couldn't put in place. "These secret societies are like giant social clubs. Just 'cause they have the same ring doesn't mean they're on the same team. Brothers fight. Lambert wants what one of them has."

"Which means he knows more than he's letting on."

I couldn't deny that part. To Lambert, this was a bit of sporting fun. He'd already held out on me when it came to the true origins of the Crown of Aevum. He was testing me, keeping me on my toes. Just another rich asshole playing things close to his chest.

I also couldn't deny the cold hard cash he was offering me. The cash already in my safe. And here we were, so close.

"How about you stay here?" suggested Bernard. "I can go in and get it for you."

"We don't want to steal it," I reminded.

"Then I can put it back after you take a look."

I pouted at him.

"At least let me go in and give it a good smell first. I'm not a know-it-all like Feifei, but I can tell you how old it is."

"You really are worried, aren't you?"

He looked down at the street traffic. "I'm trying to avoid you getting beat up again."

I smiled at his concern. "You're just a big luvvy wuvvy bundle of worry."

He indignantly straightened. "I assure you I'm not... whatever you said."

I chuckled and let that be the end of it. Banter with Bernard passed the time, but I didn't want an endless debate. I was going in whether he liked it or not. Bernard would be my muscle, and Feifei would tag in to examine the crown. In and out in three minutes.

The silence dragged. I repositioned to the corner to watch the pedestrians below. Bernard kept an eye on the window. I stretched to loosen up, but it was more painful than relieving. My stomach and side were still tender from my tumbles down the stairs and out of the van. I zipped up my jacket to keep out the chill, fit my riding gloves back on, tucked in, and waited.

The droning of the compressors made my eyelids heavy. I didn't nod off, though I could've used a coffee to make the waiting easier. We were in place a good hour before Bernard spoke again.

"Party's over."

I hurried to the ledge and looked. Bernard was slowly descending to get a better angle without being seen.

"The guests are filing out."

"About time," I muttered, clapping my hands together for warmth.

According to Lambert, the prince saw all the guests out to the bar on the ground floor, where they all toasted to good fortune and went on their way. Al-Assaf, as always, was escorted by his security team. It left a good ten-or-fifteen-minute window when the room would be empty. Or as near empty as it was gonna get.

"Is the prince going with them?"

"Hold on." Bernard shuffled to another window.

"How many are leaving?"

"Give me a second."

I clenched my jaw in anticipation. Just because the party had gone a certain way last week didn't mean it would this week. Every job had little details you were so sure of until the moment they went sideways. I paced the roof back and forth, working myself up.

I'd want to count a minute to make sure everyone filed out and was in the elevator. I remembered the Saudi bodyguard last night returning to the room alone after seeing the prince off. We should assume something similar tonight.

The gargoyle poked his head over the ledge. "They all left," he said, but his voice was introspective rather than excited.

"Al-Assaf?"

"He was the last one out aside from his bodyguard."

We knew from Lambert's party that all the guards but one stayed in the hallway during the festivities, with only one inside watching the crown. If the bodyguard followed the prince out...

"There's no one watching the cage?"

Bernard shook his head. "The Crown of Aevum is completely unguarded."

I crossed my arms and thought about this a minute. By all accounts this was great news. It meant we didn't need to subdue anyone. But it also seemed too good to be true.

"Maybe there's a reason to worry," said Bernard, mirroring my thoughts.

"I don't know. Do you see anything troubling in there?"

"Nothing. That's the problem."

"Unless it's not a problem at all. What if Al-Assaf doesn't bother guarding the crown because it's a fake?" I grinned.

This was the best outcome as far as I was concerned. Sure, I wouldn't get the second half of the payment, but I wouldn't need to steal anything. In a matter of minutes, I would confirm the crown was a fake and my commitment would be done. Lambert would pack it in and the Knights of Solomon would clear out of my city. Perfect.

"We're still on," I said.

A chorus of laughter floated over from the tiki bar. Several festive voices could be heard over the drone of the air conditioners, which was odd because they had drowned out all noise before. A group was congregating.

"Hold on," I whispered, stepping lightly to the vinyl wall. I stuck my boot on one of the compressors and peeked over. Saudi bodyguards stood around the tiki bar. I ducked as one glanced to the pool area, waited twenty seconds, and checked again. The prince's guests filed around from the elevator and flooded the area. The soiree wasn't moving downstairs, it was moving to the roof.

I realized it had been rainy the week before. Maybe it was raining during Lambert's party so they'd transferred to the ground floor as a backup plan. Now it was a beautiful night to take in the sky.

"Does this change anything?" asked Bernard. He had snuck to my side.

"I'm not sure. It depends if everyone's up here." I scanned the crowd and pointed out Al-Assaf. "It might cut down our window by five minutes. Still plenty of time. Wait a minute."

Bernard peeked but I yanked him down and ducked behind the wall. I couldn't believe it.

"That son of a bitch," I muttered.

Bernard's eyes narrowed. "What is it, Shyla?"

I forced my lips out in bemused thought. "Aaron's out there. He's one of the prince's guests."

Rooftop

"Oh no," said Bernard. "You're not doing what I think you're doing."

"I sure am." I used the gargoyle's body to heave on top of the AC compressor but hunched low so my silhouette wouldn't be obvious to the guests.

Bernard was flustered. "You can't do this. You'll blow your cover."

"I need to know why Aaron's here. Besides, if we don't steal anything tonight, there's nothing to cover up."

"So you're just gonna stroll out there for a drink during our ten-minute window of opportunity."

"Hey, you're the worry wart. I don't wanna rush into anything that looks off. Don't move from this spot."

While the guests were looking the other way, I hopped over the wall and landed hard on my boots. The couple making out in their beach chair flinched, pulling their hands from underneath each other's clothes. I'd forgotten they were there.

"Get a room," I said.

I stood and stomped toward the tiki bar. I passed a woman with a tray of champagne glasses and snatched one, plastering a smile from ear to ear as I hooked Aaron's arm.

"Fancy seeing you here."

He stiffened, eyes flashing with surprise and maybe even anger. "Shyla? What are you—"

A blonde woman wearing a ballroom gown strolled up with two glasses of bubbly and handed one to Aaron. She was tall and leggy and gorgeous and I hated her.

"What's the Lead doing here?" I growled under my breath. I noticed they wore matching wedding bands, part of their cover.

The Lead was an actress, and I had to begrudgingly admit that she was a good one. When we needed a job that required a pretty distraction and some skillful smooth talking, she was number one on the rolodex.

She flashed me a sardonic smile. "It's Bridgett tonight." Her eyes darted to Aaron. "I thought we were a two-person crew?"

"We are," he said through gritted teeth.

I snorted. "You're working my score without me? You told me Bedrock called this off."

Which was strange for a lot of reasons. If Bedrock didn't want me on the job, what was Aaron doing here? And why did Bedrock practically urge me to figure out a way to come anyway? The whole thing didn't fit together. It was like Bedrock was pitting us against each other for his amusement.

"We're not working your score," said the Custodian calmly. "I'm protecting your interests. If you recall, that's my job."

I scowled at the assertion that I needed to be protected. I think my hackles were raised mostly because the Lead was here with him. But then, I was sure she was only here to smooth over Aaron's shortcomings with small talk.

Still, he could've told me about this instead of keeping me out of the loop. It didn't make any sense...

Unless Bedrock didn't know the Custodian was here.

That was it. Aaron was acting on his own. He must've found it suspicious when Bedrock called off the job. Maybe our employer read it in his face. Maybe that was why Bedrock asked if I trusted Aaron.

Bah. We didn't have time for office politics. Sneaking around behind Bedrock's back was reckless. Aaron was gonna get himself killed. And for what?

I was so absorbed in penetrating Aaron's cool exterior that Prince Fahd Al-Assaf snuck up on us. "A wonderful night, no?" he asked.

I spun to a dignified man with a beard across his lower chin from cheek to cheek. He said something that must've been Arabic for "cheers." Aaron followed suit with surprisingly good diction and they clinked glasses.

Al-Assaf switched to English. "And you, my dear," he told the Lead, "are even more beautiful in the moonlight." He admired her on Aaron's arm before glancing at me on the other. His eyes fixed on me excitedly. "I do not believe I've had the pleasure of meeting you yet."

I smiled cordially and pointed to the Lead. "She's the wife, and I'm the girlfriend."

"Ho, ho, ho!" boomed the prince while Aaron reddened in embarrassment.

Bridgett wore the perfect resigned smile and spoke with a cold edge in her voice. "My husband is an energetic man. He gets some outside playtime, but *Brett* always comes home to me." Wonderfully acted on her part, and she even threw in Aaron's cover name for my benefit.

The Custodian did his best to compose himself, but it didn't come naturally. "Mr. Kahn, this is Marilyn. My, uh, lady mistress."

"My pleasure," returned the prince. "But call me Ahmad."

I put on my best performance and appeared duly charmed. Between our code names, cover names, and aliases, there wasn't a real name in the house. Aaron took a nervous sip.

"Don't worry," said Ahmad, "I understand. I myself have many mistresses. I just don't bring them to parties with my wife!" He laughed again. "So Marilyn," he said, turning to me, "it's a shame you didn't come inside earlier. We had a delectable arrangement of food."

"It's okay," smiled Bridgett. "Marilyn's an outside cat. She's not allowed inside with the civilized folk. I mean, look at what she's wearing."

My charmed face was fading fast. "Excuse me a minute." I killed my champagne glass and tugged Aaron toward the pool area, leaving the Lead to distract the mark.

"What do you think you're doing?" muttered Aaron, displeased with my interruption.

"I was gonna ask you the same question. You really think it's smart to go against Bedrock? He could have you killed."

"What? I'm not going against him. He ordered us off this for a reason."

"And yet you're here."

"Yes," he said firmly, "I am. Bedrock has his suspicions about the crown. He told me to call the whole thing off."

"And what if he told me something different?"

Aaron's eyes flashed in recognition. "Did he?"

I sighed loudly and looked for the waitress. Instead I snatched the glass from Aaron's hand, took a gulp, and returned it to his hand almost empty. I wasn't sure what Bedrock had said anymore. "Not really. I don't know. But I figured I could make everybody happy."

He worked his jaw and checked to make sure no one was eavesdropping. "You were told in no uncertain terms to lay off this one."

"I was told not to steal the crown. But I got a new job from the client. He doesn't need me to snatch it. Not tonight. I just need to take a look."

He breathed hard. Al-Assaf had moved on to other guests but Aaron's eyes warned the Lead to keep her distance.

I softened my voice. "Let me do my job, *Brett*. This is good for us. I already have the money."

He frowned. "You can't."

"And why not?" My lashes flared. "What is this thing?

What aren't you telling me?"

"You seem to be the one keeping secrets."

I scoffed. "Oh, because you've been one hundred percent truthful with me, right?"

My voice came out a little heated. Some of the guests looked our way. The Lead widened her eyes to warn me I was making a scene. Luckily, a little tiff fit perfectly with my cover as the snubbed girlfriend.

"Come on," I urged, "you know something you're not telling me. I can see it in your eyes. And if you don't tell me, I'm gonna go down there and see for myself right now. I'll take my chances with Bedrock."

"It's fake," snapped Aaron. "The crown is fake. Bait for a thief."

My jaw hung open as the words faltered.

"The score is a sting," he said. "I'm betting they know this client of yours wants it. Who is he anyway?"

I shook my head absently. "Nobody."

"Now who's keeping secrets, Shyla?"

I swallowed. "This whole thing is a trap?" The wind officially left my sails.

"It appears that way. Which is why I'm protecting your ass, under orders from Bedrock. No one can go in that room, Shyla, because they'll be waiting."

My befuddlement transformed to anger. "When I get my hands on that conniving smoke devil..."

"Attention," called out the prince, standing by the bar. "Attention, everybody. As our gathering comes to a close, I'd like everybody that doesn't have a fresh glass to grab one so we can all toast to a momentous night."

I blinked several times, a sinking feeling welling in my gut. "I..." I stepped away from Aaron.

"Where are you going?" he whispered.

"I need to check on something real quick."

I broke away and headed past the pool. All heads were turned to the prince as the Custodian rejoined the Lead. I just needed to wait for Al-Assaf to turn away. I jumped the fence and found myself among the air conditioner units.

"Bernard."

He was supposed to be here. The damn gargoyle wasn't waiting.

"Bernard!"

I hoofed it to the edge of the building and looked over. He wasn't there either. I held my hand over the open air and pulled him back to me. Thirty seconds passed without anything.

What the hell was he getting up to now? I leaned over the side and peered down. The balcony window was cracked open.

This was bad. I had an unruly gargoyle walking into a trap. The prince was over by the tiki bar giving a speech that would signal the end of the night, which meant I only had a few minutes to get us out of here.

Luckily, summoners have power over their hellions. I didn't make contracts with Bernard. It was an unnecessary precaution with him. He may have been occasionally headstrong but didn't usually go against me like this. Even now he was ignoring my requests to return.

But there was one thing a stubborn gargoyle couldn't do, and that was ignore my power to unsummon him. I flicked my palm and it was done. Crisis averted.

Except it wasn't. I didn't feel the release of energy like I should have. It was like he was ignoring that command too.

But that was impossible.

With my window of opportunity rapidly closing, I set my boots on the ledge, hefted myself up, and took a breath.

"Here goes nothing."

I dropped off the side of the Commercial Exchange Building.

Room with a View

I landed on the metal with a loud clang. My boot got stuck between the iron bars making up the platform, but I worked it out. The awkward floor only reinforced the idea that these balconies were just for show. I peeked through the glass. The room was empty except for Bernard in the middle of the cage with the crown. But there was no trap. He was just in the middle there, waiting.

The window was halfway open. I pulled it up and slipped inside as it fell halfway closed behind me. The space was designed like a lounge, with earthy ottomans and low tables. The crown room had barred windows on three sides but the doorway was completely open. There was no door to shut.

"Bernard, you better have a damn good reason to—"

"Shyla, stop!"

I froze at the doorway, wall of windows to my back, glowering.

"It's a trap."

I put my hands on my hips. "I know it's a trap. That's

why I never gave you the command to go in."

He sat on his haunches and meekly lowered his head like a bad dog. "There's a circle on the floor. I'm unable to get out."

I backed up a step. The cage wall was built to hide the markings, but there was a painted line across the doorway. Blood, most likely.

I hissed. "What are you doing in there?"

"Protecting you," he said indignantly. "This was a setup and I knew it."

"Oh yeah, you knew it and walked right into a circle."

He shrugged. "I didn't know *that* part."

I waved my arm. I tried it again with my full focus. "I can't unsummon you."

"I'm stuck here, Shyla. You need to get out of here while you can. I'll take care of myself."

"I won't leave you."

"You better. Or we're both screwed."

I crouched and scratched at the dried blood. "What kind of circle is this? You think it can hold me too?"

"It was *built* to hold you. It's a summoner's snare, designed to keep you in place and contain any of your summons. It had to be for you specifically, Shyla. Why else go through this much trouble?"

The door to the hallway opened. Four Saudi bodyguards filed in. We locked eyes through the barred back window of the cage. They confidently smiled.

"I think you might be right," I muttered.

So Lambert thought he was stealing from his social club,

but it turned out the Knights of Solomon had laid a trap for him instead. But this wasn't about capturing him. It didn't make sense to think the old man would headline his own heist. No, this was made for a summoner. This was about me, my father, and a missing ring.

"Get out of here," urged Bernard.

Since they had me cornered, the guards were content to wait by the door as a last man walked in. He saw me, nodded in satisfaction, and pulled off his Saudi headdress. It was the boss from the gray van. The guards shut the door and threw their head coverings to the floor as well. More tough guys from the van.

"Apologies for the deception," said the boss. I remained still as he smarmily absorbed his triumph. He gave an order in Arabic and sent two of the men out. They posted by the door, guarding it as it closed. So I was down to three of them, at least.

The other two men remained at the entrance while the boss approached. He clasped his hands behind his back and strolled toward my side of the cage.

"Greetings, Miss Crowe. My name is Kofi Hailu." He rounded the wall and froze, face-to-face with me, confused. "You're not in the cage."

I shrugged. "I'm not in the cage."

My boot hammered his groin. Kofi doubled over on his knees. The other men flinched and reached into their robes.

I backed away to the window. "I'll come back for you," I told Bernard.

"Not necessary. They can't keep me here forever."

The men produced machine pistols. I rushed to the window. It was jammed tight. I pounded at the bottom amid their cries in Arabic.

"You must stop!" cried Kofi through gritted teeth. "The Lion of Judah commands it!"

The window slid upward. "Sorry, boys, this little lady's about partied out."

Since they obviously didn't want to kill me, the automatic weapons weren't genuine threats. And I would've liked seeing them shoot Bernard with those toys. But a girl can't always get what she wants.

I flipped through the window as the guards converged on me. Back on the balcony, I blanched at my options. This wasn't a fire escape but a disconnected string of metal platforms all the way to the street.

"The life of a cat burglar," I muttered.

As I went to climb over the railing, the clunky toe of my boot got caught between the metal bars on the floor again. I tried to shimmy it out as a hand clutched me. I batted it away. The Saudis were still inside having trouble with the stuck window. I got loose and vaulted over the railing.

Thankfully, the bars making up the wall were spaced further apart than those on the floor. My boots fit comfortably between without danger of getting wedged in. At this point the guards had gotten the window open and the first was climbing through. I wrapped gloved hands around the vertical bars and stepped off the railing, sliding to a hanging position and desperately stretching my legs. With my grip at the bottom of the platform, the toes of my boots just barely scraped the top of the handrail below.

The Saudi bodyguard reached for me and I released the balcony, leaning forward as I crashed on the platform below.

I winced. "So much for the grace of a cat."

Above me, the two guards were getting in each other's way on the small balcony, arguing incoherently. I grinned. This window, like the tenth floor and all the others not numbered thirteen, led to a hallway of normal-sized hotel rooms. It was sealed closed so I broke the glass with my elbow. The riding leather protected me. I cleared the sharp edges away and pushed inside.

It would only be a minute until the guards were on top of me. Luckily, my exit plan was handy. I hurried to the concrete stairway and burst through the exterior door. My stun gun sat against the wall. In my daze the night before, I'd forgotten to recover it.

"At least I managed to get something out of tonight."

I snatched it up and practically flew down the steps.

Outside again, the alley was quiet. No yelling, no flurry of activity. It was like the calm after a storm. The lonely alley cut through the length of a block between the back sides of buildings butting against each other. It was a straight shot to my exit on the street, with no witnesses to spy an escaping thief.

I set off at a sprint, expecting the Saudi guards to spill into the alley after me. But I could've been anywhere in the hotel. They must've lost me. As I neared the halfway point to my bike, a bystander stepped from the shadow behind a dumpster. I slowed to a walk to avoid drawing undue attention.

I glanced backward. No one was on my tail. My boot steps echoed loudly off the walls, standing out against the background hum of cars that seemed miles away. I faced forward and squinted against the hazy lighting. For some reason, the area appeared blurry. I casually ran my fingers through my hair, checking my head for bumps or blood, but I was self conscious about doing it in the presence of a bystander. I played it off and smiled.

And stopped dead in my tracks. The figure was watching me with glowing amber eyes. He was a demon, and I swore I'd briefly spotted those same eyes in this alley the night before.

Even so, the figure made no move toward me. He stood in darkness, fully silhouetted against an orange background glow.

I worked my jaw, checked behind me again, and decided to press forward. Thirty seconds, and I'd be sitting on my bike.

Besides the eyes, there was something inhuman about the figure's lithe form. As I neared, I shook off the otherworldly haze and began to make out details. The demon's face had animalistic features, thin chin scrags like whiskers, and visible canine teeth. His skin was discolored— spotted, like that of a leopard. The scent of sweet jasmine sucked into my lungs.

I kept my hands in my jacket pockets, stun gun handy, and continued forward with the intention of passing him by. Still, it was silly to pretend he wasn't there. "Why are you following me?" I demanded.

"You have something of mine," he returned coolly. His voice had the coarseness of a lifelong smoker.

"I've been getting that a lot lately. Who are you?"

"I am called Jackal."

I arched an eyebrow. I would've guessed a tiger more than a canid. Orange and red skin coloration, pointed ears, a scruff of white. Even his eyes were vertical like a cat's. But then demons were often an unsettling amalgam of creatures. In this business, you got used to it.

"You were in my house," I leveled.

Jackal shrugged. I skirted around him a healthy distance, walking sideways to keep an eye on him. He followed my pace with the meticulous gait of a predator.

"You have nothing to fear," he purred. "If I was here to kill you, you'd be looking at your insides by now."

I grimaced as we walked. He was the one who'd killed Grady. "You think, in your own twisted way, that you're protecting me."

The demon showed his teeth. "He said you were smart."

"Who? Who do you work for?"

"I thought that was obvious from the coin of power I absconded with." He angled to cut the distance between us.

"Paimon," I spat. "Lucifer. I have no dealings with them."

"The dealings are rarely yours to choose."

This was Exhibit A of why demons were so dangerous. In all likelihood, any given summoner was playing ball against a being who'd lived several ages at least. Their knowledge and reach was boundless compared to a single human's perspective. This was why the collective experience of grimoires and spellcraft were vital to a summoner's playbook. The goal was to even the odds as much as possible. And it didn't hurt to dig for extra information once in a while.

"I'm not talking about Hell," I said dismissively. "What human summoned you?"

"Who says one did?"

I clenched my jaw. "I do."

He didn't reply one way or the other. That was more or less expected with my line of questioning. Hellions were usually tight-lipped about their summoners. Jackal watched me with vertical eyes, and I realized he was closer than I wanted him to be. I glanced ahead. We were almost at the end of the double-long alley. Ninth Street was seconds away.

Jackal lunged. I tried to spin away but he shoved me against the wall. It was a downside of keeping my hands pocketed.

"Where is it?" he snarled.

"Where is what?"

He shook me against the brick. "Don't play dumb with me! What did Paulson do with the ring?"

"This again?" I jammed the stun gun into his side and zapped him.

Jackal didn't even acknowledge it as a tickle. He thrashed me again and leaned in. "What is that?" he asked, sniffing me as I grew angry. "Yes... There is a darkness in you,

Shyla."

I ground my teeth together, trying to keep my head. I didn't want to lose control. I turned my head away and Jackal licked my cheek.

"It builds within you," he purred.

I was so focused on keeping a cool head that I couldn't tell if he was impressed or afraid. But my ability to summon was tied up with Bernard in a trap. The Dark One may have been knocking, but even she couldn't come to my rescue now.

Jackal smiled. "It yearns to be free."

"Never," I avowed.

His lips twisted in disgust. "Where is Paulson?"

"He's in Hell."

Jackal paused, the information a revelation.

I reached into the neck of my shirt.

"Of course. It's why we haven't found him. It's—"

I pressed the Sigillum Dei into his face and he screamed. Jackal reeled from an invisible impact and tumbled to the cement. Smoke curled up from blisters on his cheek.

I broke out running for the street. The demon roared and loped after me on all fours. I burst out of the side street so wildly that I crashed into a young couple holding hands. We hit the floor.

"Sorry!" I cried, jumping to my feet and spinning to the alley.

"What is it?" asked the guy, helping his girl up. "Are you okay?" He looked at the darkened path I had come from, but it was empty.

I took a few harried breaths. "Yeah. Yeah, I'm okay. I'm really sorry."

I'd beamed him pretty hard, but he was young and had taken it like a champ. I hurried to the Ducati a few strides away and gunned it out of there.

Fly Trap

I was dressed in full leathers, but I felt naked as I sped away on the motorcycle.

Bernard was trapped, which meant I was a summoner without a familiar. I was a soldier with a jammed weapon, unable to reload. Completely stuck when it came to my special talents. Without demons, I was a five-foot woman with a banged up stun gun.

At a stoplight several blocks away, I finally fitted my helmet on. I needed to get back to my cell phone and talk to Trap. Then again, I was running from a demon who knew where I lived. I couldn't face him again. Not now. I detoured to the highway.

The Ducati hit a hundred on the open road. My mind was racing faster. I'd never seen the Sigillum Dei do anything like that before. The pentacle was for personal protection. A ritualistic token that amounted to little more than a staple of demonic etiquette. I'd expected Jackal to shy away from it, to respect the bounds of an established and skillful summoner, but not be sucker punched across the alley.

I could only figure his allegiance to Paimon, and in turn Lucifer, had given the seal a bit of extra juice. The diagram had its origins in the medieval church and was inscribed with the holy names of God and His angels. But that stuff might as well have been myth. Summoners didn't have inroads to the so-called Celestial Planes. We didn't know the secrets of the universe. We just had a knack for communication with the World Below.

Whatever had happened with the Sigillum Dei back there, it was exactly what I'd needed in that moment. Not a victory, but a successful retreat.

I took an exit in the Valley and found myself among suburban ranch houses. A few straightaways and turns later and I rode down an idyllic tree-lined street. I revved my bike lightly in warning as I pulled to the curb. It was late and the neighborhood was quiet so I was being anything but sneaky. Trap opened the door when I was halfway down the walkway.

"Uh-uh. You are not walking toward my house right now."

I cracked a smile. It was good to see a friendly face.

Joseph Trapper was a lean-built man. Squeaky bald even though he'd only just had his thirtieth birthday, he compensated with a full, well-groomed black beard and mustache. In his current peach collar and plaid sweater-vest, he looked like a GQ model. Another decade and he'd be the black James Bond.

"I need a place to hide, Trap." I sighed and pushed past him.

He closed the door after me. "You know this is my house, right? The bed where I sleep is here."

I rubbed my forehead to rouse my senses. "I'm sorry. I can't go home and I needed to see what you found out."

He licked his lips and nodded. "So that's why you didn't get back to me."

"You have something to drink?"

He waved me to the couch. It was a green velvet Chesterfield beside an antique bookcase loaded with volumes of every size. This living room was *so* Trap.

"I'm surprised you don't have any doilies," I called out to the kitchen, where Trap was getting me fixed up.

"Says the girl who listens to records every day," he shot back.

I snorted. The last thing I needed was a reminder of my age. Life has a way of feeling more like an emergency countdown than a bountiful accrual of time. I kept my snide remarks to myself until Trap handed me a glass of whiskey with a single ice cube and sat beside me with his phone.

"I made a mistake, Shyla. Prince Al-Assaf isn't Prince Al-Assaf."

I widened my eyes at the one-two punch of bad news and strong drink.

"In my defense, they wanted us to think he was Al-Assaf. That's why they dressed up in keffiyehs and used an alias the prince used, but he's not a prince. These guys aren't even Saudis."

Which explained why they'd thrown the fake headdresses to the floor once they thought I'd been caught. It was all an act.

"That video you sent of the limo outside the hotel? They're not speaking Arabic, it's Amharic."

"What's Amharic?"

"It's an ancient Semitic language with the oldest alphabet still in use. It's also the national language of Ethiopia."

"What?"

He cut my questions off with a curt wave of his hand. "It's not the Ethiopia you think of today: war-torn, vast hunger and poverty. Did you know they were a legitimate empire lasting seven hundred odd years until being overthrown?" He leaned forward to emphasize the next part. "In the nineteen-seventies."

I furrowed my brow. "Really?"

"They managed to modernize with a full army, navy, and air force. They were allies in the Korean War, man." Trap was actually a bit excited about the history lesson. "But they came from a full-on medieval empire. They had an emperor, monks, serfs, slaves, and even knightly orders."

"The Knight of Solomon," I said.

He nodded. "That ring you saw connected the dots. A gold cross inside a six-pointed star. They're Christians, not Muslims. They're the Order of Solomon, and it's not just a men's club and an excuse to wear robes on the weekends. There were some really powerful members in this thing. The king of England, the emperor of Japan."

He took a breath. "Look, there's a reason they hold the

Order of Solomon so holy. They believe their royal line started way back in biblical times. The tenth century BC. You know the famous story: The Queen of Sheba visits King Solomon and they share a passionate romance. Well, the Ethiopians claim a son from that union, King Menelik, who founded a dynasty. Their latest empire claimed the same lineage, right until 1974 when the emperor was overthrown and mysteriously killed."

I took a sip of whiskey to help me process. "But Lambert's not Ethiopian..."

Trap shrugged. "Neither was the king of England." He scrolled through his phone while he spoke. "It says right here ordinary recipients can be inducted into the order if they render exceptionally meritorious services. Your client is probably a low-level knight and they're using him to find you."

Which added up. The Crown of Aevum was a setup. The Order had probably dropped hints regarding its power, whispered in Lambert's ear about Arab royalty showing it off. His hunger for immortality made him an easy target.

"So who's Kofi Hailu?" I asked. It was the only real name I had.

Trap tried a few different sites with a few possible spellings until his face darkened. "This is proof of who we're dealing with. If there was any doubt, there's not anymore."

"Who, Trap?"

"The Crown Council of Ethiopia. They were a constitutional body of advisors to the emperor. Many of them were executed along with him. A few years later, when the country formed a new democratic republic, the Crown Council became a government-in-exile. Kofi's their president."

"Then who's the Lion of Judah?"

"There is no Lion of Judah, Shyla. That's the given title of the emperor, and that spot's vacant. The Crown Council claims theirs is the only legitimate government. They're a bunch of old royalists who survived the bloody transitions. But they don't have an army. They can't overthrow modern Ethiopia. So they remain in the exile of their past."

I shook my head. "Not the past anymore. Kofi spoke of the Lion of Judah like he was a real person. The old empire is alive again."

Trap scratched his beard and frowned. "It was recent enough that there are those who still remember the old ways, who are descendants of the last emperor. From that perspective, Solomon's lineage is alive and well."

"I'm such an idiot," I muttered. "They've been asking me for a ring this whole time. My father might've been an honorary member of the order, like Lambert."

"If that's true, it means he knew your father."

I paused to consider that. It was a conclusion I should've come to on my own. It explained how Lambert knew of my particular skill set. The old man could probably fill in the blanks of my fractured past.

"This only reinforces my thinking," I said. "This whole thing is about an ancient relic, but it's not the Crown of Aevum."

Trap curiously hung on my words.

"King Solomon was a summoner, and it wasn't pure skill. He was gifted a ring with the power to command demons."

"The Ring of Solomon," whispered Trap. "That can't be real."

"If a whole bunch of people are willing to die for it, does it matter?"

"Die?" asked Trap. "Who's dead?"

My face darkened. All my little visits were beginning to make sense. These people had been ready for me. They were ready for Bernard.

Trap raised his voice. "Who's dead, Shyla?"

"No one," I said dismissively. "A stupid biker who messed with me was killed last night. I think it was the same demon who broke into my house this morning. The same one I ran away from..."

Trap's eyes widened. "These guys, the Order of Solomon, they're summoners like you, Shyla. They're after you, they know where you live, and now you're telling me there's a demon on the loose?"

He stood and abruptly stormed away. I sat up and tried to calm him. He returned with an RF scanner wand and waved it over my jacket and pants.

"Trap, come on."

"How'd they know where you live?"

I shook my head. "I don't know. I'm always careful of being followed." I thought it over. "The Crown Council tailed me after I met with Lambert today. But I stopped them before leading them to the loft."

Wait a minute. Lambert had been having brunch with an

associate. I'd interrupted him. Told him I needed a sit-down because I was pulling out of the job. If he was meeting with Kofi, the Crown Council would've thought they were losing their opportunity to snare me. That's why they followed me from the cafe. That's why they came at me hard.

"Your bike," said Trap, dissatisfied with not finding anything on my person. He rushed outside. I took a sip of whiskey before setting the glass down and going after him. It took less than ten seconds for his scanner to beep. He crouched down and searched the battery area.

I was red-faced at my lapse in security. "The fuse box." I pushed him aside, opened the plastic cover, and staggered in place. A small tracker had been plugged into the Ducati's active power.

"Now they know where *I* live too." Trap's nerves were electric. "This is why I don't take walk-ins."

"I shouldn't have missed it," I offered weakly.

He stood up straight, not mad but pragmatic. "I've been meaning to take a vacation anyway." He stomped back into the house and I followed. "Vegas isn't too hot right now. I can practice my poker face."

"Trap, do you really think that's necessary?"

He rounded on me. "I'm blown, Shyla. You may only be alive because you know something, but I don't know anything. I'm collateral damage, like that dead biker. I need to get far away from here."

I trailed him to the bedroom. He grabbed a suitcase and flung it on the bed. It was already filled with supplies for just such an occasion, but he added some personal effects. Ten minutes later, we were on the front porch as he locked his deadbolt. He loaded up his Jeep and closed the driver-side door.

"I forgot to pull that tracker out," he said through the open window. I stood on the street. "It's easy to disconnect."

"I can handle it," I said. "I might keep it in and set a trap myself."

"That's smart. You're gonna need to be." He looked forward and set his jaw, concerned. "My advice? You need to watch your back. This whole time you've been focused on the score, but someone out there's running a game on you. If you don't see them coming, you have no chance of stopping it."

The Jeep pulled away and I felt lost. Aaron had lied, Bernard was stuck, and now Trap was gone too. Everybody I completely trusted in this city was taken away, leaving me with a jumble of clues to solve all by my lonesome.

I sat on the actively tracked Ducati Monster and slipped my gloves on, figuring out a plan for what came next.

Rally

The first thing I did was burn off some gas. I rode west, past the dam. Circled south and zigzagged through the hills. When I had to think through something, sitting in one place was such a drag that my mind followed suit, churning without going anywhere. It was easier to work through a problem with the wind in my face.

And hey, I was just being a good host. If someone *was* following me, I was giving them a tour of the city.

I thought over all the options available to me, even if just to dismiss the impossible ones. Stuff like talking to the police. That wasn't gonna happen. Rule number four: don't talk to the law. At least I thought it was rule four. I always lost count after the first three. The rest were common sense anyway. The point was, the police were staying out of this. Which was fine by me. Even if I wasn't laughed out of the department, any officers I recruited would be woefully in over their heads.

After all the pipe dreams were discarded, what was left

boiled down to two options: leave town or stay and fight. I didn't like either if I was being honest. I wasn't a runner but I wasn't a fighter either. I faced my problems, though rarely head on. I preferred to play the elegant thief who relied on her network and wits. So going Rambo on everyone wasn't a solution, but neither was meeting Trap for drinks in Vegas.

When I realized I was riding back into the Arts District, I knew I'd made my decision. I couldn't leave my father to Bedrock, or Bernard to the Council. And I did have a network. I needed to get them in my corner.

The same went for my client. Lambert was being played just like I was. He possessed considerable resources that we could leverage to get out of this mess.

And while I was getting to the heart of things, there remained the little matter of discovering his business with my father, Paulson, and how that tied into the Crown Council.

The long ride was really a way of getting my head straight, of assessing my priorities, and deciding, demon or no demon, I needed to get into my house and recover my phone. It was the only way I could contact Lambert.

I approached the entrance to the parking garage and noticed the interior light of a parked Mercedes across the street. It was Aaron. I waved and he waved back. Instead of pulling inside, I kicked up the Ducati on the curb, crossed over to the car on foot, and sat inside the passenger seat.

"You shouldn't be here," I said. "It's not safe."

"That's why I *am* here," he said sternly. "I dropped the Lead off after the party and wanted to follow up with you.

You're not answering your phone."

"I was at a safe house."

"Where?"

I smiled slyly. "Nice girls don't kiss and tell."

"Mm-hmm, and what about you?"

I snickered. "Did you just make a joke?" I laughed and stretched the seat back. After straddling the cafe racer for the last hour, my ass appreciated the comforts of the luxury interior.

"Just trying to lighten the mood," he said, face solemn. "It looks like you've been played."

"Not entirely. I still got two hundred K out of the deal. All I need to do is report back to the client that the crown's fake."

The corners of his lips curled. "You sly dog. You convinced him to pay you without a theft?" His mouth went straight. "I don't think we can trust him, though. What's the client's name?"

"I wouldn't worry about him. Our problem is Prince Al-Assaf and his gang. They put on a good little show for us. Speaking of which, you did too. I didn't know you spoke their language."

He shook his head. "It's nothing. I picked up rudimentary Arabic when I studied abroad."

My brow furrowed. "I thought it was Amharic."

He flinched. "What's the difference?" he muttered. "The toasts are the same."

I nodded slowly as I pulled the seat up. I was no longer comfortable. Aaron was too precise a person to hand-wave a difference like that. I was getting the sinking feeling he was purposely keeping me in the dark about things. First it was him going to the soiree without me, and now this. At the same time, there was no doubt he'd protected me from the trap. I licked my lips as I carefully thought over his motives.

"They're actors," said Aaron, convincingly enough that I believed he believed it. "It's a long con, and I would put good odds that it's your client who set the whole thing up."

I swallowed. He was brushing off the Ethiopian connection. I wanted to tell him about the Crown Council, the Ring of Solomon, and the whole thing with my father. Now I wasn't sure I could trust him.

And then I remembered the strange questions Bedrock had for me about the Custodian. And I wondered what Bedrock had asked Aaron about me.

"Shyla," he said, "I need the client's name."

"You're wrong about the Saudis," I said, keeping their fake cover intact. "They trapped Bernard in a summoner's snare."

"They what? I told you not to go in there!"

"He did it without me. Bernard's a little headstrong. He was trying to protect me."

Aaron worked his jaw.

"It gets worse. There's a demon in play. I think one of the prince's soldiers. He ransacked my loft this morning."

"Shyla..." Aaron was going red with anger now. I'd never seen him like this before. He was ready to explode but was honing that anger into careful planning. "You need to go upstairs," he said, calmly but forcefully. "Tell the client you want to meet tomorrow. Then talk to Bedrock. Tell him all about our conversation and how he needs to watch your house tonight."

"Tell Bedrock," I repeated, sounding out how ridiculous it was for me to order my employer.

"He'll protect his investment," assured the Custodian. "He has no choice. He's not about to let some two-bit demon destroy everything he built."

I blinked, surprised at the determination oozing from Aaron right now. He was angry and decisive and so sure of himself. Taking charge was kind of a turn on.

I reddened and looked away. What the hell was I talking about? Aaron? I appreciated his protectiveness, and I'd use his easy confidence as inspiration, but I was far from a swooning princess in need of saving. We were a team. He was just keeping up his end.

"You'll need to tell him about Bernard too," he said. "It's unfortunate. He'll think it makes you weak, but it needs to be done. Bedrock should be able to free Bernard from the other side."

My eyebrows shot up. "From a snare? There's no way."

"He can do it, Shyla. Now hurry upstairs. We don't have time. We take care of the demons tonight, and then your client tomorrow. Okay?"

I nodded, feeling put off that I wasn't contributing to this plan. But wasn't that what I wanted? This was me, leaning on my team. The Custodian's job was to look after me.

I opened the car door and exited, looking both ways and

leaning back in. "Watch your back, Aaron. These guys have put a tail or two on me. Don't let them follow you home, too."

He nodded. "Just tell Bedrock and you'll be safe tonight."

I shut the door and watched him pull away.

I had a strange feeling, like I wasn't carrying my weight, like I was leaving too much unsaid. I could've told Aaron about Jackal, how he was looking for a ring I didn't have. But could I trust Aaron when he was lying to me too? That was the problem with conning people for a living. Sometimes you got a little paranoid they were conning you right back.

I felt a little break between us, right then and there, and it was nothing like when Trap had pulled away. Trap was my guy, an old friend who was scared for his life. Aaron was an old friend too, but his own motivations were peeking through lately, and I wasn't sure where I fit in anymore.

So I needed to play things close to my chest, tucked in like the Sigillum Dei. Deal with Lambert and the Order of Solomon on my own. At least until I got answers about my father. That was it. He had to be the key.

I returned to my bike and pulled it into the garage. It had a tracker on it, but the Council already knew where I lived anyway. Besides, with Bedrock watching the place, it wasn't me that had anything to worry about.

Apocrypha

I tiptoed through my dark loft with the stun gun in one hand and my pentacle brandished in the other. Netflix autoplayed what was probably the fifteenth episode in a row of *Friends*. Ross pining over Rachel wasn't a lot of action, but it was more than anything else going on in here. This place was empty.

I picked up the remote and turned the TV off. My cover night of binge watching was complete. I turned on a few lights and went back to the couch to check my phone. Several messages from Trap and Aaron. None from Lambert. I dialed his contact and waited through the rings. No answer.

I hissed. All that trouble and they were ghosting me again.

I pinched the bridge of my nose and wished I'd had the presence of mind to stop for coffee. But it was late, almost midnight. I put on a pot of water and readied a tea bag in a mug. There was a little time before I could check in with

Bedrock.

Out of nothing more than habit, I went into my safe and pulled out my grimoire, *Semitas Daemoniorum*. Everything was untouched this time. I sat on the bed and kicked off my boots, forlorn that Bernard wasn't coiled up nearby. Then, like I did every other time I prepared myself to speak with Bedrock, I went through the list of notable demons and henchmen, brushing up on signs of anything familiar.

But my concentration was suffering. I wasn't thinking about the demons, I was imagining all the possible histories that had brought me here. That had trapped my father in Hell. That had put me in the crosshairs of more than one demon...

I jumped when the kettle whistled. I went over and steeped the tea, absently pondering the things that went bump in the night. It wasn't until I added sugar and a spot of milk that I took a sip and relaxed my brain.

The mug too full and the tea too hot, I carefully shuffled back to the bed and set the drink on a coaster on the nightstand. I gazed at the open grimoire, at the page I'd been studying without being conscious of it. I inhaled sharply.

I now knew this wasn't about a gold membership ring. The Order of Solomon wanted the famed Ring of Solomon. That's what Jackal had searched my loft for. Everyone was searching for the mystical artifact, and no one knew where it was.

But there was one particular hellion tied to the famed magician king, and I'd already been browsing his details without realizing it. The story has several iterations, and all apocryphal, but they say Asmodeus was one of the demons Solomon commanded to build his great temple.

The tale goes that, somehow, Asmodeus tricks Solomon into giving him the ring. The demon kicks the king out of his kingdom and rules in his stead for forty days until Solomon, through blessing or chance, finds his way back, recovers the ring, and reclaims his kingdom.

But the story doesn't end there. Biblical stories rarely do, because history is the past but life is the present. Solomon went on to start an Ethiopian dynasty, and the demons must have likewise continued their machinations in Hell.

According to the *Semitas Daemoniorum*, Asmodeus was cast down, put in chains, and locked in a dungeon in Dis.

I blinked. If anybody might know of the power and ultimate fate of the Ring of Solomon, it was Asmodeus.

I sipped some tea and studied the text. I looked up publicly available sources from my bookshelf and the internet on my phone. Asmodeus was one of the most fictionalized demons in recent history. Once figures like him entered into the world's collective imagination, factual accuracies trended toward zero.

My phone chimed, signaling the approaching midnight. I smiled, expecting Bernard to complain, before bitterly realizing I was alone. I'd gotten so drawn into the investigation that I forgot my predicament. I sipped tea but it had gone cold. I returned the grimoire to the safe and pulled off my clothes, upset I didn't have time to take a shower and wet my hair. Priorities, I reminded myself. I actually needed Bedrock's help this time.

I opened the wardrobe and pulled the bathrobe off the mirror and over my shoulders in one smooth motion.

"This is a pleasant surprise," crooned Bedrock. "I didn't expect to hear from you tonight." His fingers hungrily traced his furred chin.

"This isn't a social call," I said with detachment. "I've spoken with the Custodian, and we have a matter that needs your attention."

He smiled. "This should be good."

"The Crown of Aevum was a trap. I didn't steal it, as you asked, but Bernard was caught in a summoner's snare. The Custodian seems to think you can do something about that."

His lips curled. "Does he now?"

"It gets worse. There was a demon rifling through my place. They know where I live. Can you watch over the loft tonight?"

Bedrock leaned close to the glass. "You mean, can I watch over *you*?"

I swallowed and cleared my throat. "Yes. To protect your investment."

The demon leaned his head back and licked his lips. "You've never invited me into your home before."

I grimaced, trying to keep this as business-oriented as possible.

"It would be my pleasure, Shyla. Truly. But I suppose I should see to that pet of yours first."

"Don't hurt him," I pleaded. "He protected me. That was his job."

Bedrock looked me up and down. "Then he did it well. I suppose all this urgency leaves no time for dear old dad."

I tightened the silk robe around my waist, relieved to be foregoing that part of our arrangement. "There is one more thing. A... favor."

"Your favor is my pleasure, my dear. What did you have in mind?"

I pursed my lips. I had to tread carefully here. I didn't want Bedrock knowing about my grimoire or my business with the ring. "Is it possible for you to put me in touch with Asmodeus?"

His eyes flashed. He twisted in a circle, tail whipping around him. "Now, that would be a trick. What could a little girl like you want with a notorious demon king like him?"

I ignored the jab because I needed his help. "I think he might be the key to the people coming after me." The statement was true enough, but not the whole truth. Hell was a vast and complicated place. I was hoping Bedrock didn't figure the possible link between Asmodeus and the Crown Council and my father.

"You would make me jealous, my dear. Getting in bed with Asmodeus while refusing me."

"This is just business. It's nothing more than that."

"Shyla, dealing with a devil is *never* just business."

I worked my jaw but held firm. Either he would help me or he wouldn't.

My conviction eventually wore him down. Bedrock softened and pulled away from the glass, giving me space to breathe. "Alas, I am unable to do what you ask. Even I have rules to follow, and Asmodeus is quite important down here."

"There has to be a way to get word to him."

He ignored the statement. "Not only am I unable to assist you, but I really *must* discourage this idea to the fullest. It is not for you or me to ask, Shyla, and we both *always* follow the rules."

"But—"

"Sleep well, my dearest. Be comforted by how closely I'll be watching over you. Leave the wardrobe open."

And then his image winked out. Instead of infernal blackness, the pane of glass reflected the room and me, staring back at it and huffing in frustration.

Glass

I retreated into the bathroom to put my clothes on. With that mirror open tonight, I'd be sleeping fully dressed. The mug of tea went into the microwave to nuke for forty-five seconds and it was piping hot again. Then it was a matter of finding a record to match my rebellious mood. I went with the restless guitar work of Jimi Hendrix.

The music and tea centered me, but they didn't get me all the way to calm and comfortable. How could I be with Bedrock having a peep into my inner life?

I didn't feel safe here. Not without Bernard.

I abandoned the empty mug, returned to the bedroom, and pulled on my boots. I half expected a protest from a demonic spy, but no one interrupted. That was it. I was doing this.

All suited up in leather, I stuffed a crowbar under my jacket and zipped it shut. A few text messages later, a quick jaunt down two flights of stairs, and I was at Josalie's door just as she was sneaking out.

"Let's go dancing at the club!" she whispered excitedly.

"If only," I muttered as I fought off a smile. "Thanks for this." I held out my hand for her car keys.

"Uh-uh," she protested. "You're not taking the Kia without me. I'm driving."

"Is that why you're all dressed up? You know I'm not going out dancing, right?"

"I know that. I'm going anyway."

I sighed. "You can't, Josalie. I don't want to involve you."

"Shh!" She put her finger to her lips and dragged me away from where her husband and kids were sleeping. "What is that?" She pointed to the bulge in my jacket. "That better not be a gun."

"What? No. It's..." I unzipped the jacket and showed her the crowbar.

She smiled mischievously. "Damn, I knew you were into some janky shit, girl. It's about time I saw for myself."

Josalie pushed the elevator call button. I didn't say anything as we waited. The door opened and she entered, and I followed with a melodramatic breath.

"This could involve some criminal activity," I admitted.

"I can be your getaway driver. Why aren't you using your motorcycle? Oh, too visible, right? You figured a silver Optima would be less noticeable?"

I chewed my lip. "Actually, it's because my Monster has a location tracker on it and I don't want the people who put it there to know I'm coming."

She stared at me dumbly for a few seconds until we both broke out in laughter. "Are you serious with me right now?"

"Dead serious, unfortunately."

"Damn. I need to find a word to describe this worse than janky."

We exited into the garage and loaded into her car. She asked a few questions as I directed her to the hotel, but it wasn't like I could answer many of them. Josalie may have seen a few tarot cards lying around my place, but she had no idea I was a summoner. It was enough for her to know that there were some bad people around I'd rather not tangle with.

That was why I needed Josalie's car. I didn't want the Crown Council to see me coming, and there was a chance if I disconnected the tracker, they'd know. Better to leave it and the bike and, presumably, me back at the loft. They'd never be the wiser.

"Isn't that crowbar a little, you know, low-tech for you?" asked Josalie.

I looked at her, surprised. The comment showed a surprising amount of insight into my burgling activities. I wondered how accurate her suspicions about me were. "It's for a door," I answered.

"You see? You need to be prepared. Open that." She pointed to the glove compartment.

I suddenly had the feeling Josalie was strapping. I hesitantly opened the swing door and caught the small tube that rolled out. "Josalie, why am I holding a purple vibrator right now?"

"Dayum, I've been looking for him!" She snatched it and stuffed it into her lap.

I chuckled. "Watch out, you're gonna make Marlon jealous."

"Who do you think operates this nuclear device, huh? You ever tried having sex with a house full of kids? Sometimes me and Marlon need to park somewhere discreet and make do."

"Too much information."

"Oh, we fog up the windows in here."

"Too much information!"

I dug through the glove box and found what she'd been pointing me at. A can of pepper spray. I left it inside and swung the door closed.

"What?" she asked, offended. "That's good stuff. I only used it once or twice."

"I bet you have. But I have my own battery-powered device."

I reached into my jacket, pulled out the stun gun, and pressed the button. A jagged bolt of blue electricity cracked. Josalie jumped and then, embarrassed by her reaction, laughed uncontrollably.

"Okay, you win. Yours is bigger than mine." She rolled her eyes as I put the stun gun away.

"Wait, turn here. Go around this way."

I directed her to Olive Street. We parked on the curb next to the parking garage at the back of the hotel. This was a lot more visible than my previous parking spot, but there was no way I was walking down that dark alley again. Not with Jackal on the loose. As it was, the hairs on my arms were already prickling.

I scoped out the scene for a minute and then turned to Josalie. "Okay, this is the deal. I'm gonna go in through the out door. Someone has something of mine—don't ask what it is 'cause I can't tell you. I might come running back to the car, so be ready."

My neighbor stared at me, wide-eyed.

"You sure you're up for this, Jo? Because I can take you home and come back with the car."

"Hell no! I am *so* up for this." She leaned over and traded the pocket rocket with the pepper spray in the glove box. "Just in case."

I shook my head absently. "Okay, stay here."

I stepped lightly past the sidewalk and into the back walkway. A streetlight cast the area in a cold LED glow. I hugged the wall and warily eyed the long perpendicular alley adjoining this one. The one where Jackal had confronted me.

I just had to be quick and discreet. I checked if the exit door happened to be unlocked. No luck. I leaned against it with my back to the street so I could take a better look. Anyone passing on the sidewalk would just see someone waiting at the rear of the building.

Which was good because I'd just hit a stumbling block. The metal door closed tight enough into its frame that the crowbar couldn't get a good grip on it. And a metal plate prevented me from pressuring the spring bolt. I put the crowbar away and pulled out my traditional picks.

After feeling around the lock pins for twenty seconds. I checked over my shoulder and smiled at Josalie in the

Optima, eagerly watching me, missing only a bowl of over-buttered popcorn. I usually didn't do this sort of thing with an audience and it was distinctly embarrassing. Especially since this lock had been upgraded along with the hotel retrofit. It was gonna be a tough one to spring.

Josalie had just discovered her neighbor was a professional cat burglar, and here I was having trouble with a lock.

I focused on the mechanism, closing my eyes and going by feel. A burst of air rushed past and I went lightheaded. I stumbled to my knees, leaning on the door for support. I was relieved somehow, like a great weight had been lifted, but I was also dizzy from one hell of a head rush.

Hell was exactly right, I realized. But it couldn't be, could it?

I pulled the picks away and waved my hand. A second later, the door opened from the inside. Bernard and a burst of sulfur greeted me.

"Shyla!"

I forced him back and pushed inside, the door shutting behind me. "You *are* free! What happened?"

The gargoyle frantically glanced upstairs. "I've never felt power like that. Someone burst into the room, ripped right through the summoner's snare like butter, and banished me back to Kur."

"Someone's in the room?" I asked. "Bedrock?"

"I don't know, Shyla. It was a presence I didn't recognize... A force of nature."

"And it helped you?"

"It wasn't there for me. Let's get out of here."

I pursed my lips. I'd been wondering how Bedrock had intended to free Bernard, but knocking on the hotel room door hadn't made the top of the list. Demons couldn't enter the Material Plane on their own or they'd be free to ravage people. There were rules in place, rituals, that kept hellions from running loose. It was why it was important to keep them on a tight leash.

But Bedrock here, in the flesh?

"This might be my chance," I said. "To see him in action. It could give us a clue to his identity."

"We can't risk it," said the overprotective gargoyle. "I'm telling you, we're in over our heads."

The metal door behind me banged loudly. I flinched away and Bernard growled.

"Shyla?" called Josalie. "Shyla, you in there?"

I rolled my eyes, this time without the slightest bit of mirth. "Okay, Bernard. I'm getting out of here." He nodded and I waved him away. I opened the door. "What are you doing here, Josalie?"

"Let's be honest," she said gruffly. "I was never going to wait in the car." She held her can of pepper spray at the ready. "Who were you talking to in there? Any trouble?" She peeked around me.

"Um, just a phone call."

She wafted the smell of sulfur away from her nose. "Ooh, smells like you let one rip, too. No wonder you're single." I shoved her outside and she began speaking a mile a minute. I chalked it up to nerves. "How'd you get the door open? I was watching you and didn't think you had it until—"

I shut it, locking us both outside. "You were supposed to stay out of this."

"I was trying. I really was! But then I saw you fall on the ground. You should have your blood sugar tested. Maybe with all that adrenaline—" She started when she realized the door was closed. "I thought we were going in."

"I changed my mind," I said. "The job's done."

"That's it?"

"That's it. You were a big help." I nudged her toward the car, but she was still trying to make sense of things.

A crash sounded high above our heads. A man briefly screamed. As I turned to look, Kofi Hailu splatted on the cement right in front of us. Blood spattered on my jacket and Josalie's face. She trembled in shock while something heavy rammed my shoulder.

I dove away from the blow and rolled on the ground, bringing up my arm and ready to call Bernard back. Glass rained down and struck the pavement like hail. We shielded our faces, but it was already over.

I looked up, aghast. Kofi had been thrown right through the window.

"You're bleeding, Shyla!"

I sat up with pain tearing through my neck. The shoulder of my jacket was sliced open. A heavy pane of glass had landed right on me, damn near taking my arm off. If it wasn't for the heavy leather, it might've.

"Let's get out of here," said Josalie.

Despite witnessing something truly horrible, her trauma

training kicked in. She dragged me back to the car and tied a towel around my shoulder. I bit down to avoid screaming out.

"Just hold on, girl."

Patch

The ride back to the loft was a blur. Not because I was in triage, but because we'd seen a man die right in front of us. The possibilities vexed me. Further distracting was having Josalie here, a witness to it all. She had now been exposed to my world. I was running on a complex cocktail of emotions. Anger and shame, neat, with a wedge of fear.

We slid a chair away from the dining table. The polished cement floor would withstand blood better than the rug. Josalie helped me out of my jacket and shirt. The gash in my shoulder was a long cut, but it wasn't deep. While Josalie went to her place to retrieve a medical kit, I put on some Steve Miller Band to mellow the mood.

"We should take you to the ER," she urged as she returned with supplies. "I'm not a doctor."

I tried to wear a smile through the pain. "You said it wasn't that bad. You can fix it up. I trust you."

The worry on her face was evident, but she nodded and went to work. Josalie soaked away the excess blood and washed the wound. She used a disinfectant spray on the area.

"No major arteries?" I asked.

She scoffed. "If this had hit your subclavian, you wouldn't have made it back to the car. I can't believe how lucky you are."

"Not lucky enough to not get hit."

I was bracing myself for a medieval needle and fishing line, but Josalie instead used some quick glue to close the skin. Strips of medical tape reinforced the glue, and she wrapped it tight with gauze. I stood to walk it off. My shoulder was stiffer than it was supposed to be, but I chalked it up to tension.

I uncorked the open wine bottle and poured the last glass. I took a cool sip and closed my eyes. Next thing I knew, Josalie snatched the glass from my hands and upturned it to her mouth.

After patching me up, she deserved the wine more than I did. I waited as she chugged the entire thing and set the empty on the table. "Should I open a new bottle?"

"Nope," she replied. "Alcohol thins your blood. Get at least one good night's sleep first, okay?"

I sighed.

Josalie jutted her lower lip out and studied me. She was more introspective than usual. Given the circumstances, that was perfectly understandable.

"What is it?" I asked.

"I have questions."

I shook my head lightly. "I don't know that I have

answers."

"I know. Believe me, I know."

My eyes narrowed. "What *do* you know?"

"I see things, Shyla. I see the way you handle yourself. Some of the stuff you leave lying around." She was mostly assuring herself that she wasn't crazy, doing her best not to be pushy. There was a vulnerability about the way she said it, like she was afraid of being left out. Like she wanted to be one of the crew.

"You're my best friend, Jo."

"You're mine too."

"Is that sad?" I asked. "Not because of who we are, but because we've only known each other five years. Aren't people supposed to have best friends from childhood?"

"Screw that. The people in my school were a-holes. Five years or fifty—it doesn't matter." She rested her hand on my uninjured shoulder. "Because we know, right?"

I nodded. I didn't know how I knew, but I knew. Josalie was a good person. I trusted her. She would do anything to help me, and I would gladly return the favor.

"But what if..." I started softly. "What if I'm not who you think I am?"

"You're not hearing me, girl. I *know* who you are. The details are just noise."

I smiled and gave her a one-armed hug.

"You need a new bra," she said as she broke away. "Blood's a turn off."

"Good. I got other things on my mind these days."

She rolled her eyes. "I'll leave you to it." She headed to

the door.

"Don't forget your medical kit."

"I think I should leave that one here." She opened the door and watched me with a heavy sigh. "One day, girl, we're gonna need to talk about what you do."

I tried to acknowledge her with a grin, but I stopped short of nodding. She shut the door.

"Are you hurt?" asked Bernard. He twisted the deadbolt on the front door and hurried over to me. I showed him the wound dressing and he frowned. "I thought I told you to leave the hotel."

"We did. Someone threw Kofi Hailu through his thirteenth-story window. The glass nicked me."

"You didn't see anyone then?"

I blinked. "I didn't see anyone. You?"

"Nothing, Shyla. Everything was quiet, and then it was like searing, orange heat. The circle was broken before I could turn around. What makes you think it was Bedrock?"

"Asked him for a favor." I pointed to the open wardrobe in the bedroom. "We have company tonight."

He bit down. It wasn't possible to scheme against the demon while he had a window into our conversation. Bernard knew it was best to drop it for now.

I hugged the stone gargoyle. "I'm just glad you're back."

"Me too."

I slipped another shirt on, if only to keep Bedrock from creeping. We were under his protection tonight, but I was comfortable again for an entirely different reason. Bernard had my back. He was my rock. Literally.

He stayed by the bed, leaving only when the record ended. He lifted the stylus, shut off the player, and returned to my side. I slept like a baby.

In the morning, I felt better than I thought I would. Nothing had happened overnight, which was exactly the kind of uneventful slumber I had hoped for.

I ran a bath so I could sit without wetting my shoulder. Bernard paced the loft like a good guard dog. I dressed and tried Lambert's phone again. Someone picked up this time.

"Put him on," I said.

Lambert breathed heavily. "Do you have the crown?"

"You know I don't. I got a look at it, though."

"Did you?"

"We need to talk."

He waited a moment. I was getting a weird vibe from him but couldn't be sure over the phone.

"Is the Crown of Aevum real?" he asked.

"There's no such thing, Lambert. I'm sorry."

"Ah." The exclamation carried the bitterness of an old man who knew better.

"Can we meet?"

"Isn't our business concluded, Miss Crowe?"

"Not by a long shot. I know about the Crown Council. I saw your gold ring." I noticed the wardrobe was still open. I threw the bathrobe over the mirror and shut the doors. "Your Ethiopian friends sent a demon after me."

"A demon!"

"Cut the crap, Lambert. You're in the Order of Solomon. You've at least heard the stories."

A beat. "So I have."

He went silent and I idly shook my head. The old man was playing hard to get all of a sudden. It was possible he'd heard about Kofi. I didn't want to bring it up in case it spooked him.

Still, fear was a good thing. For all of us. By all accounts I should've cut ties with Lambert. He'd paid me cash and I did the job. The contract was done.

But there was the dangling tie of my father's involvement. Like Trap had deduced: Lambert knew my father. That wasn't something I could leave alone.

"Can we meet?" I asked a little too eagerly. "You're being used by your friends. We can put our heads together and get to the bottom of it."

And there it was. The only thing I had to offer him. It wasn't a lot, depending how much he could put together by himself, but it was something. And I had one thing going for me.

Men like Lambert didn't appreciate being played. If there was any piece of the plot that I had and he didn't, he was sure to meet.

"My associate will give you the address."

I smiled as he handed the phone over. Teegan directed me to a location an hour outside town. I told her I'd be there.

It was a delicate matter getting my armor on. The boots required some force to pull on and the jacket was tight around my shoulders. The tear in the leather wasn't obvious with my arm in a resting position, but I was gonna need a new jacket eventually.

I fixed up eggs and toast and a cup of coffee to get some of my energy back. Somewhere in there the Custodian sent me a text message reminding me to get in touch with Lambert.

I didn't like lying to him, but the last thing I needed was Bedrock getting involved again. The demon was cleaning house. I was afraid what happened to Kofi would happen to Lambert, and then I might be in the dark forever.

Club

In my condition, I had to handle the Ducati a little more tenderly today. Thankfully it wasn't a sport bike that required an aggressive lean. On the other hand, the cafe racer wasn't really built for long distance comfort. I kept it easygoing and prepared to tough out an extended ride.

My destination was an hour outside the suburbs, a small satellite town in the desert past the hills. It was a strange place for Lambert to be. I figured he was aware of things going south and was ready to skip town.

I pulled off the highway twenty minutes in and found a parked pickup to toss the GPS tracker in. I was disappointed I hadn't found a more clever use for it, but I couldn't lead the Crown Council to Lambert's safe house. I wasn't sure if it would broadcast a location until it ran out of power or if the disconnection would be immediately obvious. Either way, my objective was achieved. The Ducati Monster was invisible again. I popped back onto the highway and continued north.

The heat kicked in past the hills. The land opened up, grass yellowed and growing wild. I finally exited on the outskirts, past the track homes and walled developments, and pulled up to a ranch with several long buildings. Beyond the gate were rows of parked motorcycles. I'd found the local clubhouse.

A prospect swung the gate open for me. I rolled up closer to the other bikes but parked separately, with easy access and a straight line to the gate.

Teegan approached, eyes smarmy under thick blue eye shadow. "Looks like someone finally wised up and lost their tracker."

I winced as I struggled off the bike and slipped off my helmet. "That was you?" I recalled the note she had left when I was first hired. Nice bike. The club had been tracking me from the start.

The biker hiked a shoulder. "Who else?"

I stepped into her pierced face. "Don't touch my bike again."

She waited until I moved toward the building. "Tough talk from a woman who doesn't fight her own fights."

I worked my jaw. It was unsettling that she knew that. I wondered how much Lambert had shared with her, or how much she had seen while spying on me. But in a way the knowledge made me comfortable she wouldn't try anything. Not if she knew what I could really do.

But something else was bugging me about the biker club being the ones who were tracking me. That meant the Crown Council didn't know where I lived. Last time they'd followed me, it had been from the meeting with Lambert. I confronted them before reaching the loft. And at the same time I was dealing with Kofi and his pals, Jackal was already rifling through my safe.

"Is that what you do?" I asked. "Fight your own fights? Compete with the rest of the bikers?"

She snorted. "I hold my own."

I eyed several of the boys in the yard. They prominently displayed black eyes and Nazi tattoos while Teegan had neither. "Why do you roll with these lugheads, anyway?"

Her lashes fluttered in momentary unease. "They're not as bad as they look," she said firmly. "Not all of them."

I decided it was useless trying to see inside her head. I definitely wouldn't take her word for it about the MC. She led me up the steps to the front porch and waited by the door. I stepped from the bright sun to the dim interior and squinted as my eyes adjusted. Three men stood in my path.

"You were right, Teegan," laughed one of them. "She *is* that stupid."

Teegan shut the door behind me. "I said she'd be brave."

"Same thing, no?" The guys laughed. "Look at the ovaries on her."

I repositioned so my back wasn't to any of them. "What is this?" I spat.

"What do you think it is?" asked one of the guys. "Grady's dead and you're still standing."

My lips twisted to a scowl. "Look, I'm sorry about what happened to him, okay?"

Teegan snorted. "You're sorry you got caught, you

mean."

"It wasn't me."

"Try again."

All four of them wore accusatory scowls. This was planned payback. A little more coloring outside the lines from the biker club. So much for them being scared of my abilities. "What are you guys gonna do?"

"What we owe him," swore Teegan.

"Come on. You don't owe these guys jack."

"Where's the cross?" she demanded. She pulled a silver cross pendant from under her jacket and showed it off. "It was a matching set. You don't know the first of what I owe Grady. He meant something to me."

"Get out of my way." I shoved one of the guys aside.

Another grabbed my arm and twisted it. "You wanna kill club members?" he growled.

"I didn't kill anyone yet." The tone of my voice suggested I might change my mind. The other two guys held off a moment.

"Don't worry, boys," smirked Teegan. "The old man says she's declawed."

It took me a second to realize she was talking about Bernard being trapped. That meant Lambert knew about the first half of last night, but not the part about Bedrock.

The guys came at me. I retrieved the stun gun with my sore arm and zapped one. My heel dug into the shin of the man grabbing me. I spun free and brandished the weapon to keep them at bay.

One of the bikers was hunched over grabbing his leg.

The other was still twitching on the floor.

"How's that for fighting my own battles?" I mocked.

Teegan stared knives at me.

"You little cunt," swore the biker, rising to his feet. "You're gonna pay for that." He reached for his back.

"No guns," warned Teegan.

"Fuck you. You're a cunt too."

As his pistol came out, a gray blur streaked past me. It caught the biker's arm and tugged him across the room until he hit the wall. The bones in his hand snapped and the gun tumbled to the wooden floor. The man whimpered in the fetal position as Bernard growled, sharp incisors inches from his cowering face.

"Let me eat him," pleaded the gargoyle. "I bet this one's meat is well marbled."

"And probably pumped full of poisons too," I said with casual disdain.

The other two men scurried away as Teegan backed against the door. She was scared, but she didn't run. She held her hands ready before her.

I glared and stepped her way, slipping the stun gun back into my jacket and getting in her face. "Are we done here?"

She swallowed nervously and nodded.

Still, I had to give her credit for standing her ground. That was something the two larger guys hadn't done. The silver cross she wore glinted in the dim light.

"Where's Lambert?"

"In the back."

I spun around, dismissing her, and stomped toward the

back room. "Bernard?"

"Just one pound of flesh, Shyla. That's all I ask."

"No killing."

He scoffed and hurried to my side.

Teegan shook her head. "No. The beast doesn't go in there."

"Try and stop him."

Bernard pushed the door open and we shoved inside.

Lambert

We found ourselves in a community room with tables and lamps and a long wooden bar. Mismatched neon beer signs dotted the walls. A stained-glass lamp hung above the pool table. It was the epitome of eighties dive-bar deco.

Lambert sat on a leather couch in the back while the bulk of the bikers waited outside, just like the meeting in the warehouse. Only Teegan pushed into the room behind me.

"Wow," I said, making a show of looking around, "you kicked the biker gang out of their own clubhouse. You really must be paying them a fortune."

"They have the building surrounded," he said flatly, coldly. "Are you here to kill me, Miss Crowe?" Bernard's eyes glinted at the question.

"I told you, I'm not a killer."

Teegan snorted. I shot her a glare of warning, but she just rested against the door with her arms crossed. I motioned my head to the side and Bernard broke away and paced the room, searching for an ambush.

"You know," commented Lambert, clearing his throat, "it's unseemly to allow that thing to strut around in plain sight."

"It's fair play after you left your bikers off their leash." I leaned on a table ten feet away from him. "You heard about Kofi, then?"

"Not two minutes ago. It wasn't just Kofi, it was half the Crown Council. I do hope no one followed you here."

"Very funny. You were the one who put a tracker on my bike."

"Just protecting my investment."

"It's over, then? Your interest in the crown? You fully realize the fool you were played by your group of Ethiopian royalists?"

He sniggered. "Miss Crowe, I am no fool, and I was never interested in the crown."

My eyes narrowed. "You knew it was a trap?"

"Of course I did, dear. It was practically my idea."

Bernard returned to my side with a low growl. Lambert shifted uncomfortably but retained his calm.

"So I was wrong," I realized. "You *had* thrown in with a doomed cause. I figured you for more than that."

The old man's lips curled. "Ah, but you're sharper than you think. Those idiots have a wealth of information but haven't the slightest idea how to put it to use."

"Siccing a demon from Dis on me isn't enough?"

"Here's where your judgment is clouded." Lambert's eyes flashed as he reached for the gold ring. A little rub from his finger and the corner of the room darkened. Yellow eyes radiated from the shadow, but it was the sickly sweet smell that I recognized first.

Bernard bared his teeth.

"You're the summoner..." I whispered. "You're the one that had the biker killed."

"He was interfering with the job, was he not?"

Jackal grinned. "His liver was delectable."

Gunshots burst at my back. I dove behind the table. Bullets pounded the wall behind Jackal. The demon stood there, unfazed, as puffs of dust clouded behind him. It was unnerving that his eyes never left me.

Teegan's revolver ran dry. "You bastard! That was you?"

Lambert's eyes fluttered in annoyance. "My dear, you must control yourself at once."

"Fuck this, I'm out." She turned and threw the door open.

"Teegan!" he yelled.

"Leave her," I said. "This isn't her battle."

He swallowed his anger and focused on me. "Neither is it yours. Even I am just a soldier here. I serve a king far above either of our heads. A king who will soon return to this world and shine his favor upon me."

I stared at him in disbelief. "You're a Luciferian."

"That's right. The quibbles of the Order of Solomon are nothing compared to my calling. A greater calling. A new world order."

I snickered. "And I thought the Crown of Aevum was a fairy tale."

"Laugh if you like. Your opinions little concern me. But

there is the issue of the ring."

Bernard circled to shield me from Jackal. The hellions aggressively stared each other down, though neither took action yet.

"The Ring of Solomon?" I asked pointedly.

"That's what this is all about. I used the Order's resources for a time, and we set this trap together, though I had hoped to recover the ring before them."

Which explained Jackal trashing my loft before the heist. The summoner's snare was always his backup plan, his cover to make it appear he was playing nice with the royalists.

"And the Lion of Judah?"

He grinned slightly. "They actually believe they're hiding an emperor. Imagine that, an emperor without a lick of power."

"Not without the ring," I concluded. "It was once held by the wisest of kings."

"Wise?" scoffed the old man. "Solomon was a fool whose rule ended with a fall from grace. It makes one question the value of seeking grace in the first place."

"So what, you're switching teams? You're gonna bring the power of the ring to the devils?"

"You can be instrumental in that." He waved to the gargoyle. "You know just as I do that devils and demons are just words. There are good and bad among any peoples. Why should they be relegated to Hell?"

"That answer's above my pay grade."

He shrugged. "You can have your crisis of conscience later. For now you can tell me what you know of the Ring of

Solomon. I'll pay well for it."

"What makes you think I know anything about it?"

"Because," he growled, leaning forward in his seat, "I hired your father to steal it for me. Except, once he got his thieving, treacherous hands on it, he presumed it belonged to him."

I flinched at the accusation. My father wouldn't have done that. He was a professional. He never would've broken his own rules.

But Lambert's distaste was plain. He had a history with my father, and I couldn't deny his conviction. "Paulson was a middleman without honor," he spat. "I'd hired him for several jobs. He always came through. I believed him to be reliable—upstanding even—but I had mischaracterized him. Such is the folly of trusting thieves."

I bristled. "What did you do to him?"

He sat back, confusion evident. "Do with him? My dear, Paulson absconded from Phoenix with my property many years ago. I haven't seen him or the ring since. But the infernal grapevine is vast. I was recently tipped off to the location of an acquirer of antiquities, a daughter who took after her father. The crown was a ruse all along; I hired you to get to him."

I steadied my anger, recognizing my overreaction. "Then I'm sure your devil told you my father ended up in Hell."

"An unfortunate turn of events. But that doesn't solve my problem. Paulson must have passed the ring down to you, for such an object cannot permanently reside in Hell. It was an Earthly gift delivered by the angels."

I snorted condescendingly. "Look at everything that's happened, Lambert. Do you honestly think I knew anything about this?" He worked his jaw, eyes darting from Jackal back to me. "You don't know anything else about my father?"

Lambert frowned. "I brought you here to tell me."

Great. We both wanted the same answers from each other. I shook my head. "I'm leaving."

"You are not."

"I never had your precious ring."

"Perhaps, but you're still culpable. There is no immaculate conception. You carry the sins of the father. If Paulson is indeed in Hell, then it's the ring that put him there." He straightened at our impasse and quietly assessed me. "You're being protected. Someone didn't let you walk into the trap at the hotel, called you off the job. Someone mauled the Crown Council members and freed your familiar. If it wasn't you, who was it?"

"And if I don't tell?"

He lifted his chin. "Jackal?"

The spotted devil took a step, and so did Bernard. I held him back by his neck.

"Think about what you're threatening, Lambert. I *am* in hock to another demon. My whole life is set up to keep my father safe from the devils who bind him. There's nothing you or Jackal can threaten me with."

"Then let us help each other. Tell me of your contacts."

"I do that and my father's dead. Me too, maybe."

His face contorted. "You don't tell me and I guarantee

your life will be even shorter."

Jackal leaned forward eagerly. I pulled the Sigillum Dei from my shirt.

The old man chortled, fully amused. "That pentacle is nothing. A show piece."

I gestured to the black mark on Jackal's cheek. "Ask your little pet just how showy it can be."

The demon hissed. "It's true, Lambert. She wields the seal with power."

"Nonsense," he barked. "It's magical humdrum."

"In the wrong hands, maybe."

Lambert glared angrily at the insolence of his demon. "I want her in chains. Now!"

"As you wish." Jackal's eyes met mine and he pounced.

Dogfight

Jackal bounded our way, covering the distance in a second. The darkness painted the floor around him, a physical presence all its own. It crashed into me and Bernard at the same time.

I tumbled to the floor, landing hard on my bandaged shoulder. My vision went white and swam in circles. Dizziness took over, almost like I was hit with my own stun gun.

Somewhere overhead, the two demons crashed into the pool table. Balls spilled to the floor. I pulled forward to get a better view, still reeling. The collision with the stone gargoyle left the table in splinters. Bernard, for his part, looked fine. But Jackal was standing over him, raking down with blurred claws.

Jackal struck the back of Bernard's neck and yipped in pain, favoring his hand as he pulled it back. The gargoyle's tail swept Jackal's legs out from under him. On the floor too, his head was now in reach. Bernard swatted but Jackal drew away with preternatural speed.

Bernard's face snapped to me. "Shyla, watch out!"

While I was still on the floor, a metal link clicked around my wrist. Familiar with the tactic, I clamped my legs around Lambert's and rolled over, twisting him to the ground. I elbowed him in the ribs for good measure.

A pair of handcuffs dangled loosely from one arm. Like the summoner's snare but a lot less arcane, the cold iron was not only a way to bind me but to contain my magic. It didn't much matter with Bernard already in the Material Plane, but Lambert was probably covering his bases against future tactics.

I supported my weight on the table beside me and pulled to my feet.

"Call him off, old man." I raised my boot, ready to curb stomp the veteran summoner.

Jackal brushed past me, whipping the old man away. He deposited Lambert at the far wall and faced me.

"Leave him be. A warning from the master."

I took a backward step. "Are you confused here? You're the ones coming at us."

Jackal paced to me, but Bernard collided into his side and took him down. They fought violently, limbs slashing, inflicting pain but causing little visible damage. It was why summoners let their demons do the tussling. A human getting tangled up in that carnage would end up in pieces.

Lambert recovered himself as I worked at the cuff on my wrist. It hadn't been tightened all the way down. With a bit of work, I could almost squeeze it over my hand, but it was stuck.

Green neon popped as Jackal's head slammed into a sign. Bernard pulled the demon's head back and pounded it repeatedly into the wall. The room shook, but Jackal was smiling.

"You fight well for your master," he said snidely, "even while facing insurmountable odds."

"Keep talking," returned Bernard. "It makes this more —"

Jackal's body flared with darkness and the gargoyle staggered. Jackal put his hands together and pounded Bernard's chest with open palms. The resulting explosion flung him across the room. Bernard hit the back wall and dropped behind the bar.

Jackal licked his lips and his gaze flicked to me. "As amusing as this is, there is a point to it. We're here to discuss terms."

Bernard boldly hopped onto the bar top. "Could've fooled me." His pose was inspiring and brave, like that of a true statue, but a gouge was missing from his stone chest.

Jackal's eyebrow arched, and he sighed at the ongoing distraction. "Stay down, dog. For your master's sake."

"Are you threatening Shyla?"

"I'm threatening you."

Bernard spread his wings and leaped through the air. His opponent raced to meet him. I had to make my move while Jackal was occupied.

"The keys," I demanded, pulling the stun gun from my jacket and stepping toward Lambert.

The old man reached into his vest and pulled a pistol. "I think not, Miss Crowe."

"What are you gonna do, shoot me?"

"I have considered it."

"You won't get answers that way."

"I have a weak heart. You could kill me with that thing. Now drop it."

The hellions grappled savagely. Jackal twisted around Bernard's back and pinned his head to the floor. The gargoyle's claws and teeth couldn't reach their target. Jackal pounded Bernard with his free hand.

"Drop it, Miss Crowe."

I released the stun gun and kicked it over to Lambert.

"And the cuffs. If you would be so kind." He motioned from one hand to the other.

"I'm not gonna cuff myself. And you're not gonna shoot me if I don't."

"It isn't me you should be worried about." He motioned to my familiar.

Bernard's growls had turned to yowls. He was still pinned by an arm and a knee and was taking a beating. Jackal's tongue hung from his mouth in a wild rage, and he was just getting started. His free hand pulsed with dark energy and raked Bernard's back.

"He won't last long," prodded Lambert. "Banish him and he'll live."

"If I unsummon him, I'm dead."

"And he is if you don't."

I gritted my teeth, flinching at each of Bernard's howls.

"Don't do it, Shyla," he cried.

A small explosion resounded and chunks of rocks cratered off the gargoyle's back. Jackal smiled at the tortured screams.

I lifted my hand to the air.

"No!" urged the gargoyle. "I won't leave you alone."

I swallowed as more energy built up in Jackal's fist. "You don't have a choice." I waved my hand and Bernard erupted into a cloud of ash. Jackal braced the ground hungrily, disappointed at the loss of his prize. His gaze snapped to me in anger.

A blow hit the back of my head. I stumbled over the table. Lambert pulled my arm around and cuffed my hands behind my back. I panted on the table, watching the ashes disappear in a swirl.

"Now," barked the old man, spinning me around roughly, "let's have a chat about who you're working with."

I braced my hands on the table behind me, lifted my legs with a backward lean, and kicked high. My boot pounded Lambert in the jaw, sending him flying into the couch I'd found him in. The pistol tumbled to the floor. I lunged for it, trying to sit on it and clasp it behind my back. Jackal got there first and swiped it away. The pistol slid across the floor and ended up under another sofa.

Lambert coughed and leaned over. "You little..." He spat blood on the floor. A yellowed tooth bounced on the worn wood.

The old man stood, weakly at first, then stomped over and slapped me. I flung my face back at him and sneered.

Lambert lifted his arm for another blow.

Jackal stepped between us. "She is subdued, master."

"Get out of my way!"

"She. Is. Subdued."

The old man trembled with rage. He turned to his familiar, but his harried face softened. He lowered his arms. He straightened his vest and composed himself.

I blinked back and forth between the two, intrigued by the power dynamic on display. Lambert didn't seem the type to take suggestions. Then again, they both served Lucifer. They both believed they had a higher purpose.

"What do you want from me?" I spat.

The old man's chin lifted indignantly. "We will talk." He eyed Jackal in warning. "And *you* will do as I say."

The devil's head bobbed slightly in acknowledgment. "Of course... master."

"Check her pockets."

Jackal leaned close, checking my jacket first, and then sliding his fingers into my pants, sniffing my neck as he did it. I turned my head away. He had the stench of a sickly perfume. Jackal pulled away with my cell phone and handed it to Lambert.

"You have a message," noted the old man. "Who is the Custodian?"

I shook my head. "The whole point of using that stupid name is to keep his identity secret."

"What's your password?"

"I must've forgotten it when you knocked me on the head."

He glowered. "If you don't do as I say, I'll have Jackal take your fingers off, one by one."

I studied the demon a moment before locking eyes with Lambert. "You sure about that?"

He worked his jaw. As far as I could tell, the demon was in favor of information gathering without torture. I was just playing a hunch based on what I'd seen, but it was about the only card I had to play. For his part, it seemed to give Lambert pause.

"We can still help each other, Miss Crowe. Tell me what demon is holding Paulson captive."

I scowled. "I can't do that."

"He's your enemy. He's our enemy too." By Jackal's eager eyes, it was likely the truth. The old man parted his hair with his hands and smoothed down his mutton chops, coming to terms with a new idea. "I have acted partly out of revenge, Miss Crowe. To Lucifer, revenge is a virtue. However, I am ever his servant."

I rolled my eyes. "The greater good, huh?"

"Not good, not evil, but greater, yes."

I winced. My arm stretched behind my back wasn't helping the gash on my shoulder. My neck was wet. That must've been what Jackal was smelling.

"I'll make you an offer," proposed Lambert. "I'll abandon my revenge against your father. If, as you say, he's been in Hell all this time, then we'll consider it time served. As long as the Ring of Solomon is returned to me, I won't seek retribution."

"What if we don't have it?"

"I know you don't, my dear. I believe you. You wouldn't have come here empty-handed otherwise. I see your play in this unfolding tragedy is a bit part. You're a victim of your father's malice. And he's a victim of his own ambition. But he's also a victim of the demon holding him captive. Had it not occurred to you that if Paulson was stripped of the ring, it is your demon who now possesses it?"

The Ring of Solomon. In the hands of Bedrock. No wonder he was able to so easily control an empire. Cause havoc at will in the Material Plane. I'd been forced into servitude under the same power my father had sought.

I wondered how long Paulson had held onto it. If he was ever in control. I'd known him to be the best thief in the world, but the same couldn't be said of his summoning abilities. Not once I was old enough to know better. At least not until we'd left Phoenix.

Perhaps he had acquired the ring. He'd grown more confident after Phoenix, but more secretive as well. How ironic if that was because my dad was trying to protect me.

"Tell us the demon you serve," urged Lambert. "Tell us the demon who stole your father's ring and snatched him into the pits of Hell."

"And then what?"

He leaned close. "I have powerful connections, my dear. Don't underestimate my ability to help you. It may be your only chance."

I thought of the nine-year anniversary, the last million dollars, and my confidence in the devil's bargain.

I laughed, madly, openly and without abandon. It

perplexed Jackal and Lambert alike. I laughed until the sound turned bitter and I nearly choked, full of defeat. "I don't know who he is," I said weakly. "He has a code name too."

Lambert's cheeks tightened and his eyes smoldered. "Are you really this useless?"

Jackal stepped back and glanced at the doorway. A second later, a gunshot cracked in the air. It came from outside. The front yard. Then more yelling, and gunfire.

Knock, Knock

Lambert turned to me. "What did you do? Who is that?"

I shook my head, stunned.

Amid a spattering of background gunfire, boots stomped down the hall and into our room. "Someone's here," a skinhead reported. "He's..."

"Not human," muttered Jackal.

"See to it," commanded Lambert.

Jackal vanished into darkness. The biker blinked in disbelief as his buddies marched past him into the room.

"We can't stay here," announced the old man. "My car's in the back. Take her."

A biker reached for me and I yanked my arm away. "I'm not going anywhere."

"Oh yes you are."

Two men forcefully grabbed me. I gasped as my shoulder jerked forward. I felt helpless. Felt the anger building up inside me. The anger I desperately tried to stave off.

"Leave me!" I roared. "I'll fight you."

The bikers looked at each other and laughed. Lambert peeked out a back door before smiling. "You're handcuffed, Miss Crowe. You can no longer summon assistance."

"I'm warning you."

He huffed angrily. "I have been harsher than I intended to be, but I will escalate this until you see the wisdom of my path."

I stomped a biker's leg just above the boot. I twisted away, but he held tight. The other one decked me. With my hands behind my back, I couldn't catch myself. My shoulder hit the floor again. I gasped, spittle leaking from my lips.

The Dark One was knocking.

"Now you listen, little lady," spat the biker. "That wasn't the first time I hit a woman, and it won't be the last. If you behave it'll be the last for you."

He grabbed a fistful of my hair and yanked me off the ground.

And I reached out to the Dark One.

Summoning, you see, is usually an external affair. You call a demon to a circle and ask for guidance. You bring a familiar into this world and send it on a task. But there's another kind of summoning that many don't know about. And of those that do, most won't touch. Either they aren't able to pull it off or they're too smart to attempt it.

Possession.

The iron on my wrists kept me from manipulating the Intrinsics around me, but the magical energies danced everywhere. Even within. My body was a temple, and I was gonna Airbnb it out to a demon.

As far as smarts, well, I didn't have much choice, did I?

My muscles went taut as strength coursed through my veins. I stood tall, shrugging the bikers away. I spun and kicked the nearest one in the gut. He doubled over and puked.

The other one reached for a knife at his belt. I growled, leaned down, and charged, ramming my shoulder into him. Somewhere behind all the rage, I winced at the thought of using my wounded arm for such an attack, but with the Dark One in me I didn't feel a thing. The man was twice my weight, and my small frame lifted him from the floor and propelled him into the wall. His breath escaped him. He fell and clawed at his chest, gasping.

"Jackal," called Lambert.

I spun around and assessed my enemies. Lambert and two bikers. I roared at them, vision going red. I strained my biceps and pulled. The handcuff links broke apart. Lambert flinched as I ripped the clasps off my hands.

"What are you waiting for?" he yelled. "Get her!"

One of the men recovered a pool cue from the floor. He advanced and swung the heavy end at me. I laughed and smashed it away, lunging forward in a smooth motion and breaking his nose. I beamed at the sight of blood.

My vision faded slightly as I fought for control. I pulled the Dark One's hand back, staying the killing blow meant to rip open his throat. Instead, my boot snapped his knee and downed him.

The other biker took a step away from Lambert, holding

his hands up in surrender.

"Jackal!" he called again, desperation evident. Lambert vigorously rubbed his golden ring.

I chuckled and the sound came out like a series of grunts, my voice no longer my own. "Jackal's got his hands full..."

Lambert searched the floor for his gun, but it might as well have been miles away.

"Miss Crowe," he pleaded, "don't do anything you'll regret." I advanced on him. "I can help you."

I struggled to hear the words over the raging emotions, the feel of the room and my instinctual leanings. Those weren't me, they were the Dark One's tendencies. Unlike me, she had no aversion to killing. I'd come too close to killing in the past, to losing control, and that was one thing a summoner could never afford. It was why I resented being forced to use her power. Why I stayed away from it. Why it made me afraid.

The firing of weapons increased in urgency and proximity. Several more gang members retreated inside, harried by the devil attacking them head on.

I saw the blood on one of them, the fear in their eyes, and I showed my teeth.

Their guns turned to me and I rolled away. I may have felt invincible but I was far from it. This body, this collection of pumping organs and fluid bound together by flesh, it held me back. To be truly free was a symphony, a triumphant dance of torture and agony. For now I would be sated with the snapping of bones. I would wet these lips with blood.

I picked up a pool ball and beamed it at a man with a shotgun. It cracked his skull and put him to sleep instantly. I heaved a heavy chair and took out another. Bullets pounded the wall behind me as I danced, toeing the line between demon and woman. Slowly, surely, losing the battle for my humanity.

"Watch out!" cried a biker. He turned and emptied his magazine outside the doorway. The entire wooden door flew off its hinges and flattened him. Bikers retreated toward the back, blindly firing over their shoulders.

I growled as a figure of glowing orange stepped into the room. I cowered in the face of the blinding light. It shone over me. It burned me. I hissed in anger and frustration and insolence.

Inside, I fought with the Dark One's boiling rage. It threatened to consume me faster than ever before. I wanted everyone at my feet. I demanded full compliance, and this interloper wouldn't get in my way.

The blazing figure turned to me. I searched for eyes on its glowing face but couldn't find any. No matter. I would taste my opponent on my tongue.

I roared and charged. Fingers pointed my way and I was hit with a bag of bricks. It wasn't pain, exactly. I was mostly immune to that. But it shook me to my core. Loosened my will.

Or strengthened it.

I jerked my head. Me, Shyla Crowe, urging the Dark One down. But she was more bloodthirsty than ever. She didn't listen. She attempted to take over again.

I clenched my jaw. "Get... Out..."

I bared my teeth as the demonic intruder neared. The orange glow began to fade as I recovered my humanity. Someone was at the center of that radiance, and I could almost see...

An arm thrust forward and I blacked out.

Eternity

My eyes fluttered open. I whined in sudden pain. Not the pounding in my temples. I could deal with a sharp hangover. It was my body that hurt. Everywhere. I twisted on the ground and the wound on my neck ripped. I almost passed out again but managed to swallow a few breaths.

I lay in the clubhouse among a wreckage of furniture and bodies. I stayed in place and breathed, listening for any activity.

There was none, and I knew what that meant.

I bit down in anticipation of intense pain and sat up. It was agonizing, but I was a tough girl. As long as I was mentally prepared, I could deal with almost anything.

The Dark One had really done a number on me. I was all kinds of banged up. I couldn't remember what happened, exactly. I went solemn at the thought that I had killed the bikers strewn about the room.

No. Please no.

Even if it hadn't really been me but the Dark One, I

deserved the blame for summoning her. But a faint vision of an intruder scraped my brain.

I stiffened and rose to my feet. I was still in danger. I waved my hand to call Bernard, but the effort of will seemed insurmountable. I was too weak. Hell, Bernard was probably weaker than me. I just hoped I'd banished him before he'd suffered a mortal blow.

I rubbed my eyes and walked off the lethargy. My body may have been my temple, but it'd just been subjected to an illegal house party. For now, a little extra adrenaline wouldn't hurt. I loosened up, head pounding but limbs feeling better. I staggered to the door and carefully stepped over a severed head.

The sun was bright. I glimpsed the glowing intruder again and flinched, but it was only in my mind. An after effect, burned into my corneas. I had never seen anything so simultaneously riveting and frightening.

I stepped outside and found more dead bikers. Half the club's motorcycles were tossed around the yard. The other half were gone, which meant a good number of club members had gotten out alive. My own Ducati Monster sat a short distance away where I had left it, facing the smashed open front gate and ready to leave.

And believe me, I was ready to leave.

But something nagged me. Something I couldn't just leave behind.

Not after coming all this way.

I turned my boots and headed back through the hall. I'd seen no sign of Teegan. She'd likely escaped the demon's wrath by leaving early. The rest were nameless bikers. A part of me figured they deserved what they got. It was a sickening thought. No one deserved this. Not really.

I trudged back into the community room, avoiding body parts and trying not to track blood. The last thing I needed were my boot prints in an evidence locker in some desert police station.

I checked behind the bar, grimacing at the small grains of rubble that had come from Bernard. I crossed the room, growing more limber the more I moved. With my boot, my butt, and a lean, I slid a couch away from the wall. Lambert's small pistol was on the ground.

I didn't especially like guns, but I knew when I was facing long odds. As much as I hated the chance of someone dying by my hand, I hated the thought of me dying more. I bent down gingerly, checked the weapon, and shoved it in my jacket.

With a sigh I surveyed the rest of the room. I laughed when I saw it. In my haste to leave, I'd almost left my cell phone here. I went to where Lambert had taken it from me and picked it up. This time it really did take me a minute to remember my password.

There were two messages. One was Trap, hoping I was okay, showing a picture of his bare feet lounging at a pool I assumed was in Vegas. The other was Aaron, asking where I was. I shut the phone off and put it away.

Although the floor was spattered with blood, a single tooth stood out. I grabbed a used cocktail napkin, recovered it, and held it up to the light.

"Gotcha."

I wasn't an expert at spellcraft, but I knew a demon or two who might be able to locate Lambert with his tooth. It was gross but it got the job done. I balled up the napkin and shoved it into my pocket.

I continued to the back door, following the path the bikers had retreated through. It led to another hallway and then a sort of inner chamber. A meeting table with a desk opposite. A rich leather chair was upturned and the contents of the desk swept to the floor. And I supposed I no longer needed to locate the old man.

Lambert lay on his back, pinned to the wooden surface by a sword sticking straight through his neck. His arms were outstretched to his sides, a dagger through each palm, their tips still wet and dripping on the floor. The old man's head lolled over the edge of the desk with a blank upside-down stare.

Wrapped tightly around his crown of white hair was a golden funerary wreath. Metal leaves of laurel. Lambert wore the Crown of Aevum.

I shivered at the grisly scene.

On the blank wall behind the desk, where the primitive weapons had no doubt been ripped from their mounts, were words written in Lambert's blood: Vita in Aeternus.

It meant Eternal Life in Latin.

But in my particular line of work, I knew the words had another, more sinister, meaning. Vita is Life, and Aeternus is the name of the first ring of Hell.

The old man had finally found his ring.

Rest

By Hell or high water, I made it back to my place. It wasn't easy. I had to stop and get off the bike twice, pour a bottle of cold water over my face, but I made it.

Josalie came up and cleaned me up again. I told her she didn't want to know what happened. Really. She took my word for it.

I responded to my text messages. Aaron came by too. He was happy to see me and even put up with Josalie's teasing. It was only after some bed rest that I felt strong enough to summon Bernard again.

He was in sorry shape too. Gouges in his chest and back. I needed pliers to dislodge a claw embedded in a hard-to-reach spot behind his ear. I locked up Lambert's gold ring in my safe. I'd thought it wise to retrieve it but, out of respect, had left the crown on his head. Despite its dollar value, it seemed befitting that he keep it.

Later that evening, Aaron stopped in again to talk business. We sat at my glass dining table while Bernard curled on the floor below, tail flicking hypnotically back and forth.

"You should've given me the heads up, Shyla," he chided in a softer-than-usual Custodian tone. "You could have died out there."

"I'm sorry. It's just... I'm a professional." The word sounded hollow after discovering my father's betrayal. I didn't mention that part to Aaron. There was a lot I wasn't talking about. I sighed. "I just thought it was the right way to finish the job."

"Well it almost finished *you* off." He sipped the tea I had made. "I don't envy your next conversation with Bedrock. Luckily he wants you to rest. For what it's worth, I put in a good word."

After everything I'd just been through, I couldn't bring myself to squirm over the threat of facing Bedrock. I was an asset to him. It was the demon who'd counseled me to try to make everyone happy. Maybe I failed at that by keeping my actions secret from the Custodian, but it had worked out in the end.

And now I knew a little something extra about the relationship between my father and my so-called employer.

"At least you're safe from the demon," offered Aaron, now referring to my limited account of Lambert and his devil. "Without a summoner, he's stranded in Hell, wherever he came from. But if you're still worried, you can sleep with your wardrobe open."

"Hard pass. I have this little guy to watch me." The toes of my sock rubbed Bernard's back. "Besides, I'm confident you're right about Jackal."

Aaron leaned back and fixed the sleeve of his sweater. "Jackal, huh?" He chuckled inwardly. "Everyone has a code name."

"Not Bernard."

"No, well, you got lucky with him."

The gargoyle purred in satisfaction.

Aaron set his empty mug on the table. "So what now? Rest, I imagine? A vacation, perhaps?"

I smiled at a distant memory. "Sounds nice, doesn't it?"

"It's not just nice, it's smart. It'll be better if Bedrock cools off before you talk to him. But whatever you need. I know you can't stand to be away from work for long." He grinned. "Just take some time. Call me when you're ready for something else." He stood and sighed. "I'm glad this is over with."

"Is it?" I asked absently. "It feels like there's more left undone."

He straightened his glasses and studied me quizzically. "Like what? You finished the job. You were smart enough to take payment in advance. And since the crown was fake, you weren't going to squeeze any more juice from that fruit."

I swallowed my tea and frowned. "I'm not talking about the job, Aaron."

He pressed his lips together, mollified, and gave me a nod. "What happened afterward... with your client... He brought that on himself. Lambert was no innocent bystander. The man was a summoner; he knew the depths he was treading in. Anyone with infernal dealings knows the risks."

"And the others?" I asked, still sitting, still staring into my unfinished mug. "I figured out about the Crown Council."

He smiled. "Ethiopian royalists. It was the Amharic, was it not? It surprised me that you identified that." He crossed his arms waiting for an explanation, but I only shrugged. "I will admit, they have some odd beliefs. And long odds, if they think they're getting their country back. I understand, now, why you believed you were safe from Lambert. You thought Jackal had been sent by the Crown Council. I probably would've come to the same conclusion, if I knew what you did."

"You don't think they're the real deal?"

He mulled over the question for a moment. "It's hard to say for sure but, don't forget, I met the self-styled prince. He wasn't really summoner material."

I understood how Aaron had that impression, but summoners didn't go around advertising their profession. As skilled as I was—and I'd seen a lot more than Aaron ever had—Lambert had caught me totally off guard.

"You don't think they'll come back?" I asked.

"Maybe one day, but not soon. In fact, they already left town. Apparently Bedrock made quite the impression last night."

The wind seemed to leave me at that declaration. It was like I'd lost something without knowing what it was.

Aaron placed a gentle hand on my good shoulder.

"Listen, Shyla, I won't pretend to have all the answers. But I will say that it's my job to assess these things. To be a neutral third party. In my report to Bedrock, I'm going to theorize that Lambert wanted to recruit a worthy summoner for some crackpot cause, and that he enlisted the Crown Council for assistance. I haven't heard anything else that makes sense, and that's all Bedrock needs to know."

It was a good shine. One that was, after all, in my interests. I didn't want Bedrock to know the information I uncovered on Paulson, Lambert, and the Ring of Solomon. I didn't want anyone to know for that matter, not even Aaron.

I thought he suspected something, but he wasn't pushing, he wasn't forcing. He was giving me time and space while spinning a good story for our employer.

"Thanks, Aaron." I was earnest but my voice came out dejected.

He gave me a pat. "You should relax, Shyla. You're in good hands."

"I'm in hock to a demon."

"I'm talking about us." He took my empty mug, and his, and set them in the sink. He leaned on the counter and regarded me coolly. "I like to think of us as friends. And Josalie is... a little outgoing for my tastes, but she's good for you. Some positivity to negate your cynicism. And who can forget Bernard? You're surrounded by a safety net. It's okay to rely on us sometimes."

I knew he was right but didn't say anything. He understood me enough to know nothing was needed. Aaron strolled to the table and picked up his jacket from the back of the chair.

"You're leaving?"

"I wish I could stay but... I need to be diligent about managing Bedrock's empire. He really put himself out there for us, and he didn't do it out of the kindness of his heart. I'm afraid there are going to be consequences. The best we can do is keep our heads down."

I snickered. "You mean behave like his good little operators."

"I do," he returned, softly but without a smile.

He was his serious self again. The Custodian. Already thinking about the next play. "What kind of consequences?"

He shook his head. "Let's worry about that when we get there."

I nodded in thanks and he nodded back and saw himself out. I sat a little longer, my foot rubbing Bernard's back, dwelling on my trademark cynicism again.

I could already see Bedrock calling on more debt, upping the amount we owed him, lengthening our servitude. That was the thing about being in hock. It was infinitely easier to get deeper than to get out. And when you were dealing with Hell, the word deep became profoundly literal.

The next day was more or less the same. Me lounging, in bed or otherwise, listening to the entirety of my mom's record collection. Josalie visited when she could, but she worked long shifts and had a family to care for. I was alone most of the time.

Well, I was never alone. Bernard paced the loft, always at

foot, always watching out for dangers I knew wouldn't come.

For some reason, the possibility of never seeing Jackal again disappointed me.

It was over. At least if I wanted it to be. And that was what Bedrock wanted. For Shyla Crowe to be his good little operator.

With me laid up, it was an easy plan to wrap my head around. Half my body was sore, my headaches came and went with abandon, and every hour I slept was another hour of peace. I didn't completely mind it.

But I was a mass of inertia inside, teetering on the edge of something steep, continually poised to snowball downhill no matter the path. It was like trying to rest when you were about to fall.

And, it turned out, I only needed the slightest of nudges to get going.

Trap sent me a text. "You're never going to guess who the newest high roller at the casino is."

The attached picture showed a covert snap of a casino interior. The man pretending to be Prince Al-Assaf had fled to Vegas.

Road Trip

I flipped the Ducati Monster 821 into touring mode and revved the L-Twin engine out of town. I was fully geared up. The Corse Carbon helmet had splashes of red, like the bike, but besides that I was dressed in black from head to toe. Calfskin leather gloves, Icon boots with shin plates, tight-fitting pants, and a hastily stitched up leather jacket.

Riding the open road across a sparse desert landscape was a biker's dream. Everything seemed miles away. There was nothing to do but set your sights and throttle.

It wasn't lost on me that I was finally giving myself something to do, forcing my body to join the workout of my hyperactive thoughts. Vegas was mind and body coming together, and I was amped the entire ride.

Chasing down the fake Saudi prince might not've been what Aaron had in mind when he'd suggested a vacation, but it was the medicine I needed right now. I was a workaholic. It was how I relaxed.

As for Bedrock, well, what he didn't know wouldn't hurt

him. His intent for how I spent my R and R wasn't my problem. I was getting out of town, obeying the letter of the law if not its spirit. If anyone understood loopholes like that, it was a demon.

The heat wasn't bad as I kept a lightning pace, and before I knew it the evening was setting in. A little over two hours and I pulled into the parking lot of the Venetian, texted Trap that I'd made it, and entered through the food court.

I'd come to the conclusion that the Ring of Solomon was everything. Its existence wasn't knowledge I was supposed to have. My father had obviously been bound from mentioning it. Bedrock kept him on a tight leash, which was why my visits with Dad were social rather than strategic.

If it hadn't been for Lambert finally tracking me down, and him and the Crown Council stumbling over each other trying to get to me first, I might've been in the dark forever.

But even with that golden nugget, that forbidden fruit of knowledge, my understanding was incomplete. I was ninety percent to the truth, just on the cusp of winning it all or losing everything. It left me both excited and terrified to discover the rest. It also left me determined.

All my skills, all my dark deals, all my hardship and suffering had led me down this narrow path. There was only one way to go and I was gonna ride it till the end.

If I died, I died with the truth.

Trap discreetly waved me over from the bar. I sidled up without greeting him. A glass of honey-colored bourbon waited for me. I picked it up and leaned my back against the bar, observing the maze of gaming tables. Trap faced the other way, leaning on his elbows, hunched over a rack of multi-colored poker chips and sipping a drink matching mine.

"This one's smoky," I said.

"It's cherrywood, it's expensive, and you're buying."

I chuckled. Trap was a connoisseur and he deserved it.

"Our prince likes the card tables," he said slyly into his glass.

I scanned the distant poker room and found him. No longer wearing the head covering, he didn't stand out from the crowd. It was the two bodyguards some distance at his back that had drawn my attention.

"What a coincidence for you to land at a casino with him."

"It's the best cardroom in Vegas."

"Mm-hmm," I dubiously hummed.

He shrugged. "Okay, maybe I did a little digging on my own. Looking out for you. For old time's sake."

I grinned. "You're a workaholic, Trap. Just like me. You can't run from a good score."

"That's where you're wrong, Shyla. I'm running just fine. This isn't me getting involved. I'm giving you a friendly nod and that's all." He turned to study me for the first time. "You look beat to shit. How'd everything play out down there?"

"Pretty much how you were afraid of it going down."

He snorted and shook his head. "Well, it's good to see you breathing."

I dropped the secret-agent act and gave him a hug. Trap returned it for a second, and then we pulled away and settled back into not knowing each other. I sipped the bourbon, sweet on the nose and smoky down the throat, eyes back on the card tables. Our impostor pulled a stack of chips to his pile.

"His real name's Kato Selassie," reported Trap. "He's a descendant of the deposed emperor." My eyes widened at the implications. "And the only coincidence is Vegas being the closest international city. I tracked them down the same way I tried back home, by checking flight manifests from local airports. I found a jet owned by Ethiopian royals that came in three weeks ago."

"They flew into Vegas to stay off my radar."

"Which made them much harder to find, especially since we were looking for Saudis. But once I tracked the jet, finding them was a piece of cake. I'm assuming you can take it from here."

I nodded. "There's even an open seat next to him." I pulled away from the bar.

"Wait," he said, sliding his rack of chips over. "Take these. I'm not getting cards today anyway."

I clinked my glass to his and took his chips, which I was sure he would bill me for later. I headed over to the cardroom, going with as direct a strategy as possible. I figured I could follow their crew around all night and not get a better opportunity. In a public casino, his bodyguards wouldn't try anything. Anyway, what was a poker table if not a war table, neutral territory for opposing generals?

I set my chips down, surprised to see the enhanced buy-in. These were high rollers. I added some cash from my pocket and the dealer chipped me in. Everyone at the table simultaneously appraised me. Was I a regular, overconfident, a bimbo, easy money? No one made obvious expressions except for Selassie. I winked as I sat beside him.

His eyes flitted to his men.

"Relax. We're just playing cards."

He swallowed, lacking the cool confidence from the night of the party. The dealer asked for his blind. He hurried a chip forward as our cards were dealt. Continuing Trap's luck, I got an eight-three. I folded the hand and turned to the royal.

"I think I know you from somewhere," I said with a smile.

"Yes. I'm—"

"Kato Selassie," I cut in, before he had a chance to introduce his third alias.

He stiffened. The bet got back around to him. He double-checked his cards and called. The dealer dealt three community cards: a king, a jack, and a deuce. Kato made a modest bet. Two others at the table stayed in with him.

"A king and a jack," I mused aloud. "That reminds me. I ran into your friend after you left. Not sure where Jack went off to, but things didn't turn out well for his handler. I don't think we'll be seeing him again."

Kato blanched at the mention of Lambert's death. But he put on a good poker face. "He was no king."

"I was talking about you." I leaned close and whispered,

"Lion of Judah."

He watched the next card dealt. An eight. He repeated his bet. The other bettors raised, and he went over the top on them. Double what they put in.

"I'm not the Lion of Judah," he said as his opponents pondered their responses. "But he will need what's his one day."

"Not interested in rings anymore without Jack around?"

"Jack's allegiances may be questionable, but he knows jewelry. This new player? No one knows him. It's like cards, Shyla. You must understand when the risks outweigh the reward."

One of the men folded but the other called. One on one now. The river came, an unexpected queen. I widened my eyes. "That might've just made someone's day."

"It has," he announced. He slid a large bet into the pot.

"What makes you think your king is ever gonna get what he wants?"

The man sitting opposite stared Kato down through sunglasses, trying to determine what he had, playing cool and aggressive at the same time.

"It was ours to begin with," explained Kato, growing comfortable with speaking freely. "Lambert worked with us to find the ring, but we knew of his ulterior intentions for some time."

"The big L," I muttered.

He chuckled. "If you can believe such a thing. But then Paulson stole the ring."

The man opposite went all in, giving Kato pause.

"Perhaps it was for the best," I said. "To avoid collateral damage."

Kato shook his head. "That was never a worry. The ring cannot be used without Solomon's son. This is why it's ours and ours alone." He faced the dealer. "Call."

She counted his chips over. Kato Selassie had more than enough to cover his opponent.

My brow furrowed. "That's not what the old stories say. Asmodeus took the ring and used it in Solomon's stead for forty days, didn't he?"

"He did, but he made a fatal mistake. He banished the king from the kingdom, separating the power from its source. The demon's rule waned until there was nothing left."

All eyes were on us, a healthy mix of interest in our conversation and in the outcome of the sizable hand.

"The Lion of Judah has time," he said confidently. "And there are always more kings than one. Remember that." He placed his cards on the table. Another king with a queen. Two pair. That last queen had helped him, but maybe not as much as he thought.

His opponent quickly showed his hand. Ace-ten. He'd scored a gutshot straight. He flashed a cool smile and dragged his winnings over. Kato frowned, worried more about losing face than his chips. Money wasn't much to him.

I stacked my chips back in the rack and whispered to him. "Don't come after me. I don't have what you want."

"Perhaps," he said with an astute grin. "But the Lion of Judah will return one day to claim his property. It's the destiny of the line."

"Destiny?" The guy with the big payday laughed as he organized his winnings. "Doesn't look like luck's on your side, brother." He turned to me as I picked up my rack and stepped away from the table. "Don't leave, lady. You just got here. You're good luck."

My eyes fixed on him. "That all depends in what context you run into me." I leaned toward Kato and patted him on the shoulder. "You slow played that hand. It was yours all the way but you waited too long to go for it." I marched away from the table and right past the hard-staring bodyguards.

Tooth and Nail

I booked a room in disappointment. The Crown Council didn't know anything. In fact, they were cutting their losses. A few of their own dead, Bedrock on the loose, and their ring nowhere in sight. I'd been hoping they could help me, but once again I needed to do that myself.

Before heading up, I made sure to get myself a nice dinner. A rack of lamb with a spicy Syrah. Then I went to bed.

In the morning I had crepes and hit the hotel spa. I didn't see Trap again. After announcing myself to the royalists, there was a possibility I'd be under surveillance. Which was fine by me. If a couple of goons wanted to wait on my deep tissue massage and facial rejuvenation, more power to them.

Aaron texted and I told him I was in Vegas. I sent him a selfie of my mud mask with cucumber eyes. If that surprised him, he was doubly surprised when I said I'd be on my way back.

"Rest didn't last long, did it?" he joked.

Rest was good, but all good things come to an end. Rest wasn't what I needed. I was energized now. I was after answers. And it just so happened, in my line of work, humans weren't always the best source for them.

I gassed up and rode home. It was the early afternoon by the time I made it back to the loft. Pleasantly quiet. Everything was where it was supposed to be. I locked the doors and got my grandmother's grimoire. This time, instead of sprawling across the bed, I set the book on the dining room table and slid it aside, exposing the hexagram on the floor.

"Are you thinking things through?" pressed Bernard. "You've never summoned a hellion from Dis before."

The sixth ring of Hell was a famed penitentiary. Instead of humans it housed monsters of the worst kind. It was a place where Hell's Order held sway. Dis was the front line of hellion royalty. Those from the Material Plane had no business at its gates or beyond.

And yet, Jackal was there, and maybe even more.

"His claw's not going to last long," I explained. "I preserved what I could, but it's already breaking down." The decrepit remnant of Jackal's nail sat in a bowl beside me. "With it I'm almost guaranteed a successful invocation."

"Getting him here isn't the problem," said Bernard protectively. "You were deceived by a smoke devil from Stygia. It's not safe to go deeper."

"Thanks for the vote of confidence," I muttered. "You're just upset because I need to banish you before performing another summoning. You hate being on the bench."

"It means I can't defend you."

I exhaled sharply. "I need to do this, Bernard. I know it sounds stupid, but I feel like this is my fate."

His jaw twisted. "It doesn't sound stupid. But might I remind you fate isn't always kind? Many famous men and women were fated to suffer horribly and die."

"I need to know." I pressed my lips tight as I dressed the circle with candles and scented oils. "I need to know why my life is like this. Why I'm surrounded by demons."

In light of the severity of my actions, I was going full bore with the ritual. I reinforced the alloy circle with protective powders. I fortified each candle with blessings. Six points in each of the star's valleys. It was Solomon's star, recreated with a blend of traditional spellcraft and modern science.

I used a pair of tweezers to pick out Jackal's nail from the bowl and gently set it in the center of the hexagram. Then I recovered the cocktail napkin and poured Lambert's tooth out beside it.

"It's showtime," I announced.

Bernard watched with his chin on the ground like a patient pet. He was behind me, several paces from the circle. He didn't ever cross over. I scooted over and put an arm around him.

"If this backfires..." I said softly. "If I don't make it through this, I want you to know you've been the best hellion a summoner could ask for."

He turned his head away, refusing to acknowledge the

potential goodbye. When I hugged him, he did hug back. I turned to the circle and wiped my eyes. With a casual wave, my companion disappeared.

I was alone in this, but not for long.

"Hear me, Bornless One."

I used an invocation from the *Semitas Daemoniorum* this time. One hand on the Sigillum Dei, the other pointed to the star before me.

"Come thou forth, and follow me."

The yellowed tooth and bloody claw shriveled as if speeding through time until they were dust. The loft darkened and the powder flared like a match, forming a ring of fire. The hellish light cast long shadows and winked out.

For three seconds, I was in total darkness, unable to see my hand before my face. I didn't waver, release the pentacle, or bungle the ritual. I had located the demon but he wasn't coming.

"I invoke thee, Jackal."

I pulled Lambert's ring from my pocket and rubbed the smooth gold. Lambert had used it as a fetish of sorts, a way to focus his spellcraft. I hadn't needed one for summoning since I was a kid, but I was going deeper than I'd ever been.

But the ring wasn't just a tool. It was a sentimental link from Lambert to Jackal, from human to hellion. He wouldn't ignore its pull.

"I invoke thee, Jackal."

The hexagram glimmered into view but remained dim. None of the lights from my loft remained, nor the lights from the windows. In fact, the polished cement faded to black a few short steps away, the metal star the only source of illumination. It was a lonely circle surrounded by oblivion.

In the center of the star sat a man with animalistic features, cross-legged, bearing the spots of a leopard.

Jackal

A rough tongue tickled sharp incisors. Cat eyes the color of shining amber took in the scene, gazing into the blackness as if something was there, as if they longed for it. Delicate white flower petals swirled around the figure as if suspended in a lazy dust devil, ever spiraling, their sweet floral scent in the wake of each pass.

"This place smells of sulfur," muttered the demon, nose wrinkling in displeasure. "Your pet was recently here. You saved him after all."

I scowled at his casual attitude over the incident. "It looks like you escaped a similar fate."

"Indeed. Though it seems I left a piece of myself behind." Clawed hands scrubbed his orange-red coat. One of his fingers was already regrowing a claw. His eyes snapped to the golden ring I held. "I didn't take you for the sort who kept trophies."

"I'll take that as a compliment, coming from you. You took Grady's silver cross when you killed him."

He grinned and produced it, chain dangling from his hand. "I love the irony of the cross, don't you?"

"I want it back."

"Ah, but we each possess something we shouldn't. You can have it in return for the ring."

I frowned. "I'll think about it. I want to talk first."

He shrugged. "So be it. It was a risk invoking me, you know. But then, Hell has underestimated your holy trappings for some time."

If Jackal had a specific meaning, he didn't clarify. I supposed he'd meant the Sigillum Dei. The blackened spot on his cheek was faded now. Bernard was also mostly recovered. Hellions healed fast.

I decided to offer what little sympathy I could before I requested help. "I didn't intend for Lambert to..."

Jackal's eyes glinted. "He was a true believer. His death was unfortunate." The devil frowned. "There aren't many willing to fight for us."

"For Lucifer, you mean." I snorted. "I don't know why Paimon declares his allegiance so, but don't count on recruiting me to serve a fallen angel."

Jackal grinned. He grinned until he could bear it no more and laughed with amused disdain. "You humans are forever puzzling out such references. Chasing tails you don't even have. Who is what. What is who. You desire the simplest of answers when it's apparent, even among your kind, that no such simplicities exist."

I waited patiently with my pentacle brandished, letting the demon say his piece.

"In the antediluvian days before the Flood, the Earth was a playground for demons and man. This was a time of nephilim and giants, of Gilgamesh and Humbaba. Their whispers are both familiar and foreign, invoking names upon names: for pagan gods, Jewish angels, and Christian demons. And the thing of it is, many of them reference the same beings. They come into and fall out of favor with each age and as each slant of theology defines them."

He smiled inwardly. "Those times witnessed a deluge of disagreements. It is never mankind with the answers, just the questions. No single human text does justice to the complexities of who was what and what was who. Many of those truths are beyond even me. But I do know this: Lucifer was never an angel. The king of Hell is a hellion, born and bred."

"Was he not cast out?" I asked.

"He was, along with many. The receding waters of the Great Flood marked the beginning of ancient times. A cleansed Earth. Christians began to teach that some of my kind were angels fallen from grace. It was their way of asserting dominance and order, God's hand in creating Hell." Jackal lazily shook his head. "In truth, He never touched the place. Hell sits outside Creation. It's why we live there."

I had seen references in various grimoires about demons living outside of grace, exterior to the confines of God's kingdom. According to Jackal, God and the angels ruled the Material Plane but not the World Below.

"There are stories," I said, "of angels visiting Hell."

"Aside from the truly fallen, many spend vast amounts of time there. That's the greatness of Hell—we're not picky. This Earthly Steppe has rules and regulations and lines that cannot be crossed. The only lines in Hell are territories, the only rules contracts. But the sign says Open and the doors are unlocked." He blinked suggestively. "You are welcome anytime you like."

"No thanks."

"It's an open invitation, Shyla Crowe."

I squirmed slightly. I had known, of course, that Jackal knew my name. With Lambert as his summoner, he knew much of my history. It left me at a disadvantage.

"Instead I invited you to my world," I said firmly. "You're here, now, under my power. I invoked you."

He returned a bored breath. "And here I hoped your unfortunate handling of the smoke devil would have taught you a measure of humility."

My eyes narrowed. "Did you have something to do with his lies?"

Jackal chuckled. "Does a Stygian devil need my persuasion? You know their reputation. They sit in the center of Hell and are quite proud to represent it."

"But I compelled him with his archon's coin. King Balam —"

"No longer rules Stygia. Balam was deposed and killed a short time ago. An incident with aftershocks already being felt in your world, I believe." Jackal assessed me like a tutor admonishing a student, gifted but cocky. "You set the smoke devil loose with a blank slate. He could've done almost anything he desired. Be lucky he chose merely to deceive his summoner about a snare."

My heart rate quickened as I learned of my error. The *Semitas Daemoniorum* would need to be updated. Either Estever had gotten it wrong or, more likely, the Greek hell had changed leadership extremely recently. "Who's the new archon of Stygia?"

Jackal clicked his lips and showed the faintest shake of his head. "Is this the puzzle you truly seek to unravel? Is this the information you wish in return for your payment?"

"What payment?"

He pulled a round piece of metal from the darkness. "One coin of iron, to my liege, Paimon."

It was Estever's sigil, the one he'd stolen from my safe. Instead of absconding with it, the demon was taking it as payment due. He was putting himself in my debt.

"I will give an answer truthfully, Shyla Crowe, but you must fashion the question. Humans always have questions." He licked sharp teeth and pondered his bargain. "We'll keep this simple so as not to run counter to any cross-interests. I will only answer to what I have seen with my own eyes."

I blinked, taken aback by the offer. Perhaps Jackal needed this to truly possess Estever's coin. Maybe he'd taken it in the first place with the intention of paying off its debt. The motivations may have differed but the end result was the same, and I believed him.

Jackal would answer one question truthfully.

There was so much to ask. Lucifer's role in this had philosophical ramifications, but my quest was much more personal. My father, on the other hand, was outside Jackal's jurisdiction. I'd witnessed his surprise at being told Paulson was in Hell. Lambert and the devil had both hoped to catch him hiding with me.

Which meant that line of questioning was useless.

But it did lead to the Ring of Solomon. Did I dare ask about that, knowing Jackal himself may have never laid eyes on it? I already knew of its legend, its power. Everyone was fighting for it, but the ring itself wasn't the single key to my enlightenment.

It was the demon who wielded it. Names upon names.

I took a slow breath and locked eyes with Jackal, daring him to defy me. "What is the true name of the demon who killed your master?"

He snickered once, then smiled. "An admirable question, if profoundly flawed. But I did witness the bearer of the ring. I did feel its power against my being. I was banished to the depths of Dis before lifting a claw in defense of my master." Jackal leaned forward slyly. "But not before identifying the interloper."

"Who was it?"

"The Great Destroyer," he answered with a playful smirk. "The Angel of the Abyss. The Lord of the Pit."

"I demanded a true name, Jackal."

"And so you shall have it, but you will wish you haven't. For he is Abaddon, the Scourge of Hell. Not because he is a demon, but because he is an angel."

My throat closed up. Bedrock wasn't a demon but an angel. "Is he fallen?" I asked quickly, the first thing that came to mind.

"His grace is intact, as far as I know, but I am not one to judge such things." He watched me intently as I processed. "It is as I said, the Celestials effect their power in many places, even outside Creation."

Which made sense, considering the ring was supposed to have been a gift from the angels in the first place.

"Is this about Lucifer warring with Heaven?" I asked.

He snorted. "Forget your antiquated stories, the simplicities you tell yourselves to make sense of the world. The ring is power. That alone is enough reason for many to desire it."

I reached for my grimoire and paged through. Abaddon didn't have a listing. *The Path of Demons* didn't track angels. Though I recognized the name from *Revelation*. Other texts sometimes cast Abaddon as a villain for his role in Armageddon. But as far as current motivations, current simplicities, I was empty.

"What could Abaddon possibly want with me?" I asked inwardly. I was another lost human, puzzling away at ancient secrets, barely a scratch on the surface.

Jackal lost interest in me. Instead he gazed intently at the coin with Paimon's sigil. "This piece is well fashioned," he said idly. "It has your family's touch on it." He jutted his lips out, coming to a conclusion. "There are two sides to this coin, so I shall give you two answers. One for the mystery facing outward, which you have already solved. Next for the mystery within."

I shook my head. "But what's the question?"

"That is for you to ask." His fingers toyed with the coin. "Abaddon holds the ultimate power against my kind, the Ring of Solomon."

"But it can't be used without a son of Solomon."

His amber eyes flashed. "Once again, a flawed understanding. It is true that Solomon's blood is the source of the ring's power, but there's no rule that only Solomon's blood can wear it. All it requires is a ritual. Regular contact."

"Like if a son of Solomon was being kept prisoner..."

My jaw fell. Jackal was implying that my father was being held captive for a reason. In Lambert's service, Paulson had come across the ring and found it to be his birthright. Except he lost it to Abaddon, who keeps him tucked away to recharge its holy power.

But if my father was a son of Solomon, then the reason I was surrounded by demons was because...

"I'm next in the bloodline," I whispered.

"And there," announced Jackal with relish, "is your second answer. Even with your question unasked."

I thought of the Ethiopian royalists, the ones with the claim to the holy lineage, and then I thought of Paulson and Estever before him. I was a nobody, and yet I wasn't.

Jackal touched his cheek. "I feared the truth when you wielded the Sigillum Dei against me. The power was inherent within you. All this time you've been treated as a sidelong player, but you're more central to this conflict than you realized."

I took it in, speechless. I finally had answers. I finally knew who I was. And it didn't simplify things *at all*.

Jackal placed the cross on the metal hexagram. "And now for our trade. You must allow the circle to share our physical space. I pledge not to betray your trust."

My eyes narrowed. "I wouldn't let you if you tried." I pushed my hand inside the circle and set the ring down. I grabbed the cross and pulled back without consequence. Jackal smiled devilishly and scooped up his prize.

"And that," said the demon, "concludes our business. Repayment for the coin is complete. When we meet again, and we will, there will be no more debt between us. Remember that, Shyla, for your sake."

Jackal leaned forward and exploded into a rush of flowers. The petals clumped over the hexagram and powders and spilled into the room. A whoosh of air rushed me and the light of the world returned.

Uninvited Guests

I was still taking it all in and imagining my future confrontation with Bedrock when someone knocked on my door. I jolted up.

"Aaron?"

"It's me, bitch!" called Josalie.

"One second."

Crap. I scooped up the six candles and shoved them into a kitchen cabinet. I grabbed the rug and slid the dining table right over the leftover flowers and powder, throwing the edges down. I'd need to do a more thorough cleanup later.

"What's the holdup?" asked Josalie. "I've seen you naked before. You finally got a man in there?"

I rushed to the door.

"Bernard, the book."

The gargoyle puffed into existence and grabbed my grandmother's grimoire. He scooted off to the bedroom to lock it away. I opened the front door and my neighbor pushed in.

"You're looking better," she chimed. "What is that, a new perfume?"

"I'm good," I said, clearing my throat to buy time. "Actually, I stayed in Vegas last night. I was in a spa all morning."

"And you didn't invite me?"

I shrugged. "It was a business trip."

"Mm-hmm, the business of getting your nails done, it looks like."

I admired the deep scarlet. "I can do two things at once."

"At least we know you're feeling better." She hung her hands on her hips and looked around. "How long have you had this?" She went to the coffee table and picked up Lambert's revolver.

"Watch it!" I snatched it from her. "It's loaded."

Josalie pressed her lips tight. "I can't say I blame you. I'd be scared too."

"It's not mine," I grumbled, shoving the weapon into the small of my back.

She took a long breath. "Actually, this is why I came. I've been thinking things over, and they're more serious than I thought."

"You think?"

"Yeah, and I was hoping we could talk. About what you've been up to."

My face fell. "I don't blame you one bit, but things are a little precarious right now."

"I get that, it's just—"

There was another knock at my door. My brow

furrowed. Josalie went to open it for me. Aaron looked surprised to see her. He held two coffees in to-go cups.

"Ohhh," said Josalie knowingly. "*That* kind of precarious."

I almost denied the implication, but the misunderstanding helped the situation along. Instead I chewed my lip and hiked a shoulder.

Josalie winked at me. "How's it hanging, Tom?"

"Um, it's hanging."

"It sure is. Did you know our girl went to Vegas? Wait. You didn't go too, did you?"

I laughed. "He didn't go. I just needed a change of environment to clear my head. You know me. Any excuse to hit the road."

"I hear you. You needed a little fresh air. Too many pheromones in here. Speaking of which, I'll get out of your hair. But let's talk soon, okay?"

I nodded and she saw herself out. My eyes turned to Aaron, trying to straighten his glasses with his hands full. I grabbed one of the cups to lighten his load.

"Actually," he said, "that one's mine. Hold this."

I chuckled and accepted the other cup. He pulled his leisure jacket off and hung it by the door, straightened his cashmere sweater, and adjusted his wire frames.

As he made himself comfortable, I realized I still wore my full leathers. My armor. The jacket was on but unzipped, and the Sigillum Dei hung loose over my shirt. I handed him his coffee and tucked the pentacle back in.

"What did she want to talk about?" asked Aaron.

"You," I blurted out.

I didn't enjoy lying but it was part of separating work and my limited personal life. Aaron had introduced himself to Josalie as Tom, after all. I was merely extending my neighbor the same distance.

Except now that I had voiced the cover story, my face reddened.

"It's a little embarrassing actually, but you know Josalie. Everything's about sex."

He swallowed uncomfortably. We both turned to our coffees and took long gulps. My eye flitted to the ring on his hand.

"Look, don't worry about her. I respect your situation with your wife. Trust me, I get that more than anybody."

He nodded and took another sip. I wandered to the far window for a break. This was why I didn't do relationships. Because I was bad at them. Because, at the drop of a hat, I wanted the freedom to shrug off the world and go to Vegas.

But I wasn't free, was I? Not in the slightest. My whole life was one scam after the other just to get out from under.

That was why I was a stickler for control. I often ran my own jobs, met my own clients. Hell, control was a summoner's business.

That was also why I was sometimes shaken when jobs veered in unexpected directions. Unexpected was bad. Unexpected meant I wasn't really in control. The enlightened part of me knew that. But just like an alarm clock going off at five a.m., while necessary, I really hated getting the reminder.

So I opted back for full control, away from unexpected things and diving full bore into work.

I spun around. "I'm ready to talk to Bedrock."

His mouth crooked. "That's fortunate, because as soon as I told him you were back in town, he demanded an end to your bed rest."

"Suits me. I'll check in tonight."

"Actually, he wants to talk now. And, I confess I didn't just swing by to bring you a coffee."

I arched an eyebrow. "He wants you here too?"

"I'm afraid so. I think..." Aaron tapped his plastic coffee lid a few times. "Well, neither of us has been entirely truthful with him. He wants us to clear the air. Together."

"That's bullshit, Aaron. I'll take the blame—"

"This is about both of us," he asserted. "Let's face it, I've been covering for you."

"No. I never asked you to do anything."

"And yet I did."

The statement punctuated the point and there was nothing more to say. But it made me worry for Aaron. Bedrock had been asking strange questions about him. And in the role of Custodian, I wasn't sure he'd always been acting in the demon's interests lately.

No, not demon. Bedrock was an angel. His identity was leverage of a sort. I would use it if I needed to.

I idly scratched my shoulder under the bandages. "Should we get our stories straight first?"

"There's nothing to get straight, Shyla. We never conspired against him, or acted counter to his interests.

Convince him of that, tell him what you know, and that will be the end of it."

I snorted. It would never be the end of it. Not with what I knew. But maybe I could mold the predicament into a new beginning.

"No time like the present," I said.

He smiled and nodded. He set his coffee on the end table and strolled into my bedroom. I followed him in, still sipping. It was strange to see Aaron charge into my personal space so confidently, but he'd been doing that the past couple of days while I'd been confined to bed. It was another one of our professional walls, cracking and crumbling.

Aaron stopped and turned his head toward the dark bathroom. He waited a moment and said, "Very well, Bernard, but if you must stay, please remain out of sight."

The gargoyle's silence was his answer. I was surprised Aaron had noticed, but he knew my tricks and Bernard wasn't hiding from him anyway. I nodded to the blackness and Aaron opened the wardrobe. He picked off the silk bathrobe gently, giving it a strange look, like he was slightly confused and slightly embarrassed. I took it from him and stuffed it in the drawer of the nightstand.

The Custodian cleared his throat. "We're here," he said, stepping away from the mirror.

I hooked a hand on my pocket and sipped my latte, strangely exhilarated.

Abaddon

The mirror flickered and Abaddon appeared. His thin flesh was especially sullen, with his ashen hair throwing his appearance into a muted black and white. He stared at me and loosened his neck with some bobs of his head.

"Bedrock," I said in cordial greeting.

"Why are you dressed?"

I briefly turned to Aaron, but held firm. "The Custodian's here."

"And that concerns me how?"

His glare was withering. I reminded myself that his concern was dressing me down in the metaphorical sense, not the literal one. It was time to face the music. Bedrock scratched a finger to his chin and waited.

"As you can see," interjected Aaron, "Shyla's well rested. The Crown Council has fled, Lambert is dead, and the job, from our perspective, was a success."

"A success?" snarled the ghostly figure, serpentine tail flicking at his back. "In what sense was this a success?"

Aaron opened his mouth to answer. "Silence, Custodian. I'm speaking to my Handler."

I cleared my throat. "For one, I got paid. That's what you care about, isn't it?"

"And how much money is my anonymity worth?" he returned. "There were other demons involved and you walked into a trap."

I furrowed my brow. "You—"

"Do not presume to tell me about your lack of awareness, Handler. You are the summoner. Spellcraft is your jurisdiction." He lowered his head within his abyss. "But we're not speaking of the Crown Council besting you. I gave the Custodian specific orders to rein you in." He turned to Aaron. "How well done is your job when the girl is running off on her own?"

The Custodian's eyes flashed with indignation. "I did my best."

"Sir," said Bedrock. He watched Aaron's confusion and then said, "You did your best, *sir*."

The Custodian grimaced. "Yes. I did my best, sir."

Bedrock peeled back from the mirror's surface and took us both in. I got the feeling he was deciding which of us to execute.

"You tied off the loose ends," I placated. "There's no exposure to us."

He made a show of nodding his head and considering it, playing the debate opponent. "That's for me to judge, isn't it? In fact..."

Bedrock approached his side of the glass and stepped

through the mirror, right into my bedroom.

"Isn't that why we're all here?" he asked snidely. "In the flesh?"

"Bedrock." I stepped backward and set my coffee on the nearby bookcase.

My employer was here, in my bedroom. He was with us.

Aaron pulled my arm and stepped between us. "Sir, we can talk about this."

Bedrock gallivanted forward, stretching his arms and feeling out the space. I pulled Aaron backward with me, not wanting him to do anything stupid on my account.

Bedrock sniffed the air and grabbed my latte, taking a sip and dropping it in revulsion. "Cow's milk," he muttered. "I'll drink something a little more dignified."

He stomped toward us. I pulled Aaron away and flashed a palm toward the bathroom to signal Bernard to stay put. Bedrock didn't notice and wasn't even coming for us. He strolled past to the windows and the wine cooler.

I glanced into Aaron's gray eyes. He nodded encouragingly. "This is just a scare tactic," he whispered.

I loosened my shoulders and stepped out to follow him. "The one on the bottom is the best," I announced coolly. "It's a 1967 Cheval Blanc I pilfered from the cellar of a rich drug dealer who wouldn't appreciate it."

Bedrock plucked out the bottle and admired it. "Yes. This is the one." He lobbed it underhand to the Custodian, who flinched and caught it. "Would you be so kind?"

I grew nervous when Aaron knew exactly what drawer my corkscrew was in, almost like he'd done it before. If

Bedrock caught on he didn't show it. The Custodian poured three glasses. I held mine up to toast but Bedrock put his hand to my glass.

"Why don't we decide if we have something to celebrate first?" He swirled his glass and sniffed at it. "But feel free to drink in the meantime. I may be a demon but I'm not cruel."

The taste of the wine was a welcome distraction from the situation. Even though it needed a few minutes to open up, the flavor was rich and complex, though a bit on the alcoholic side.

"It's fitting," said Bedrock after a long pull at his glass, "to have you both here, together. If it's not clear, you're my two favorite operators."

Neither of us were asked a question, so neither answered, which seemed to please Bedrock.

"But the two of you have grown confident in yourselves, haven't you? Confident in your... positions." He leaned close to Aaron and bared his teeth. "Is it comfortable being my Custodian?"

Aaron stiffened but didn't flinch. "Yes, sir. Of course."

Bedrock was immediately at my side, nose brushing my hair and sending shivers down my neck. "And my Handler, do you think yourself indispensable?"

I shook my head, bothered by his proximity. "I wouldn't think that."

Bedrock lingered longer than he should've, taking in my scent. I imagined grabbing the gun from my back, sticking it up his nose, and letting him sniff that. But I held off for now.

He pulled away and shrugged. "Well, then. It appears my misgivings were unprompted. I have two loyal subjects before me."

Aaron nodded.

"I'm not your subject," I said with distaste. "I put up with you because I have to, because we have a deal. You employ me, I pay off my debt. That doesn't make me your subject."

Bedrock pulled his head back at my proclamation. His widened eyes flitted to Aaron in amusement before landing back on me. "Well, now, such fire. But I've always known that about you, *Shyla*." He grinned at my discomfort. "Oh, no worries, I'm aware the Custodian knows your name. His attention is obvious. The question is, do you know *his* name?"

Bedrock chuckled inwardly and Aaron flushed red. I couldn't be sure what they'd discussed in the past. Just like Aaron couldn't know the times Bedrock and I had spoken of him. Once again I got the feeling the employer was playing the employees against each other. Divide and conquer. The only thing I could do was go with my gut and soldier forward.

"That would be against the rules," I said with a smile.

"Rules," he repeated. "Very good. Don't ever believe a demon who tells you Hell has no rules. You put two living creatures beside each other and rules automatically spring to life. Even among hounds. *This is my bed. This is my food.* Rules separate the strong from the weak, and those who know from those who don't. Isn't that right, Custodian?"

Aaron worked his jaw and nodded. "That's why we're here. To give you everything we know. To prove our loyalty."

Bedrock's eyelids fluttered at the dull pointedness of his Custodian. "Very well," he sighed. Then he sized me up. "You went after a rogue summoner, on your own, without word to me or my Custodian."

My cheek twitched at the accusation. "I was concluding the job in as professional a manner as possible. I had no reason to think he was a summoner, that he—"

"Had his own demon lurking in the shadows? Rifling through your loft? Nosing about my business?"

"I figured the hellion had come from the Ethiopian royalists."

"A misplaced assumption, but understandable for a human. Did you ascertain what the Crown Council wanted?"

"No. I mean..." I glanced at Aaron standing silent. "Obviously, they wanted to lure me with a fake artifact and trap a thief. The Custodian believes they may have been after me for my talents."

"Your talents that didn't see them coming?" He frowned. "And who was the demon?"

"He announced himself as Jackal, as I'm sure the Custodian relayed to you."

"Yes, but I want to know *who he is*." Bedrock paced between us. "Look around you. Is anyone here who they really say? Does anyone have only one name? You're an old hand at this business."

"I don't know his true name."

He rounded on me. "Is that so?"

I didn't want to reveal everything I knew. The grimoire, my birthright. But I had to give a little to keep the pressure off us.

"Lambert was a Luciferian," I told them, figuring, if even the Crown Council knew of it, the knowledge was public enough. Bedrock would discover it eventually. Bedrock and Aaron traded concerned glances, but I chortled. "Don't worry. The old man had a romanticized version of Hell in his head. He liked to reference the *Inferno*. I doubt he ever whiffed anyone who'd ever been in Lucifer's presence."

That last part was a bit of an overstatement, but if I played Lambert off as a kook, they'd be less inclined to look into the details. That Paulson had worked for him. That we used to live close to his compound. That, because of our history, the old man had tracked me down. And that, although Lambert was dead, Jackal now knew Abaddon's true identity.

If there was infernal retribution headed his way, I wanted it to be the last thing on his radar.

"Forget the demon," said Aaron. "He was just a servant."

"My thoughts exactly," said Bedrock. "This Lambert Pemberton is an interesting, if misguided, fellow. I find it strange to believe you had further business with him after the crown was revealed to be fake." Bedrock paced around me in consideration. "I think it's unwise to write him off as an ignorant. Did he not, after all, manage to fool all three of us?"

"What do you want me to say?"

"I want you to tell me what Lambert wanted."

"Me."

"But for what?"

My eyes defiantly met his. "Maybe you should've asked instead of impaling him to the desk."

He snarled in return. "Maybe you should tell me what I ask!"

Bony fingers were suddenly around my throat, squeezing. I clutched his hands but his strength was formidable. A human couldn't fight him off. Not directly.

I felt Bernard stir. It was a sense, the Intrinsics connecting us, rather than any physical sound he made. But Bedrock's grip loosened. I waved Bernard off as Bedrock leaned close, the hair of his thin mustache scraping my cheek.

"Prove your loyalty, Shyla," he growled. "Prove you are what you say you are."

As he released me I kicked my boot into his hip. He stuttered back a few steps, utterly surprised.

"And what about you?" I hissed. "Who are *you*, really? Did you forget that I saw you in that clubhouse?" I stepped toward him. "Have you considered that I know who you *really* are?"

Bedrock snorted in contempt. "Don't be a fool."

"I'm not a fool. Not anymore. You want to come clean? I know your true name. I finally know you for who you are, Abaddon the Destroyer."

The Custodian tensed. I chugged my wine glass as

Bedrock stood listless, stunned. Surprise overtook his face, then concern, and then Bedrock set his glass down. His dark eyes pooled with shadow.

"By the very makings of Hell," he said solemnly, "I am compelled to deny this. A hellion cannot claim to be celestial in nature. One of those rules I spoke of. I must say this isn't true."

And then Bedrock waited and watched me. For what, I wasn't sure.

I fumed. I wasn't sure what I'd been expecting. Obviously the pronouncement wouldn't completely upend the power dynamic—he still had my father—but I'd hoped for some measure of notice. Of respect. Instead I was rewarded with calm denial.

I trembled with anger. I wanted to kick him again. To call him out for his lies, for bearing the Ring of Solomon.

But I realized I had never seen a ring on his finger. Not that he couldn't possess it without wearing it.

Aaron, beside me, was also silently fuming. At what I didn't know. I thought it strange, even though I could hardly explain my own emotions.

"Where is it?" I asked Bedrock. "Show me the ring that's cause to enslave my father."

It was my turn to get close to Bedrock. I broke his personal space, patted down his chest and waist. I pulled his sleeves up. No pockets, no jewelry.

"Where's the Ring of Solomon?" I growled.

I spun to Aaron in desperation, for help. His calculating nature would think of something to say. Some way to twist the revelation to our advantage. Or at least defend me one last time.

But all I saw was him try to hide his hand behind his back.

I froze and stared. Then back at Bedrock. How had he stepped through the mirror? A demon couldn't enter the Material Plane without a summoner, and I damn well sure didn't do it.

"Let me see your ring," I said quietly.

Aaron blinked, gray eyes pleading in confusion.

But I wasn't sure if I trusted him anymore. Aaron had been the one I told about Bernard being trapped. He'd been the one concerned with Lambert's whereabouts. I'd always presumed his questions were in service to Bedrock, but what if I'd had it backwards?

"Aaron," I said calmly, "let me see your ring."

It was the ring that reminded him of his wife. The one he wore facing inward, with the signet hidden. The one he kept just out of sight so it was always an afterthought.

The corner of Bedrock's mouth crooked, and the truth was plain.

I staggered in place, legs momentarily failing me.

Oh my God. Bedrock was just a demon, as he claimed to be. It was Aaron who had the Ring of Solomon. It was Aaron who was really Abaddon.

The Custodian's face went flat. He swung and hit Bedrock right in his smirk. The demon landed on the floor beside the sofa.

I recoiled, amazed and horrified at the power it must take

to do something like that to someone so strong.

And then I stepped away from Aaron in fear.

No. Not Aaron. Abaddon the Destroyer.

The angel smoldered as he approached, an orange glow washing over his skin as he was consumed by a heavenly rage.

Destroyer

Abaddon's eyes flared into great orbs of fire, sweater and hair bristling with invisible current. His countenance took on the warm hue of firelight, but it wasn't blinding as it was before. I figured me being possessed had something to do with the difference.

"You couldn't leave well enough alone," boomed the angel.

My back butted up against the bookcase divider. Abaddon closed the distance between us and leaned close. My neck was hot at his nearness.

"She's worth more to you alive," reasoned Bedrock, hunched on the floor.

Abaddon spun to him. "You pushed too far!"

"You asked me to find out all she knew!"

"She wouldn't have figured it out without your prodding."

The demon cowered. "What could I have done? My denial was required."

Abaddon paced around Bedrock, nearly prostrate before his master. It was a mindfuck seeing the switch. After nine years of serving Bedrock, seeing him wholly subservient to someone I considered a friend. The being that had really enslaved my father.

Abaddon mulled over the whimpering demon at his feet. He leaned close with suspicious eyes, voice turning calculating. "Did you have something to do with this?"

"I swear," he appealed. "I did not! I followed your commands to the letter!"

The angel kicked Bedrock's ribs. "That's what I'm worried about."

The demon sputtered on the floor, pulling himself away from the alpha in the room. "I did everything you asked! She wasn't to make an attempt on the crown. She was to coordinate with you. How could I be blamed for the Luciferian?"

The Custodian stepped slowly after the pathetic excuse for a demon. As their attention was turned away, I wrapped my fingers around the gun at my back.

"And how do I know you had no hand in that?" Abaddon spun the signet ring around and brandished it over Bedrock's head. "You think you deserve this, don't you? Third time's the charm? Why shouldn't I smite you down right here and now for your betrayal?"

"I didn't betray you!" he pleaded.

Bedrock's eyes went wide. He frantically sniffed the floor. "Look!" He pointed to the stray flower petals peeking from underneath the dining table rug. The demon slid over and upturned the edge, revealing more flowers and protective powders. "Look at this!" he cried. "The cloying fragrance of Dis. This was Paimon's doing!"

Abaddon stood over his defeated opponent and stayed his trembling hand.

"I would never conspire with the likes of them," Bedrock continued. "Not after what they did to me. You know that to be an indomitable truth."

The angel frowned and turned his back on the quivering demon. His fiery eyes locked onto mine. "You've been operating behind my back this whole time."

"You're one to talk," I scoffed.

He set his jaw and came for me again.

I drew the gun, still backed against the bookcase bordering my bedroom. "Stay away from me!"

He was too angry to be amused, but he slowed his approach. "You crossed me, Shyla."

"What do you care? Bedrock—you—gave me free rein to work as I saw fit."

"As long as you didn't counter my interests, girl."

"What interests? You said the job was a success. I'm giving you the money."

"This is about more than money. It always has been."

I shook the gun. "Keep back. I'm serious."

Abaddon lunged. The gun barked. He was on me before my eyes tracked it. The second time I pulled the trigger, my hand was twisted toward the ceiling.

"You're mine!" he growled, holding me close. "Do you see that? You're mine just like your father is."

He held my gun hand high above him. I twisted my wrist to point the revolver at the side of his head, but the angle wasn't good.

"Just because I work for you doesn't mean—"

"No, Shyla, you're mine. You said it. It's time to be a good little operative. If you want to live through this, you'll say yes master and do my bidding."

I turned the revolver and stuck my thumb over the trigger. It was horrible firearm technique but it did the trick. I pressed the trigger.

Abaddon's head hammered to the side. He stiffened and shook me savagely. He roared while the gun fell from my hands. The anger welled inside me, that savage side I tried to keep hidden deep down.

"Little girl," he spat. "Who do you think you're dealing with?"

He raised a fist. The Ring of Solomon was proudly displayed over his knuckles now. It was brass and iron, with a relief of Solomon's Seal on its bezel.

Before he could strike, Bernard launched from his hiding spot in the bathroom and slammed into Abaddon's side, peeling him off me. The angel spun and heaved the gargoyle sideways. Three hundred pounds of solid rock slammed into my mother's record player. Bernard skidded to the floor, dazed.

"No!" I yelled. I dove for the gun and emptied a few bullets into Abaddon's back.

The angel didn't bother to pay me any attention. He walked to Bernard and shrugged. "There's your loyal pet,

Shyla. Your most faithful and true hellion. Did you think he would stand a chance against an angel, even if I didn't have the ring?"

I turned to Bedrock with pleading eyes. He sat on the floor, silently watching events unfold. I set the gun down and spread my hands in surrender, tears in my eyes. "Don't hurt him."

"Oh, I have no intention of hurting him. It's almost impossible to find a reliable subcontractor these days. But you do need a lesson." He turned to the smashed record player and admired the drawers of vinyl.

"Please," I said. "Those are my mother's."

"No. This loft is mine, Shyla. Everything in it is mine."

His fist plowed through stacks of vintage records. I recoiled at the blows as if they connected directly with my ribs.

Bernard growled and readied to pounce.

"You can go now," said the angel. He waved his ring hand and Bernard vanished. The hellion was gone.

Abaddon continued his destruction. He tore the sleeves, smashed the records to pieces, and wrecked the shelves for good measure.

I tried to resummon Bernard—maybe we could escape through the window—but the ring's power prevented it.

As I watched him destroy the last bits of my record collection, the anger welled in me again. I didn't care about giving into it. I didn't care about losing control. Just this once, I wanted to set myself completely free.

My body jolted as the darkness flooded in. My limbs

went taut and my face went feral. I charged forward just as the angel idly glanced over his shoulder, unsuspecting.

His hand waved and the Dark One fled. It happened so fast I couldn't get my feet under me. I tripped to the floor, wracked with residual confusion over being both possessed and exorcised within a matter of seconds.

"Foolish girl," he growled, angered by the affront. "I am the Angel of the Abyss. Do you hear me?" He leaned over me. "I wield the Ring of Solomon. I command all stripes of demons. There isn't a thing you can do to me." He grabbed my jacket collar and lifted me off the ground. "Do you understand?"

I weakly pulled the gold pentacle from around my neck.

Abaddon's eyes glowed with holy fire and he grinned with chiseled lips. He shook me violently, and the press of the Sigillum Dei did nothing.

"You have no power over me!" he declared. "Neither spellcraft nor hellions can harm me. To you I might as well be a god."

I peeked at Bedrock. He watched with no intention of interfering. The demon valued survival more than any attachment he had to me. He was out of this for good.

I faced Abaddon, wearing a proud mask against the heat of his fire. "You can't hurt me, either. I know who I am. A daughter of Solomon. And without my line that ring is useless."

His eyes smoldered.

"And what happens to you then, Abaddon? Do you lose your control of Bedrock and the others? Do you lose your

Earthly empire?" I leaned toward him. "When you return to your Pit, will there be payback waiting for you?" I panted hard, with confidence, nearly spitting in his face. "You need me more than I need you. I have nothing to lose. You have everything."

He released me and I crumbled to the floor. "Yes," he said, remaining calm. "You put it all together, but your assessment is only half right. I still have your father. Don't think I won't hurt him to get to you."

"You don't want me to be the last one left," I muttered. "If I was, I'd kill myself just to strip your power."

His orange eyes twitched. It was a slight flinch, a momentary lapse of his shielded exterior, but it was enough to prove I was onto something. It was enough leverage to save me and my father, but I wasn't sure it was good for much more. It was clear who had the power here. Bedrock and I were hunched on the floor at his feet.

The warmth bathing the angel faded. His eyes returned to their dull gray. The Custodian adjusted his glasses and smoothed his cashmere sweater, displaying a cool smile above his cleft chin.

"I wanted to see how much you discovered," he stated, oozing confidence and control. "It disappoints me that Lambert told you so much, but it is what it is." He considered Bedrock and myself, pressing his lips together in satisfaction. "There now, we all know each other a little better. Our secrets are out in the open. But there will be consequences."

Abaddon recovered his jacket by the door and slipped it

on as he returned to us. "No more speaking with your father," he said flatly.

"No."

"It's the price of your insolence."

Bedrock inched forward. "Master, if I may, Paulson is bound from speaking of the ring and other sensitive matters."

Abaddon shrugged. "Don't worry, you'll still have your check-ins." He turned to me. "Starting tomorrow, you'll check in with Bedrock every night this week. Make sure you're in town and accountable for every action you make. And we're upping your contribution to a cool quarter million. You can handle that, can't you?"

My eyes flashed defiantly but I remained silent.

"Good. Bedrock, you'll report the slightest wavers in her honesty. Don't think I can't find another hellion."

"I live to serve," he answered with a bow.

Bedrock and I slumped on the polished cement, defeated subjects before our glorious king. Abaddon picked up the wine bottle and filled the three glasses, setting ours on the floor at his feet.

"It turns out we do have something to celebrate." He took a small taste and rolled the wine on his tongue. "The past is behind us. We should forget it and move on. Forget about the nine-year anniversary. Forget about the million left in debt. This act of defiance is setting you back another five years at least." He held his glass in the air. "To forgetting our past and looking to our future."

Bedrock took his glass and drank with the angel, but I

couldn't bring myself to play along. All this time I'd hated the demon, and he was underfoot just as I was.

Abaddon leered at us. "Please, please, this is a pathetic display. Rise to your feet. At least pretend to be festive."

Bedrock and I stood. The angel looked pointedly at the wine glass I'd left on the floor. Bedrock picked it up and handed it to me.

Abaddon smiled. "I'm not a sadistic employer. Serve me and you'll be rewarded. Do well and I'll even let you see your father one day."

He clinked our glasses and drank. I was shivering so hard I took a sip just to hide it.

Maybe it was an angel I was in hock to, but it was still an infernal deal stemming from the literal pits of Hell. And just as I'd feared from the beginning, I was worming myself deeper than where I started.

"There," said Abaddon, taking the demon's wine glass and setting it down with his. "You may leave us, Bedrock."

The demon bowed his ashen hair and vanished.

I breathed hard without moving, eyes darting to Abaddon's every casual move.

"It's nice to have a moment alone, Shyla." He squared up to me and placed a gentle hand on my cheek. "I know it might seem like it now, but things haven't changed. You'll still have autonomy to choose your jobs. I'm still the Aaron you knew."

I shook my head. I couldn't say that name anymore. "You're just the Custodian to me."

He sighed, disappointed by my distance, but resolve

overtook his face. "I *am* the Custodian," he said intently. "Remember that. It's my job to watch over you, to care for you. Whether you like it or not, I'm not the enemy you think I am. It was your father who toyed with the ring and had it swindled away. Believe me when I say, Paulson was lucky I discovered him being tormented by demons."

He stepped close and I was too tired to back away.

"I have your money. I have your allegiance. And I have your family. *Always*."

I scowled. "You need to know, Abaddon. I'm gonna fight you, tooth and nail, until I'm free. Until me and my father are miles away from you." I swallowed down the anger. "I want you to know that."

The Custodian blinked at me a moment, and then he nodded in approval. "That's why I like you, Shyla. You'll work till the bitter end."

Closure

That was a long night. I spent most of it reverently cleaning broken records, at times crying so hard I made the mess worse. Each vinyl shard, every tattered sleeve, was full of memories. Of all the times I'd listened and felt her warmth. Of all the dreams of knowing my mother. The music was the only time we'd ever spent together.

I woke up the next morning determined to put the sob story behind me. I didn't make it this far in life by feeling sorry for myself. There was some final bookkeeping to take care of before it was time to move to the next thing. More work. I was Shyla Crowe, consummate professional and summoner for hire.

I gave Trap the all clear to come back home. He decided to stay in Vegas a while longer. Wait for his cards, he said. I went to the bank and got him a cashier's check for what I owed him and dropped it in the mail.

I stopped by a couple of stores for some shopping too. I realized the Custodian had likely tracked my phone to the clubhouse. I bought a burner and copied the relevant info over before dumping my old phone in the trash.

I dialed a number on the new phone and waited out the rings until it went to voicemail. "I'll be at the clubhouse," I said, and I hung up.

The sky was unusually overcast, with layers of gray as far as the eye could see. It made for a cool day. Great for a long ride. I hit the highway and made north for the desert.

I wasn't sure what to expect, but there hadn't been anything in the news about the grisly scene at the biker clubhouse. I wondered if the Custodian had managed to clean it all up. I weaved through the suburbs on my approach. Engines rumbled in the distance, growing louder. Three Harleys converged from behind.

I bit down and approached the clubhouse. A biker pulled on either side of me, with Teegan behind. We slowed at the front of the property. The building had burned down. There wasn't a single motorcycle or vehicle parked outside.

I pulled over across the street and took off my helmet. The smell of charred wood still filled the air. There was no point going inside. I wouldn't find anything.

The Harleys pulled over ahead of me. The two men straddled their bikes, keeping an eye on me. Teegan tapped them lightly and pulled off her helmet as she approached.

"The MC packed up," she said. "Headed back east." The dash of blue above her eyes seemed to glow in the gloom.

I didn't get off my bike. "And you guys?"

She nodded to her escort. "This is Chip and Turkey. They're cool." She crossed her arms and studied the burned clubhouse a moment. "We're not in anymore. I'm done following that train wreck."

I arched an eyebrow. "Is that safe? To up and quit like that?"

"Given what happened here, no one's worried about us."

I chuckled. "Teegan, Chip, and Turkey, founding their own MC."

"Gotta start somewhere." She pouted. "I was never like most of those idiots, you know. I grew up around them. Where I come from, you're either predator or prey."

I nodded. "You don't always choose who you get mixed up with."

"Ain't that the truth." She sighed. "Grady was an ignorant asshole, but he looked out for me, you know? He got himself killed and I was riled up about that. I thought it was you. Sorry."

I reached into my jacket and handed her his silver cross. "I tracked this down for you."

Her fingers went to her neck where her matching pendant would be under her jacket. "I don't..."

"You don't need to say anything."

She pressed her lips tight and nodded as she accepted the gift. "What about... the thing that killed him?"

I exhaled softly. "Sometimes real justice is a little too much to ask."

Teegan eyed her friends waiting on us and seemed to want to say something. She pocketed the cross and almost backed away but paused. "It's not so easy, you know. Going out on your own."

I didn't say anything. She rejoined her friends and rode out.

I did know. But I also knew being on your own was a choice.

Growing up in the company of trouble, having other people's problems thrust on you, starting behind the eight ball from go, that was life.

Riding out with Chip and Turkey was a choice.

It was time for me to take control of my choices, too. To shrug off the weight on my shoulders or carry it proudly. And, ultimately, to live my life on the terms I set.

I hit the kickstand and steered the bike out of there.

"Raw deal," said Josalie, sitting on my couch waiting for her toenails to dry. "Sometimes the quiet ones are the biggest assholes."

I'd mentioned the falling out with the Custodian, but couldn't even begin to approach the details. Sometimes being an asshole was enough explanation.

"Unfortunately," I groaned, "we still need to work together. He's pretty much my boss."

She hissed. "I should give him a piece of my mind next time he comes by."

All mirth left my face. "You need to stay as far away from him as possible. You understand?"

Josalie locked eyes with me and nodded. She turned her attention back to her toes and waved her hands to help them dry.

"What about the other thing?" she asked idly.

"What other thing?"

"Have you decided if I'm cool enough to be promoted to the inner circle?"

I sighed. "It has nothing to do with being cool, Jo."

"Sure, but I've proven I can handle myself, haven't I?"

"I'm not even sure I can handle it, sometimes."

"Don't start being a buzzkill on me." She put her feet down and scooted closer to me. "Shyla, if my advice is worth anything, you shouldn't work with someone who's gonna screw you over. That's a bad situation you need to get out of."

"Believe me," I said firmly, "that's the next thing on my list."

Josalie had to go back to her family for the night. I wanted the time to clean up. I relaxed in a piping hot bath, soaking while Bernard sat vigilant on the wool rug.

"Daily check-ins," grumbled the gargoyle. "Who does that angel think he is?"

I popped bubbles on the water's surface. "I think you answered your own question."

He snorted. "With the Ring of Solomon, no less. You know it's your fate to get that ring."

"Weren't you warning me about fate just yesterday?"

"That was before we knew you were a daughter of Solomon." Bernard scratched his ear and watched me curiously. "I always knew you were special. There was something that drew me to protect you. Except I didn't *actually* think you were special."

"Thanks for that."

"I'm serious. This changes everything. We're playing in a whole new league. Jackal, the Lion of Judah, Abaddon. These are players with formidable assets and power. It makes one wonder."

I raised my eyebrows expectantly. "Wonder what?"

"Well, how we're going to deal with them."

I leaned over the edge of the bath, resting my chin on my soapy hand. "That's easy. We're gonna play them against each other. And it's not just them. There's one more."

Midnight

I dried off but didn't overdo it with my hair. I put on a faded Jim Morrison shirt, pulled my pants and riding boots on, then my leather jacket, zipped all the way up. I capped the ensemble off with the Sigillum Dei pentacle outwardly visible.

I'd been studying the *Semitas Daemoniorum* a lot lately and didn't bother pulling it out now. I didn't have the time anyway.

It was midnight.

I stepped around the bed, opened the wardrobe, and tossed the bathrobe to the floor.

Bedrock waited, eager excitement turning to disappointment as he saw me in my leathers. "You're dressed," he said flatly. A warning.

"And my hair's wet too. You notice that?"

Bedrock's already pallid face went somber. I stomped my boots away from the mirror and leaned on the far wall.

"Just because you're no longer allowed to see your

father," he stated evenly, "doesn't mean you can forget about our arrangement."

"It seems my arrangement was never with you in the first place."

"About that. I was to propose it cause for us to turn a new leaf."

I crossed my arms. "Couldn't agree more."

"Then why are you choosing to anger me?"

"This is my new leaf. I hope you like what you see 'cause this is all you're gonna get."

His face tightened and his tail flicked in agitation. These fidgets only increased as Bernard strolled by.

"Oh, we're not alone," I added. "I know that's what you prefer, but I wanted to bring a friend along so you didn't think this was a date."

"Shyla," he warned, "must I remind you I still have your father."

I laughed. "Abaddon has my father. You're just a babysitter. You've probably been treating Paulson better than I thought, considering he's the one generating power for your master's ring." I put a painted nail to my lip. "I hope you don't mind me calling him your master. That's what he is, you know."

Bedrock sneered, a mix of appreciation and confidence. "So this is to be a renegotiation then? That's what you believe?"

"Honey, I'm not some naive damsel who's never been around the block. I know exactly what this is. And I know exactly who you are, Asmodeus."

He flinched at the name.

I stood off the wall and showed my teeth. "Abaddon said it himself. He fears you want the ring a *third* time. Which meant you weren't innocent in this. *You* were the one that stole the ring from my father. Abaddon saw the imbalance and took it from you, didn't he? Which means you took my father captive in Hell."

He growled in frustration. "I was only teaching Paulson a lesson. Giving him a sampling, if you will, of the hellions he dared insult by attempting to master. But it's true, I could not contend with the Lord of the Pit." The demon scowled. "He took the ring as his own and left me to serve him."

"Which is why you want it again, a third time. Which leads us to the first time. You were the one thousands of years ago who tricked the ring from Solomon himself."

I stepped closer. "You swore you would never conspire with Jackal and Paimon, with Dis. And why? Because when Solomon wrested the ring back, you were banished to Dis and imprisoned. I know your story." I chuckled. "There's even reference to you hating water, like my wet hair, because it reminds you of God. It's clear now, especially given who I am, that you are Asmodeus, usurper of Solomon."

His face twitched in annoyance, but after a moment the tension eased. "This much is true, Shyla Crowe. I cannot deny this." Asmodeus leaned forward in a bow, introducing himself for the first time.

I finally knew his name, who he was. The usurper of

Solomon, and I a descendant. That was a small power over the demon, in a way.

"It seems we are on equal footing," he said, resigned.

"Oh no, honey, not equal, because I'm not done. I know something else about you."

His eyes narrowed. "And what is that?"

"That you were the catalyst for everything that just happened."

He blanched.

"You took the ring from my father almost fifteen years ago. After thousands of years in an infernal prison, you finally possessed the power to free yourself, but the ring was snatched away before you could enjoy it. You weren't a prisoner anymore but a warden, in service to an angel. An angel that later found me. Abaddon kept me around as insurance against you, to curtail any cute ideas of you withholding Paulson. And that's when the charade started. The Custodian, the Handler, Bedrock."

Bernard yawned and settled his chin on his paw, keeping one eye open on the demon.

"It was all shade to throw me off the scent. My true nature and the existence of the ring. And it worked for nine years of my life."

The last sentence came out like an angry growl. I took a moment to compose myself and lifted my chin.

"So we were both slaves, of a sort," I said quietly. "And you waited for the perfect moment. You and my father were bound from revealing the ring, from directly telling me any of this. But it was in your interests for me to find out. So you found your perfect moment. With my father as a confidante, you'd probably known about Lambert for some time. Maybe the plan took years. Maybe your restrictions prevented you from outright telling the old man about me. But somehow, you found a workaround. You found a way to tip off Lambert to my existence. He said as much. You knew he'd find me because he wanted the ring. You knew he'd track me down and ask about it."

The demon's face was animated. "It was the clearest way to fill in your knowledge gaps without going against my master, his letter of law."

"It was clever, even if it could've gotten me killed. But I'm sure that part wasn't your concern."

Asmodeus accepted the accusation. "Even after that," he added, "the angel was suspicious."

Abaddon had called off the heist, and Bedrock had urged me to make everyone happy. Again, a loophole. Not directing me to go against his master's wishes, but still prodding me into contact with Lambert.

I smiled. "And the thing of it is, I know why you did it too. It goes without saying that a depraved angel bearing the Ring of Solomon needs to be dealt with, but there's more than that. You want *me* to take the ring from him. You want *me* to be the bearer of Solomon's Ring because you're confident you can swindle it out of my hands, just like my father and Solomon before me."

His eyes glinted devilishly. Color returned to his flesh. Asmodeus was excited. For everything to be out in the open. For the next stage of the plan to begin. "I, of course, cannot conspire to overthrow my master. I will give you no assistance."

"To the letter," I countered. "Because I not only know your name, Asmodeus, but I know of your betrayal against Abaddon. So we are *not* on equal ground. For your treachery, you are *mine*. Because, if you do not assist me within your every power..." I took a long breath, crouched over Bernard, and rubbed the scruff on his neck. "Then I'll tell your master what you did, and I'll beg him to let Bernard chew on your bones."

The gargoyle's stomach growled, and the whites of Bedrock's eyes stood out from the shadow of his brow. He watched me calmly, carefully, without saying a word. And that was it. I knew I had him.

Which was a minor victory, in the grand scheme of things. Asmodeus was a big player, but he was never in charge, never my true employer. Abaddon was the true Custodian, of my world, my father, and me.

"We are not at cross purposes, Shyla," he said encouragingly.

"Maybe," I said. "For now, I'd like to speak to my father. And I'd like to do that whenever I see fit, without restriction or requirement."

The demon nodded his head. "It is possible. Abaddon's statement was a threat to you. He gave me no such command. But realize I can only do so much under his word."

"You're dismissed," I said. "Chop, chop."

Asmodeus stifled a scowl. The mirror blacked out and

cut to my father.

"Shyla!" he cried, eyes wrinkled with joy. "I was afraid I wouldn't see you for a while." He cleared his throat and looked his daughter up and down with pride. "The biker leathers look good on you, honey."

And I told him how I'd been doing and what had happened. We spoke freely and without a timer, but when I came to the subject of the ring and the angel, my father tightened up.

"I was ashamed," he admitted, "to tell you I stole the ring. That I ripped off a client." He frowned, not only at that moment but at all the events that had transpired since. "So much for me being a consummate professional."

"Don't be too hard on yourself, Dad. We might be in the middle of a different story if Lambert managed to acquire the ring."

He accepted the sentiment with a nod of thanks, rubbed the salty scruff on his chin, and put his hands in his pockets. "So, you know about Abaddon, Asmodeus, the Ring of Solomon, and most importantly, our lineage. It's a start, but I'm bound from revealing anything that might help you or subvert their will. I'm barely a sounding board."

"I know, Dad."

"And be careful with Asmodeus. He's shiftier than he lets on. Anything you tell him may be relayed to Abaddon. In fact, he'll be required to report any counterplays you have in the works."

"I know, Dad."

He chortled, stopped, and shook his head proudly. "Of

course you do, my dear. I can't believe how far you've come."

The next day was a new beginning. Not because the work was any different, but because I knew exactly where I stood. As I geared up to meet the Custodian, the Lead, and the Wire for a new job, I pushed in ear buds and scrolled through the new music library on my phone.

All my mom's classics, restored in digital form. The music lacked some of the range of the vinyl format, but the warmth had never come from the instruments and the voices. Not for me.

The more things changed, the more they stayed the same.

I straddled the Ducati Monster and strapped the helmet on, feeling pretty good about things. You can learn a lot about demons once you know who they are. Angels too. Apparently, the same holds true for yourself.

So I was still in a prison of sorts. Still serving higher powers. But I was armed with knowledge now. I would do it my way, on my terms, and only as long as I had to. From here on out, every job I pulled, every dollar I earned, and every mile I rode was a step closer to my eventual freedom.

-Finn

If you're reading this, it means you demand more from your urban fantasy. Demons and heists are a riot, but they're nothing without a layered cast of characters and realistic plot drivers. *Summoner For Hire* is my stab at a cut above the rest: non-stop intrigue, true friends banding against impossible odds, and themes that hopefully make you put the book down and ponder, if even for only a minute.

My writing process demands quality control at every step of development. I hope you agree *Summoner For Hire* is the premium product I strive to make it. Unfortunately, doubling down on originality and quality in an on-demand world has drawbacks. It's simply not possible for me to get you a brand-new novel every month or two. The process takes time.

That's where you come in. If you want to be part of building a better book, consider one or all of the following shows of support. The best part? These displays of true fandom don't cost you a penny.

- Join the Outlaw Underground.
  (www.facebook.com/groups/dominofinnfans/)

- Leave an all-too-important review on Amazon. Each one helps more than you know.

- Recommend this book to your buds. Link it on social media.

- Join my reader group newsletter, get a free story, and only hear from me when I have new releases or important news.
  (dominofinn.com/newsletter/)

Simple, right? Five minutes of your time makes a world of difference to me and Shyla. Thank you for your heartfelt support. I'll keep writing as long as you keep reading.

- Domino Finn

Also Try:
Black Magic Outlaw

Did you know Shyla Crowe first appeared in the *Black Magic Outlaw* series?

Did you know she's part of a shared universe with a too-cocky-for-his-own-good necromancer in a tank top?

Did you know Cisco makes a guest appearance in *Summoner For Hire* Book Two?

You absolutely do not need to read *Black Magic Outlaw* to continue your journey with Shyla, but if you want to know his backstory and the details about how they met, you can't beat following along with Cisco too.

And trust me, you're gonna want to see how they met.

Shyla and Bernard have heavyweight roles in Book 4 of the series, but everyone knows the best place to start is the beginning.

Dead Man

Black Magic Outlaw Book One

Waking up dead is the worst. Trust me. I know these things.

The last time I woke up this hungover I was naked, soaking wet, and wrapped in a Cuban flag.

This time, at least, I had clothes on. I couldn't see them in the pitch black, but I could feel them. I could feel other things too. Raw pounding in my head. Enough tightness in my chest to make every breath a chore. I was in ten kinds of pain. Apparently that wasn't enough because my leg was asleep too.

There was more. Cold, wet, grimy more. Flies buzzed around my face, circling the stench of death. My arm was slimy. I shifted my weight and something crunched beneath me. My hands and feet pressed against the tight confines of a box.

Smell of death and decay. Check. Some kind of giant coffin. Check. I'm no mathematician but things were starting to add up.

Despite the evidence of my apparent death, I didn't panic. You see, I'm a necromancer (among other things) so I know a little about the subject. I couldn't tell you where I was or what happened the day before to get me here, but I had an inkling I was still alive. Even if just barely.

I tried to sit up. A stabbing pain pulsed through my body until I relaxed again. Request denied.

Okay, deep breath time. I focused inward to calm myself, then reopened my eyes. A thin sliver of light crept through the seam of my crypt overhead, but it was too weak to illuminate the interior.

Good thing I knew a trick or two.

I stared into the darkness, more deeply than before. Not into the box or any physical place, but into a place within me. The pupils of my eyes leaked and my green irises filled with black, and with a blink I could see.

And you thought the necromancer thing was all about wearing black and growing your hair long. I hate to burst your bubble but I'm not a walking death metal stereotype. I don't wear a trench coat and I have a crew cut. I live in Miami, for fuck's sake. It's hot and humid *in the winter*. No sense getting a heatstroke to appeal to northern sensibilities.

Not only that but Cisco Suarez (that's me) isn't just a necromancer. He's a shadow charmer too. That's the magic I just called on. The darkness all around me, it was still there—I could just see through it now.

The thin razorblade of light now stung my eyes. I avoided looking directly at it and checked the rest of the tomb. Crushed cardboard boxes. Stuffed plastic bags. My accommodations weren't as morbid as I'd feared. This wasn't a coffin but a dumpster.

Maybe I wasn't dead after all. Just down for a nap. A bed made of beer bottles. My pillow? A dead sewer rat.

That would've made most men jump, but remember: necromancer. I scrunched my nose and reached for it.

The simple act of limberness was a battle of pain. My muscles were sore. Dry and withered like the old husks of a toppled tree. My bones creaked and my joints were half-dried cement. I stirred up more dust than the Mummy. But I pushed through the agony until I dangled the dead rat by its tail.

It had been decapitated. A tribute. Sacrificial magic, and not mine. That spelled trouble.

I checked for other signs of ritual or binding. Charms. Runes. Burnt sacraments. Scanning the contents of the dumpster, I spied a couple of dark-red cowboy boots on my feet and literally hopped in place. (I almost knocked my head on the dumpster lid.) You see, the rat I could handle. My wearing a bona fide pair of alligator boots was unacceptable.

Don't get me wrong. There was nothing magic or cursed about them. It's just that the modern Cuban doesn't wear cowboy boots. Cisco Suarez doesn't wear cowboy boots.

That's me again, by the way. Shorter and catchier than Francisco, it always reminded me of a comic book name. What kid didn't want to be a superhero? I liked the sound of it so much I picked up referring to myself in the third person. My fatal flaw.

Enough about my name. Let's talk spellcraft. I'm what you call an animist: an everyday human who happens to tap into spirits for magical energy. Wild, huh?

I know what you're thinking: A cleric deals with gods and a wizard with books, right? Well, put the Player's Handbook away and forget everything you think you know. Gods and books have plenty of overlap. (The most famous book in all history is a notable example.)

Fact is, magic is a universal force in the world, pure energies known as the Intrinsics. They're the building blocks of all creation. People like you or me can only manipulate them through spirits. That makes us animists.

Everything else is just a title. Wizard. Cleric. Learned men like to use mage (it's more sophisticated). You see shaman or witch doctor applied to primitive peoples. Or if you wanna vilify animists, call them witches and warlocks. You get the idea. I'm sure some academic somewhere compiled a list of unofficial "official" definitions—but you'd have a hard time running into that terminology on the street. And the street is where the real stuff happens.

Case in point: the dumpster I was lying in.

Some alarm in my head screamed that I was hurt. Maybe fatally. The thing was, besides stiffness, there wasn't anything wrong with me. I wasn't dying, anyway. I kinda felt like a homeless vampire more than anything else. Which would be a lot funnier if I didn't know vampires actually existed. After all, right now I had a hangover from hell—maybe hell was where I came from.

You're probably bored by now, right? Sorry. I think too much. It's a problem I'm trying to address.

With a strained kick of an alligator boot, the lid of the dumpster flew open. Blinding light engulfed me and seared my senses. I literally hissed and uselessly threw my hands up in defense. Maybe I was a vampire after all.

But I didn't burst into flames. After I took another second to get my head on straight, I realized I was still drawing upon my shadow sight. I drained the darkness from my eyes, my lids pushing out black tears, until it was safe to look.

A blue sky. Fluffy clouds. Palm trees.

I was in South Beach.

Not the pretty coastline with white sand they show on TV during football games. That was never far in Miami Beach, of course, but the back alleys were far less picturesque. I was just off Washington Avenue somewhere, outside a dive bar. The alley was empty. I heaved myself over the dumpster wall and landed on the concrete with a thud. I wouldn't win any vaulting medals but it got the job done. Standing and walking involved entirely new kinds of pain, but either it was wearing off or I was getting used to it.

Normally I'd assume this predicament was my doing—it wouldn't be me if I didn't go big—but the dead rat was a bit much. It was also a dead giveaway that someone else was involved.

I padded at my jean pockets. I had a cell phone but no wallet.

Was I robbed? It seemed unlikely given the evidence of spellcraft. A beatdown, then?

I frowned. I'd annoyed people, sure. I'd had minor run-ins with gang tough guys and stirred up the local talent, but that was life as a small-time hustler. I was too young for real enemies. No reason anyone should wish me dead.

The preternatural fog in my head wasn't going away. I couldn't think clearly. No amount of head-scratching helped.

With my head on a swivel for danger, I staggered to the pink sidewalk. (Miami Beach, remember?) I was ready for anything. What I didn't expect was to be ignored.

Small groups of shoppers strolled up and down Washington Avenue. Horns honked and cars inched forward and came to a stop at the light. I got a few odd looks but nobody confronted me or threw any blood curses my way. It was just your average whatever-day-it-was in South Beach.

A man strolled by and held his hand out to me. While trying (and failing) to make eye contact, I accepted his offering. A nickel and two pennies. He avoided my puzzled expression and continued on his way.

That was random, but I couldn't be accountable for the South Beach crazies. Cisco Suarez needed to stay on task. Since everything appeared normal outside, I considered pumping the bar employees for information.

The car that was stopped on the road in front of me clicked its doors locked. I looked and the woman in the passenger seat averted her eyes. Bitch. Then I got a glimpse of myself in the window reflection.

I would've locked the doors too.

Besides my healthy tan, nothing of my disheveled appearance was recognizable. My usually close-cropped hair hung over my shoulders in a wild mane. My eyes were permanently frantic, sporting the raised-by-wolves look. The full-on homeless beard didn't help. And my clothes. Besides my jeans and red cowboy boots, of all things I wore a yellowed and bloodied tank top.

Tank tops were never really my look but, to my surprise, I actually filled this one out. My chest strained against the thin fabric and my bare arms looked carved from marble. Still in disbelief, I flexed a bicep at my reflection. Maybe the car windows were made from magic fun-house mirrors.

This warrants an explanation. I may be a little cocky and reckless at times, but one thing I'm not is a gym rat. I was always that scrappy skinny kid who was too stupid to stay down. Yes, that means I lost a lot of fights. I wanted to be a superhero but lacked the dedication. What animist would spend time working out anyway? The power of the world at your fingertips, wasted by repeatedly picking up and putting down heavy things.

No, I was never out of shape, but I was supposed to be thin. Now I suddenly felt like Peter Parker after running into that radioactive spider. I was straight buff, is what I'm saying.

My jaw glued to the floor, I stared like a lunatic. The driver floored the gas at his first opportunity. In their place, a matte-black jeep slammed on its brakes. Which was weird since the light was green and the cars behind it honked. I snapped out of my shock as the group of Haitians in the jeep focused on me, anger in their eyes.

They yelled, "Dead man!" and dismounted, brandishing light automatic weapons.

I threw seven cents at them.

Thanks for reading this Chapter 1 preview.

Get the full version of Dead Man
where Domino Finn books are sold

Also by Domino Finn

SUMMONER FOR HIRE
Tooth and Nail
Hell and High Water

BLACK MAGIC OUTLAW
Dead Man
Shadow Play
Heart Strings
Powder Trade
Fire Water
Death March
Blood Craft

AFTERLIFE ONLINE
Reboot
Black Hat
Trojan
Deadline

SHADE CITY

SYCAMORE MOON
The Seventh Sons
The Blood of Brothers
The Green Children

About the Author

Domino Finn is an award-winning game industry veteran, a media rebel, and a grizzled author of urban fantasy and litRPG. His stories are equal parts spit, beer, and blood, and are notable for treating weighty issues with a supernatural veneer. If Domino has one rallying cry for the world, it's that fantasy is serious business.

Take a stand at DominoFinn.com

www.ingramcontent.com/pod-product-compliance
Lightning Source LLC
Chambersburg PA
CBHW051645180726
48284CB00006B/1869